Class Act

Thornback Society
Book One

By
Aspen Hadley

OTHER BOOKS BY ASPEN HADLEY

STAND-ALONE NOVELS:

Simply Starstruck
Blind Dates, Bridesmaids & Other Disasters
Suits and Spark Plugs
Halstead House

DUOLOGY:

Just Enough Luck
Just Enough Magic

DEDICATION

To my author friends
Without you I wouldn't have had the courage to try self-publishing.
Thank you for the advice, the random discussions, the hysterical gifs, the
questions that breed more questions, the venting, and all the ways
you remind me that I'm not alone on this author journey!

PROLOGUE

Last week of May

I listened distractedly to the conversation around the table as I stacked a perfect bite onto my fork. Chicken, mushroom, snow pea, and now to scoop some rice. There. I opened my mouth and placed the well-balanced tidbit directly on top of my tongue. Satisfied, I looked around at my friends as I chewed. The faculty break room wasn't anywhere near as dazzling as some of the places I'd eaten, but it felt like home to me thanks to the other women at my table. Lizzie was dangling a limp noodle off the end of her spoon, her nose wrinkled up in distaste. The look, so unusual for her, made me smile.

"My life, represented in food," Lizzie said. She wiggled the noodle at us until it slopped lazily into her soup. We all stopped talking to each other and looked at her, curious about the uncharacteristically dramatic mood. "School's out for summer next week, and I need to do something that makes me feel alive. I'm in danger of disappearing into the void of monotony."

Ruby was the first to reply. "I felt alive when I caught vomit in a trash can, earlier," she said with a chuckle, her dark eyes nearly disappearing as they crinkled up.

The rest of us groaned, and I pushed away my plate of leftover stir-fry. No way was I going to be able to eat now. I suppose I could forgive Ruby, a nurse who thought all that body stuff was normal and interesting. Not me. No way, no how. I'm all for keeping blood and vomit inside the body where it belongs and pretending it doesn't exist.

Lizzie sighed, which had the desired result of reclaiming our attention. "Am I the only one watching the clock tick and realizing how fast time is passing while I sit inside a school room?" She speared the four of us with a look. I sat up a little straighter as her eyes pinned mine before moving on. "I'm about to finish my tenth year of teaching here and am in serious danger of becoming a vicious stereotype."

1

She pointed her noodle-less spoon at each of us, one by one. "You should all be worried too. We're all in our thirties, never been married, and teaching school. Eventually someone is going to accuse us of being old maids. Certain parts inside of me are actually turning to dust."

I'd turned thirty last month, yes, but it hadn't occurred to me to be panicking quite yet. Of course, I was the youngest at the table, and it had taken me this long to settle into my own skin and decide how to live my life. I wasn't exactly yearning for a man to complete me. But that didn't mean I couldn't see Lizzie's point or occasionally hope there might be more in the future.

"Old maid is an insulting term," Meredith replied, her darkly lined blue eyes flashing her offense on behalf of all of us.

"I could have called us spinsters, which isn't any better," Lizzie replied with a shrug.

"Who says we need a label?" Meredith continued, pausing to pop a piece of her sandwich into her mouth before reaching up to tuck a lock of her jet-black hair behind her ear. "Labels are limiting."

I was inclined to agree. If my mom could hear Lizzie throwing around disparaging remarks and pigeonholing us that way, she'd start an intervention on the spot. I wanted to cheer in agreement with Meredith but settled for a nod and patted Meredith on the arm.

"I heard a new term: thornback," Aryn stated as she bit into her crisp salad. At our blank stares Aryn hurried to swallow and then leaned forward with a cheery, amused expression. "I read an article the other day that said the word spinster was for women who were in the age range of twenty-three to twenty-six. Thornback was what they called unmarried women over the age of twenty-six. It was some sort of reference to a hideous fish with thorns down its back—meaning those women were ugly and prickly and should be thrown back."

Ruby's brow furrowed and her lips pouted slightly. "That doesn't sound any better."

Aryn held up her hand. "I know. It was terrible. But . . . there's a movement on social media right now to resurrect the word in more of a dragon-like way. Like saying, 'Who needs a man? We're thornback dragon women, and we rule the entire kingdom.'"

The five of us were silent for a beat, something that certainly didn't happen often, before I sputtered out a laugh. I reached up and habitually smoothed my hand over my white-blonde bob while shaking my head. "It's perfect," I said. "See,

Lizzie? We're not old maids. We're a bunch of thornback dragon women, thriving without men."

Lizzie leaned across the table to give me a high five as her expression became entertained, her hazel eyes dancing. "You're right, Hailey. I love it."

Ruby squared her shoulders playfully and stated, "I'll stand with you, Lizzie, and so will your sisters of the lunchroom table." She set down the soda she'd been nursing and gestured widely. "We, the Thornback Five, must seek adventure in the great wilderness outside of this school. Each of us will find our fortunes and happiness will be ours."

Meredith rolled her eyes while the rest of us chuckled, drawing the attention of other faculty members who had been peacefully eating. Someone cleared their throat, and we shared a grin as Meredith cleared hers back, loudly. It was something that happened frequently, and we all brushed it off, refocusing on each other.

"We should form The Thornback Society," Aryn said, raising her water bottle. "To fierce women!" she called.

We all picked up our various drinks and tapped them together.

"To women who don't need men but who think they might want one someday," I said in my head as my metal water bottle clanked against the others. Someday.

CHAPTER ONE

September

I've never been one to shy away from admitting to my mistakes. I know a person can't grow without some self-awareness, after all. But ethical high ground aside, some days are meant for lying. I mean, it's not every day that you're standing in the middle of the school cafeteria, wearing gloves dripping with taco sauce, when one of your mistakes shoves itself in your face and you suddenly have to pretend you've never seen him before in your life.

In all fairness, and I promise I'm not trying to justify my behavior, I never thought I'd actually come face to face with him. Sure, I'd seen him around town but always at a distance, allowing him to maintain the same illusive mystery as a sweet bedtime story or the perfect hero in a romance novel. He was both real and imaginary.

He was never meant to step straight out of dreamland and into my real life. He walked through the cafeteria, holding hands with his eight-year-old daughter, wearing the same swoonworthy smile he always flashed in pictures. His gray suit was crisply pressed as though it repelled wrinkles, and I happened to know that it was almost the same shade as his light eyes. My own eyes were the size of ostrich eggs as he sauntered past the taco stand where I was working and came to a stop near a table of other parents, casually tucking his free hand in a pocket and joining effortlessly in the conversation.

I made a few quick assumptions about what he might be saying to them, based on an interview of his I'd read a few weeks ago in the local paper. He was big on the preservation of Earth and its resources. He also played golf. Whatever it was he said, they were eating it up the same way I had imagined I would, you know, should the entire world revolve straight off its axis and plunge into the icy depths of space.

This was not supposed to be happening.

The echoing sounds of many voices, along with the constant motion of the crowd, did nothing to hide him from my view or distract me from my staring. It all became background, soft and subtle, growing fuzzy the longer I focused in on the way his mouth moved and his shoulders shifted as he spoke . . .

"Hailey," Meredith hissed next to me, "you just dropped taco meat on my shoe."

Heat flooded my face as I was called back to the fact that I was holding a spoon full of juicy taco meat up in the air, causing the sauce to run down my hand and the meat to slip onto Meredith's sneakers.

"I . . . sorry," I stuttered, yanking my arm away from her foot and back toward the tortilla I was supposed to be filling.

"The only thing I hate worse than getting taco duty on school fundraiser night is going home wearing the taco meat. What's got you distracted?" she asked, taking my filled tortilla and adding lettuce and cheese before passing it to a mother waiting in line.

"Nothing."

"Uh-huh." She nudged me and nodded toward the tortillas. "Why don't you grab another one of those and fill it up then, Miss Laser Focus?"

I blinked a few times, eyes still refusing to budge from the man who always looked better in person than he did on my computer screen. I hadn't seen him often, but every time I'd caught a glimpse of him around town, I'd wondered if my mind was playing games. He couldn't possibly give off that level of magnetism. Tonight, however, the undeniable truth hit me straight between the eyes. That man was my personal kryptonite. His draw was more potent than I'd imagined.

And I'd done a lot of imagining.

In my mind we'd had quite the whirlwind affair including several romantic dinners, a yacht trip in the Mediterranean, attending the theater, and a particularly embarrassing bit about him feeding me chocolate-dipped strawberries. It wasn't like me to live in a fantasy world, but it had felt safe, I wasn't hurting anyone, and I was never going to actually talk to the man in person.

"Hay-Lee," Meredith sighed as she reached past me to grab a tortilla. "Head in the game, please."

"This is bad, this is so bad . . ." I muttered as his daughter spotted me. She let go of his hand and headed my way with a big smile. "I'll never survive this."

Meredith's eyes followed mine to where Hillary Whittaker was walking my way. "Hillary? You're not going to survive seeing her? Is she going to murder you with her cheer? Drag your body out from this booth and tickle it to death?"

"Her dad. She's going to want me to meet him." Without thinking, I scrubbed my dirty hands against the apron I was wearing, smearing orange across the cream color. "I can't do it."

Meredith sighed once again and bumped me out of the way with her hip. "Go meet her dad and maybe take a little bathroom break. I have no idea what has you all riled up, but I hardly recognize you right now. You are definitely not in the zone."

I finally dragged my eyes back to her. "This is a two-person job."

I needed the excuse to keep my distance. What if somehow two hearts appeared in my eyes when I met him and he could see right through me? What if he knew that I'd formed a completely unwarranted and fictional attachment to him without ever having actually met? What if my body took over and I flung myself into his arms?

"And one person has been doing it ever since you froze like a possum under threat." She nudged me again, and this time I shuffled to the side. "Go on. Say hi to Hillary. Come back when you're done."

Hillary arrived at the taco station just as I managed to come around the side. My expression was tight, my lips feeling like ice as I glanced down at her with a half-hearted greeting. I felt terrible about not being my usual, warm self, but I was going through something, and Hillary had the power to make or break me in the moment.

Please don't introduce me to your dad, I thought loudly, hoping it would miraculously project through space into her small ears.

"Miss Thomas!" Hillary called cheerily, oblivious to my hesitance. "My dad came tonight."

Yes, that I had noticed. It was as though the air had changed and something strange had whispered at me to look to the doorway the moment he'd entered.

Ford Whittaker.

My mind flashed to the previous school year. With only one month until school would be ending, I'd gotten a new student. Hillary Whittaker was bright, precocious, and imaginative, and we'd clicked immediately. She'd constantly talked about her new house, her brother, and her dad. The way she spoke about her father, though, had made me begin to wonder if any of her stories were real and if he even existed. I'd seen a nanny at pickup and drop-off but no sign of a parent or guardian in the short weeks I'd been her teacher. It made sense in a way, though. There hadn't been parent-teacher conferences or really any reason for him to have come to the classroom in that short amount of time.

One Friday afternoon, on a whim, I'd decided to look her father up online. That had led me down an unfortunate, and spine-tingling, rabbit hole. I'd spent over an hour reading articles, scrolling his social media, and researching his business. After that I began watching for news of him, which had somehow morphed into a humiliating tendency to attach his face to the heroes in my daydreams. I'd even created a personality for him. Yes, I was a thirty-year-old daydreamer and possible stalker. This was a strict secret that I'd never told anyone.

Because that type of starry-eyed behavior should have ended when I was fifteen years old. At thirty I knew better . . . at least in my mind. My stomach, however, had a terrible tendency to launch into butterfly mode and steer me down desperate paths.

At least no one else knew that I'd assigned Ford such a central place in my mind. I'd only ever mentioned him once, on a girls' trip over the summer, and not one word had been said since. I was pretty sure no one remembered.

Hillary didn't wait for any response on my part as her expression shifted to that peculiar look children get of pure delight before it morphs into scheming. Her two round, gray eyes, and missing teeth in a jumbo smile had another set of nerves zipping along my arms, but they were different than the ones her dad had set off. I wasn't sure what to expect when she opened her mouth, but it wasn't "You should come to my dad's birthday party."

Her blurted words sucked all the air out of my lungs as I slid a glance over her head to where he was still standing a couple of feet away. His body was relaxed, both hands now tucked into his pockets as he chatted with the other parents who currently had his attention. A slight wrinkle sat between his eyebrows, however, and I imagined that he was wishing he were somewhere else. I blinked and let go of the idea that I had any clue what Ford would be thinking or feeling. We were strangers.

I tore my gaze away from the silky layers of his dark blond hair and focused on the little girl in front of me. Did a tiny, irresponsible part of me celebrate a little at the idea of being invited to his birthday party? Yes. But, the bigger part of me, the introverted and less heart-eyed part, knew it would be a mistake. It would only serve to deepen my attraction and attachment, and I really needed to be moving in the opposite direction: away from possible heartbreak when reality came crashing into my fantasy world.

This was my wake-up call. My long overdue, seriously humiliating, wake-up call.

"Hillary, that's so kind of you to invite me, but birthday parties are special, and your dad has never met me," I said gently, hiding my relief at being able to turn down the invite without her father being involved in the discussion. "Do you have a friend you can invite?"

Her smile dipped, and she bit her lip as she thought. "No. Daddy says it's for adults, and the only kids allowed are me and Henry."

Henry, her ten-year-old brother, was across the cafeteria eating one of the tacos I was supposed to be selling as a part of tonight's school fundraiser fair. The sight of the taco had me looking to where I'd left Meredith alone with a tub of taco meat. The line had grown to rival Disneyland. Neither of us understood the draw, but both of us had pasted on a cheerful face and pretended the tacos weren't going to cause a bad case of indigestion later. Nothing like forking out good money for school lunch tacos and then paying all over again when it hit your stomach.

My eyes sneaked back to Hillary's dad. Ford. Even his name was dreamy. I cleared my throat and tamped down that thought.

"I'm sure you and Henry will have a good time together," I said kindly.

"No," she shook her head. "Brothers aren't that fun at fancy parties. But I think Daddy would let me invite you. You're an adult, you know." Her little nose scrunched up. "I know how to fix this. I'll have you meet him, then you aren't a stranger."

I opened my mouth to suggest, I don't know, anything else, but she darted over to her dad and tugged on his sleeve. I'd done this to myself, really. I should never had said the part about him not knowing me.

He was still speaking with another parent, so he gave her a pat on the back and wrapped up the conversation while I tugged down the front of my apron and reached up to smooth my hair. He'd never met me and now this taco princess outfit was going to be his first impression of me. It was a letdown, to say the least.

My imaginary world and the real world were not ready to collide. I needed to stop this. I needed time to prepare before coming face-to-face with those charismatic vibes he was giving off that had nothing at all to do with playing pretend.

Mr. Whittaker finished up his conversation and glanced down to Hillary. I noticed his expression soften, and I tilted my head to the side at the shift. It was subtle but sweet and told me a lot about his relationship with his little girl. I was glad. He'd been widowed when Hillary was only three years old, and although Hillary loved her nanny, I'd worried that her dad was . . . Well, it didn't matter what I'd worried about because he was looking at me and walking my way.

So this is what it felt like to have those eyes focus on me. It was almost as good as when Fake Ford . . . nope . . .

I forced a serene smile. "Hello, Mr. Whittaker. I'm Hailey Thomas. I taught Hillary when she transferred schools last year."

He reached out a hand and, oh my gosh, we were going to touch. I wondered if his hands would be soft or calloused. Would his grip be strong or that dead fish thing that I hated so much? Our hands had almost connected before I remembered I was wearing plastic gloves covered in taco meat, and I hastily stopped the progress of my hand. Then I remembered I had just smoothed my hair with this hand, and I could only imagine how taco meat juice looked strung through my short and sleek white-blonde bob. Fantastic.

"I'm sorry," I forced a chuckle even as my mind was screaming at me to run to the bathroom and fix the damage, "I almost forgot, I'm covered in taco meat."

I waved my hands at him, and his hand dropped. It was for the best. I was barely keeping from passing out as it was. My hands trembled at my side as I waited for him to speak. What would his voice sound like? Would it be like the videos on his company page, or would it sound different in person? Would it be rehearsed and professional or casual?

"It's nice to meet you, Mrs. Thomas," he acknowledged politely.

His voice was deep and easy, friendly in a way that would translate well to the boardroom to keep things from getting heated. It had the opposite effect on me. It made me want to cozy right up.

"It's Miss, Daddy," Hillary supplied helpfully. "She's not married, and I want to bring her to your birthday party." She bounced on her feet, clapping her little hands together.

He merely nodded as he held my gaze, and I was immediately weak in the knees. There was no way my expression was as relaxed as I was trying for, and it didn't help that he seemed to be sizing me up. Was he trying to decide if I should receive an invite to his party? My pits began to sweat, and suddenly the taco stand seemed like an oasis calling me to safety.

Under his thoughtful stare I felt like I had an eight-year-old agent trying to get me into the cool club in town while I stood there smelling of salsa and wishing he'd never been torn from my fantasies and thrust into this unpleasant situation.

I realized in that moment that I was going to have to rescue myself, so I plastered on a bright grin and waved a taco hand. "Oh, that's so sweet Hillary, but I'm sure the guest list is all set and that you'll have some people there to spend time with."

Ford--better make that Mr. Whittaker -- nodded down at Hillary. "Grams will be there," he said. "She's really excited to spend time with you and Henry."

"Yes, exactly." I nodded repeatedly. "You told me your grandma lives far away. I don't want to interrupt your time together."

Hillary's lips twisted in thought. "Grams is old, though. I can play with her before the party, and then you can come to the party when she goes to bed," she said to me.

I looked over my shoulder to where Meredith was slinging tacos like she was born to it. The line, though, was bogging down, and I once more saw my escape in the glorious form of tortillas. I hooked a thumb that direction and offered Mr. Whittaker a smile before glancing down to Hillary.

"I really need to get back to helping Miss Atwood, but I love that you thought to invite me, Hillary. I think you're fun and smart, and I miss having you in my class. Your dad's birthday is a special occasion, but maybe next week you could stay late one day, and we'll paint our nails together?" I shifted my focus up to Mr. Whittaker, expecting to see relief, but his expression gave nothing away. "If your dad says that's okay?" I nudged. I'd given the man an out. Why wasn't he taking it?

Hillary looked to her dad, too, her eyes exactly the same gray-blue color and shape of his. "She's trying to be nice," she said sincerely. "Cause it's rude to invite yourself places."

He grinned, and my heart tripped. "True. Miss Thomas seems to be a very polite person."

"She wouldn't be a problem at your party. She has good manners," Hillary pleaded.

I bit my lips as they tugged upward. She'd given me quite the glowing recommendation.

"I'm sure she does." Mr. Whittaker straightened a little and looked to me. "Hillary, why don't you go get your taco before Henry eats it? I'll give Miss Thomas the details so she knows how to get to the party."

Hillary squealed and wrapped her arms around my middle. I felt a little bad that her shirt was going to have grease stains, but she let go before I had time to squeeze her back. Then she skipped across the cafeteria to where her older brother was sitting with a group of classmates. Warmth flowed through my chest as I watched her. That girl was going places.

"She's something special," I said softly to her father.

"She is," he responded, his tone assessing.

I looked back to him, my face warming as the buffer she'd provided slipped away. I was face-to-face with a man who radiated something I was slightly afraid of. The pictures I'd scrolled had only hinted at who he was in person.

"I truly don't want to push myself onto the guest list. I really would enjoy a few hours after school next week to soften the blow to Hillary," I said, gathering my confidence around me.

"It's obvious Hillary likes you. She talks about you enough. I hope the two of you aren't plotting something."

"Plotting?" I stumbled over the word.

He focused back on me--like really focused--and a buzz of electricity hit from the top of my head to the soles of my feet.

A tone of authority suddenly radiated from him as he stated, "Don't take this the wrong way, Miss Thomas, but I'm not looking to date anyone or get remarried. Ever."

My eyebrows flew up, and I took a step back before I could stop myself. Instant hurt and confusion warred within me. Why would he say that? Didn't he know me better? No, Hailey, he doesn't know you at all, I reminded myself sternly.

My jaw clenched and humiliation threatened to take away my voice, but I managed to speak in barely more than a shocked whisper when I replied, "The thought never crossed my mind."

Lies, lies, lies. Fake Ford and I were getting pretty chummy. Rumor had it he'd been ring shopping. I wished he were here instead of this mannerless impostor.

"Hillary has her daydreams about getting a new mom. I just want to make it crystal clear that I'm not getting set up on dates by my eight year old."

I nodded tightly, my emotions cooling into resolve. "It's quite clear." I glanced at his sweet daughter, feeling sad that she'd be disappointed, but not sad enough to be in company with her dad again. "Please express my regrets to Hillary."

I avoided looking at him again as I walked away, head held high and blood boiling. I had a host of feelings shooting laser beams at Mr. Ford Whittaker. How rude. I hoped he choked on his taco tonight. I detested confrontation as much as the injustice of being put in my place for no reason at all. As if I'd ever plot with a child to snag her father. My bubble had officially been burst, and I firmly told myself there would be no more daydreams. My throat was thick as I returned to my place next to Meredith and started plating up tortillas and meat once more.

"Have you ever wondered what my most favorite night of the year is?" she asked as she slapped some lettuce onto the flat white disk I presented her.

"It's obviously school fundraiser night," I replied. "I'm having a hard time containing my excitement. If cartwheels were allowed indoors, I'd be doing them right now."

Sarcasm oozed with every word, made sharper by the confusion washing through me over that ridiculous exchange and the loss of something I'd never actually had.

"Exactly," Meredith stated with equal displeasure, glancing at me from the side. "When else do I get to stay late to run a taco stand and try to sneakily convince people to give us their money?"

"It's like schoolteacher Christmas." My reply was more cynical than it should have been.

She gave me more side-eye but finished serving another family before asking, "What were you and Mr. Business talking about over there?"

"Oh, nothing much," I replied as I took a few breaths and worked to shake off my mood. I wouldn't give this unfortunate interaction any control over my emotions.

"He looks like a politician, working the room. Is he sleazy?"

"I have no idea."

"You stomped away from him, which tells me you do have an idea." She sprinkled some lettuce and cheese in with the meat, handed it to a waiting mother, and asked the woman if she was enjoying herself and had had a chance to donate to the school fund. I was feeling pretty good about avoiding the rest of the our conversation, but five minutes later we'd cleared the bottleneck of taco lovers and Meredith was after me again. "I don't see you stomp very often, and that blush could have heated a hot tub. What happened?"

I told her the whole story--well, not the whole, whole story--and rather than getting offended on my behalf, which is like her superpower, she chuckled. "Obviously you have to go to his party now."

I'd rather crawl across broken glass. "Why on earth would I do that? I have a firm policy about staying away from places where I'm not wanted."

"Isn't he the guy you internet creeped last school year?"

"Maybe." I studiously kept my eyes away from her, which was a tactical error. She knew me well enough to know I was avoiding something.

"Yes. You told us he was a ten out of ten, and you'd looked more than once."

I scooped up another tortilla and filled it before passing her the plate. "An obvious misjudgment. Looks don't matter if the personality is atrocious."

Meredith bumped her shoulder against mine. "You sound disappointed by that." I shrugged, and she pushed ahead. "Are you honestly telling me it wouldn't give you some satisfaction to show up at his party, dressed to kill, and schmoozing all his guests with your fancy manners, all the while knowing he didn't want you there?"

"I'm not going." I felt like I'd just been dumped, and no one wanted to see their ex again that soon.

"Not even for cute Hillary? Imagine how lonely she must be with a dad like that and no mom?"

My stomach felt woozy at the thought, and I looked to Meredith to gauge her sincerity. She was making it really hard to work my way back to calm. "Do you really think she's lonely?"

12

"Hailey, she's latched onto you. She begged you to come to the party. Do it for the children." When she could see I wasn't convinced, she started singing a Whitney Houston song under her breath.

I cracked up. "Knock it off."

"So you'll go?"

I shook my head. "No. Going places I'm not wanted, banging down doors, making people pay for misjudging me? Those are your happy places. My happy place is far away from arrogant single dads throwing themselves birthday parties. Pass."

Which is exactly why two days later I was walking up the front steps of Ford Whittaker's mansion, wearing a knee-length, rose gold, sequin wrap dress and a smile that could give frostbite to a fire.

CHAPTER TWO

The Whittaker home was over-the-top arrogance. Of course, if I'd seen it before Real Ford had been a total jerk, I would have had a different opinion. I'd probably have said the place was one hundred percent storybook material, the kind of home I could celebrate living in with the man I loved and his two adorable children. For now, though, it only represented the bittersweet reality that we lived in very different worlds, and he did not want to invite me into his.

The front doors were opened for guests to arrive without knocking, and every arrival was ushered into the impressive circular three-story entrance. The entryway was roughly the size of my entire classroom, and it performed its function as a greeting area with cool simplicity. Stark white walls that shot sky high, a white floor, and a chandelier that would have made my mom weep with joy all worked together to impress greatness on anyone who entered.

I may have officially been in a castle, but everyone who's read a fairy tale knows that villains can live in castles, too.

The September evening air was cool, even though summer was still holding on, and I shrugged out of my black cashmere shawl when a young man in a white and black uniform offered to take it from me. I silently thanked my parents for the pricey clothing item as it wasn't something I'd have bought for myself on my teacher's salary.

A goblet of something sparkling was offered to me as I watched my shawl disappear down a side hallway, noting where it was taken so that I'd be able to duck out later. I reached for the stem of the glass and mentally went over my plan as I followed the flow of people through an arched doorway into a palatial gathering room.

The morning after my disastrous interaction with her father, Hillary had come to my classroom with a handmade invitation. She'd promised her dad had said she could invite me and begged me once again to come. While I didn't believe for a second that Daddy Dearest really did want me there, I channeled my inner Meredith and agreed to make an appearance for Hillary's sake. Then I hustled to Meredith's classroom before the starting bell rang and asked her what to do.

The plan was simple. Show up looking worlds away from the lady covered in tacos and then spend the evening with Hillary, ignoring the birthday boy altogether. (Meredith had no idea that was easier said than done, considering I'd trained my brain to watch for any sign of him.) Bonus points if I knew some of the people in his circle. Chances were high that I would, because . . .shh . . . these were my parents' people too.

According to Meredith, Ford Whittaker had no idea who he'd snubbed. I didn't see it the same way but borrowing courage and determination from Meredith had worked in the past when my tendencies toward peacekeeping rendered me mute. And if I maybe daydreamed a little about being fearless and making him question his judgment, well, there was nothing wrong with that.

The room I'd entered had the same white walls as the front hall, but it was softened with tans and blues in furniture and decor, making it feel homier. I sipped at my drink while I looked around for any sign of Hillary. Conversation topped the faint sounds of instrumental music as well-dressed guests chatted easily. There was a feeling of ease among the guests, and I tried to let it seep into me. I was confident in myself and my ability to be in this world, but I meant what I'd told Meredith about not wanting to push myself into places where I wasn't wanted. Humans are complex, and I was living proof that it is possible to be confident and shy at the same time. I was probably going to lose ten pounds tonight from the knots in my stomach and sweat tracing my backbone, but I glided through the room as though I didn't have a care in the world.

I finally spotted a flash of hot pink fluff sprinting past the couches across the room, and I smiled to myself as I began working my way through the crowd. There must have been at least two hundred people inside, not to mention the people I could see mingling out on the terrace. Lights strung from tree to tree lit up the backyard, and cheery conversation floated in through the open double doors. This was the kind of birthday party I would never personally enjoy. My thirtieth a few months ago had been ideal: me, my parents, my four best friends, and some takeout sushi. Simple and peaceful with happy conversation around my parents' large dining room table.

"Hailey Thomas?" a woman's voice snagged my attention at the same time Hillary and I made eye contact.

Hillary whooped loudly enough for a few people to glance her direction and then came barreling my way as I turned to see who had called my name. It was my dad's boss, the dean of the education and human services college where Dad was a psychology professor.

I reached out my free hand to grip hers. "Agatha, how lovely to see you," I said as I pressed a light kiss next to her cheek, careful not to leave any trace of my lipstick. "It's been a long time."

"Too long," she gently chastised, squeezing my hand before releasing it. "I hear you're an elementary school teacher now."

"I am."

I was jostled forward as Hillary bumped into me from the side, very nearly splashing my drink on poor Agatha and her stunning aqua dress.

"Miss Thomas," Hillary cried happily, "you're here."

Agatha laughed heartily. "I suppose this tells me how you know Ford?" she asked curiously.

I only had time to nod before Hillary was talking. "Daddy said I could invite a friend, and I chose Miss Thomas because this is an adult party, and she's my only friend who is a grown up." Hillary smiled brightly, her hodgepodge group of missing teeth making her even more darling, if possible.

"That makes sense to me," Agatha replied. "It's not every day your dad turns forty."

This was his fortieth birthday? Oh boy. I'd landed myself in the middle of a milestone celebration. Fantastic. It would seem my internet searches hadn't quite given me all the details about him.

Hillary ran her hand down the sleeve of my dress. "It's so sparkly."

I leaned down to whisper. "Sparkles are my favorite."

"And it's pink, too, just like my nails." She pressed her open hand against my dress to show off her nails that were painted a very similar shade.

"Looks like you're going to have a wonderful evening," Agatha said. "I'm glad Miss Hillary will have a friend here tonight." With a wave at another familiar face, Agatha bid me farewell and continued her mingling.

"How do you know her?" Hillary asked with round eyes.

"She's my dad's boss. I've known her a long time."

"Your dad has a job, too? He isn't a grandpa?" Hillary tugged at my hand to get us moving, and I followed along easily.

I assumed that to Hillary the word grandpa was synonymous with retired. "He has a job, yes. He teaches at the college, and he's not a grandpa yet."

" 'Cause you don't have kids."

"That's right."

"Do you have a brother or sister?" she asked, weaving me dangerously close to people. She was used to her small body that could flit through tight spaces, which meant I was doing a lot of apologizing and dodging. "I hope you say no, 'cause brothers can be real dummies. But maybe a sister would be okay."

"I'm an only child."

I was grateful to see a waiter passing, and I put my drink on his tray. It wasn't safe to carry it, and I'd had enough sips of the tart liquid to satisfy me.

She stopped our progress to scrunch her nose and look up at me, blonde hair bobbing in pigtails. "I think that's lucky."

I'd never felt that way myself at her age. Being an only child had made me an odd-man-out among my peers in this small, conservative town where families were large more often than not. I'd always begged for a sibling, wanting to share in what appeared to be the magic of family life. However, as a teen I'd come to understand that it hadn't been in the cards for my parents, and I was okay with it. My friends had become like sisters, and that was enough.

"Maybe sometimes it's lucky," I replied. "But it can be kind of lonely, too."

Her entire expression said she didn't believe me, and I was still smiling when she hauled me to a stop in front of her father. His back was to us, and I only had a split second to smooth my hair and dress and collect my expression before she tapped him on the back and he turned around.

He was dressed in a navy suit that made his eyes pull bluer as his dark blond hair caught the lights from above. Planted on his head was a traditional paper party hat, the bright reds and yellows contrasting against his tailored, polished look. He didn't seem self-conscious about it at all. His face was relaxed, and part of me wanted to lean in and see if he smelled as good as I'd dreamed he did. That same spark I'd experienced the other night was back, but I had learned the hard way not to trust it, so I held myself straight.

"Doesn't Miss Thomas look super pretty?" Hillary gushed to her dad.

He dipped his head in a greeting nod making the pointy part of the hat aim in my direction. "She does. I'm glad you could make it," he said to me. Unless I was reading him wrong, his tone said he meant it.

"Thank you for having me," I responded graciously, remembering that Meredith had instructed me to make him drool. Sadly, the only one in danger of drooling was me.

"Did you know Miss Thomas knows Agatha? They're friends, Daddy, just like I'm friends with both of them. And did you know that Miss Thomas's first name is

Hailey? It starts with an H just like me and Henry. Mommy's name started with an H, too."

A sinking sensation planted itself with needle-like talons in my chest as Hilary continued to prattle on about how wonderful I was and what things her dad should like about me. Heat blossomed across my chest, a sure sign it would move up to my face, as I dared a glance at her father who was listening with an interested expression and steely eyes. He may have had a point about Hillary plotting something. He could have been kinder about cluing me in to what was happening, but I was beginning to doubt that it had anything to do with me as a person. He simply didn't want any part of the game Hillary was playing.

"Yes, Miss Thomas is a good friend," he said kindly to his daughter, even though to my adult ears, it sounded strained.

"I didn't know your mom's name started with an H, too," I added as my mind spun. It wasn't exactly true that I didn't know, but I looked to Mr. Whittaker who met my eyes over his daughter's head. I read the 'I told you so' loud and clear. I managed not to make a face, but it wasn't easy.

"It did. Poor Daddy was the only one without an H name, but Henry told me that Mommy said it was fair because we all had his last name." Hillary smiled and grabbed my hand again. "We should go meet Grams now. I told her about you."

"Happy birthday," I said to her father as she yanked me away once more. If he responded I didn't hear it.

My thoughts couldn't keep up with my feet as Hillary zig-zagged me around the room and through another doorway into what must be the family space. I'd seen something about Hillary's mom during my research. (Okay that thing was her obituary.) But I hadn't really made the connection that her and her children all had H names. Mentioning her had stolen some of the color from Ford's face, and while I knew I had no right to feel protective, I didn't like my name being associated with painful memories for him.

And wait . . . wasn't the plan for Grams to be in bed by now? I wasn't opposed to meeting her but had thought I was the post-Grams backup buddy.

The room we entered next was all warm browns and tans with plush carpet and family snapshots placed on every surface. It looked lived in and comfortable, a stark contrast to everything else I'd seen so far. On one of the overstuffed chairs sat a thin woman with gray hair. Henry was sitting near her feet, and they were looking through what appeared to be a photo album on her lap.

"Grams!" Hillary yelled, her voice reverberating in the much smaller space. "She came." I was going to need shoulder surgery after this night, I thought to myself with a chuckle as she yanked once again to get me moving. "Do you see her sparkles? She's so glittery."

"I do see, dear." The older woman's voice was rough, like her breath couldn't support her words.

She made to stand, and I held up a hand. "Please don't stand for me," I said. "You must be Grams?"

Her smile was very much like Hillary's, and I immediately felt welcome in her presence, an unexpected boon. "I'm Marlene Whittaker, Ford's mother."

"Hailey Thomas, Hillary's former teacher," I greeted.

"And friend," Hillary added.

"Yes and friend." I let go of her small hand to shake Mrs. Whittaker's.

"Well, friend, come sit down. We're looking through Ford's childhood photos, and then we're planning to sneak an entire cake off to have for ourselves."

Hillary and Henry giggled at the pronouncement, and I joined in, picturing them finding a way to hide a cake as they ran for it.

"I like that plan," I said.

"Grams has the best plans. They're always fun, and we almost never get in trouble for them," Henry pronounced, looking back down at the photo book.

I didn't know Henry well, but from what I did know, he was quiet and studious, a definite contrast to his bubbly sister.

"Those are the best kind of plans." I sat on a nearby couch and watched the three heads lean together as grandmother told grandchildren about each photo.

Marlene Whittaker, from what I could tell, was soft-spoken and content to spend time with her two grandchildren in a side room rather than participate in the large event. In fact, I got the feeling that she was a bit of a sideline hugger like myself. I watched as the two children leaned closer, pressing their little sides against her legs and reaching out to place a hand on one of her arms as she spoke. It was obvious that she gave them all the love a grandmother could give. Along with being an only child, I'd had no living grandparents by the time I was five years old. Life had taken my grandparents from me before I'd truly been able to appreciate those precious relationships.

"Well, I'm afraid we've bored poor Hailey to death," Mrs. Whittaker announced, slapping the book shut and catching both Hillary and Henry's hands with it. They squealed and she joined in, a boisterous sound that did not match the breathiness of her speaking voice. "Are you ready to steal some cake?" she asked me.

I licked my lips and wiggled my eyebrows, purposely reacting how children would hope an adult would. "I've been waiting all night, Mrs. Whittaker," I replied, lightly clapping my hands together.

"Oh, no, no, no. Marlene will do fine. Any friend of Hillary's is a friend of mine." Marlene stood, placing the photo album on an end table and shuffling toward the opposite end of the room. "Come along my little thieves." Two giggling and whispering children fell into line behind her, and I followed suit.

Marlene was in stocking feet, wearing comfortable flowing pants and a t-shirt that said 'I'm That Grandma' in boxy lettering. She'd definitely stand out, big time, among the well-dressed crowd in the other room. I was guessing she didn't care one bit. She led the way through a door into a huge open kitchen, all done in the same whites as the rest of the house. It was gorgeous. I couldn't help but imagine how lovely it would be to cook in that masterpiece.

Right now, it was completely filled with servers in the same black and white outfit I'd seen bustling around in other parts of the house.

"Ma'am, where's the cake?" Marlene walked directly up to a woman wearing a black suit and headset, marking her as the event coordinator.

She bobbed her head to the left and gave Marlene a wink, letting me know the staff was in on it. "In the butler's pantry."

"Excellent," Marlene replied. "Very smart of you to give us what we're after rather than fighting a battle you would have lost." Hillary laughed behind her hand, and Henry's little eyes glowed in awe of his grandmother. The coordinator bowed her head gracefully, playing along with Marlene who grabbed one leg of her flowing pants and swept it to the side as though she were wearing a ball gown. "Onward, my dears. The treasure awaits."

The two children bounded ahead of us, aiming for a small doorway that I assumed led to the butler's pantry and the cake treasure trove. Their nearly identical blond heads disappeared from sight, and I followed along, eager to see what would happen next.

"I bribed the coordinator, of course," Marlene said to me over her shoulder. "I insisted that Ford's assistant order a variety of smaller cakes and then informed her we'd be commandeering one for ourselves. It's up to those darling cherubs to choose the flavor, but the coordinator will be glad she cooperated." I had a feeling the event coordinator would be flush with some extra cash that night, but Marlene surprised me by adding. "I'll be crocheting her an afghan starting tomorrow. She'll never be cold again."

I had to bite my tongue to keep from expressing my surprise. "I applaud your bartering skills," I said as we entered the butler's pantry to find Hillary and Henry looking closely at a selection of no less than twenty small cakes.

"You don't get to be my age without having a few tricks up your wrinkled old sleeves," Marlene grinned. I returned the grin without any hesitation. "So," she turned to her grandchildren, "what flavor stomachaches will we have tonight?"

"I was so full after the German chocolate last year," Henry moaned, patting his belly. "I promised I'd never eat that one again."

"Strawberries and cream looks yummy," Hillary stated, pointing to a pink and white creation that really did look yummy.

"Any arguments from the committee of robbers?" Marlene asked me and Henry. We both shook our heads, and she plucked the strawberries and cream cake off its stand. "Henry, dear, hide that cake stand somewhere so nobody notices we're down a cake."

Henry grabbed the stand and stashed it in the first cupboard he opened. He then stood and scrunched up his face in a move very similar to one I'd seen from his sister. "Where should we eat it this time? It has to be somewhere Dad won't think to look."

"Do you have a treehouse?" I asked.

Three sets of gray-blue eyes swung my way. I now understood where all those eyes had come from, because Marlene was squinting hers at me right now. "Terrific idea. Although, Hailey, I'm afraid you aren't dressed for tree-housing today."

I glanced down at my forgotten sequin dress and heels that were meant to slay hearts, not to climb rope ladders. "Sad, but true."

"What about the garage?" Henry suggested. "No one would think we'd be in there."

"A garage is a weird place to eat cake," Hillary giggled.

Marlene nodded. "True. Hillary, grab some forks and let's get moving."

Hillary skidded her way back into the kitchen, a blur of hot pink and flying hair, and was back before I could worry too much about sitting on a garage floor in my best clothes. I followed the jolly troop down a few different sets of stairs and finally entered a six-car garage that made mine seem like the size of an outhouse.

"Wow," I said, in awe over the reality of seeing what I'd only imagined existed.

I'd figured Ford would have a nice car, definitely nicer than my older, used model. In fact, it pained me to remember the zippy red convertible I'd imagined and how Fake Ford liked to go for rides up Logan Canyon to see the fall leaves. However, even I hadn't touched what was actually housed in that garage.

Marlene shot me a glance. "The boy was raised shopping sales and eating off the dollar menu at McDonald's."

Okay. It didn't change much in my mind, but I understood parents well enough after years of teaching to know that they cared about how the world thought of their children. I offered her a smile in return and then continued happily trailing behind her and the pink cake. We eventually found a blanket on a shelf with some camping gear and spread it out on the floor near the trunk of a sports car. Hillary passed out forks and Marlene put the cake down in the center of our little circle.

Marlene held up her fork and called, "To Ford. Happy fortieth birthday, Son."

"To Daddy," Henry and Hillary joined.

"To Mr. Whittaker," I added my fork to the cheer.

Marlene threw me a side glance. "Always call him Ford. He doesn't need you puffing him up by being formal. He's a regular man."

"Grams says he has to brush his own teeth just like everyone else," Hillary added helpfully.

I couldn't imagine telling Marlene that in my head, Ford was not a regular man. He'd grown out of proportion, and I was working hard to put him back in his proper place. I'd call him Ford in front of her, but I'd be keeping that professional boundary wall when I was around him, which I did not see happening very often.

"Interesting name, Ford," I said as I watched the two children dig in.

"It's short for Fordham. My husband was Fordham the second, my son is Fordham the third. We call him Ford to not get confused. Such a fancy name for plain folks like us. My other two boys are Joe and Rick, which are easy, simple names."

Marlene dug in, too, and I wanted to ask her what, exactly, she found plain about eating cake next to a Corvette in the garage of a mansion. She may have felt plain herself, but Fordham was the perfect name for her son.

Time flew by as I listened to Marlene and the kids chat while shoveling forkfuls of cake into their smiling mouths. I joined in a little but ate lightly and tried not to feel like I was intruding on a special tradition these three had. I laid my fork down on the blanket when I saw Hillary yawn for the second time and put my hand on her little shoulder.

"I'm so sorry, Hillary, but I'm getting sleepy. I think it's time for me to head home."

Hillary stood when I did and grabbed me around the waist, smearing frosting from her cheek across my stomach. I glanced down and had the strangest sensation roll over me. As a school teacher, I was used to spills on my clothing, but there was something oddly special about this particular smear. It was a love smear, and I found that I didn't care about my dress or keeping it clean.

"I really like that you came and played," Hillary said, her cheek still pressed against me.

I patted her back. "Me, too. You have such a cool Grams and such a fun brother. You're lucky." She stepped back, and I smiled at Henry and Marlene. "I think stealing birthday cake is my new favorite activity."

They all nodded as Marlene said, "Come see us again, anytime."

It was offered in kindness, because we both knew she didn't live in this city, and I was only here for the night. But it was still nice to hear.

With a few directions and only three times getting turned around, I was able to find my way back to the large room where the party was still going strong. The guests had ballooned to even greater numbers in the hour I'd been gone with Hillary. They were now eating pieces of cake, and the decibel level had climbed as the party grew in festive spirit. I was anxious to get home to my own place and away from the crowd. It was jarring after the quiet evening I'd shared in a garage--not to mention the quiet evenings I typically spent alone in my home.

As I made my way through the room toward the entryway where I would reclaim my shawl, I caught sight of Mr. Whittaker. He was at the center of a big group, smiling and laughing, a natural extrovert, still wearing that silly hat. It was more proof that he was nothing like the man I'd imagined.

Fake Ford had been peaceful and introverted, like me. Together we'd been content to spend quiet nights at home and keep a small group of friends. We'd talk about books or classic movies, maybe plan a European vacation or a historic tour back East. Fake Ford always waved away my offers to help pay, saying he could cover it, that I should save my pennies for myself. Fake Ford . . .

Real Ford's laughter rang above the voices, jolting me out of my thoughts right as I was getting warmed up. I couldn't hear the words he was saying, but I did understand that he was thriving in the spotlight, and I reaffirmed my plan to let go of all of it. It was messed up and wrong and definitely had the power to hurt people if it got out.

I made my way through the crowded room, occasionally stopping to say hello to an acquaintance but not staying long. I was ready to go home and put this strange series of events behind me. I was standing in the large circular foyer, waiting for my shawl, when Mr. Whittaker's voice spoke from behind me. I recognized it immediately and turned to face him.

It was completely surreal, standing here in his foyer while he stood in front of me, holding a small plate of chocolate cake. My eyes followed the movement as his mouth formed a small smile.

"I'm guessing this year it was strawberries and cream that they stole?" He sighed, but there was no real anger in it. "They have a real knack for taking the one I specifically requested for myself."

I swallowed back the butterflies that tried to rise. I was actually alone with him. "I'm sorry to report that it was delicious."

"Think they'll save me any?"

I shook my head. "I think they'll throw away the evidence."

"It looks like there's some evidence on your dress, there."

He handed me a napkin, and I lightly dabbed at the frosting. "The danger of goodbye hugs," I chuckled softly, marveling at the thought that I was actually talking to him. Him!

"Is that Hailey Thomas I see?" A booming man's voice startled me, and I looked to the left to see the very familiar form of Leonard Cox joining us in the empty room. With his height and girth added to his gregarious personality, Leonard always filled up any space he was in, and I could still hear the greeting echoing off the high ceiling. "You're outshining everyone tonight in that dress." He held out his arms and pulled me into a hug while I watched Ford's eyes dart back and forth between us. "Ford, why didn't you tell me you knew Hailey?"

Ford took note that I was hugging Leonard in return, and his expression became something like calculated interest. "We haven't known each other long," he responded.

I squeezed the large man who was practically an uncle to me. "Leonard, you can't expect him to list everyone he knows in the hopes that you'll stumble across a mutual acquaintance," I teased.

Leonard released me with a snicker. "You have a winning argument every time." He looked past me to Ford. "Well, you couldn't have picked a better girl to hitch up to than this one," he grinned.

Hitch up to? Oh, no. Nope. Had he seen something on my face? Leonard was always one to jump to conclusions, but in this instance, he couldn't possibly know how dangerous that comment was.

I nervously giggled. "Actually, we're . . ."

He threw up his hands. "Say no more, kiddo. He's been grieving for his wife a long time, and if he isn't ready to tell people he's found someone to move forward with, well, I'm happy to keep that secret. But I have to say, those two angel kids of his are sure lucky to have you around." My throat froze, and so did Ford's entire body. Head to toe, frozen in place. It was a stark contrast to the man I'd seen holding court a moment ago. Leonard laughed. "I can see I've shocked you, Ford, but don't worry. I've known Hailey here since she was in diapers. Our families are the best of friends. We've had Sunday dinner together twice a month for nearly thirty years now, not to mention vacations and get-togethers. I can vouch for her."

Ford seemed at a loss for words, and I had the impression that didn't happen often.

I jumped in. "Leonard, you have the wrong idea here," I said, embarrassment for both Ford and myself making my shoulders tighten. No woman wants to have her name and the word diapers said in the same sentence. "Mr. Whittaker and I are, well, I teach his daughter . . . actually I taught her last year, and . . ."

Once again, Leonard, true to his style, interrupted. "Worried about getting in trouble with the school for fraternizing with a student's parent? I hear you."

"No, that's not a rule in our district, but . . ."

He threw up his hands, palms out. "Okay, Hailey, I'm backing off. Last thing I'm going to say is how excited I'll be to see you at our business partner dinner next weekend. I'm going to keep it a surprise for Connie." I had no idea what he was talking about and looked helplessly at Ford, expecting him to dive in anytime here. My attention on Ford drew Leonard's back as well. "Ford, don't tell me you didn't invite your new lady to the most important meeting you might ever have?"

Ford shook his head and smoothed his expression into one of practiced ease as he held out his free hand. "There's been a misunderstanding. Miss Thomas is simply a friend of Hillary's."

Leonard looked back and forth between us, analyzing. I could see the cogs in his brain working behind dark brown eyes and thinning eyebrows. My hands gripped together, knowing the stubborn look he was getting on his face. Leonard Cox was a good man but a bulldog who dug in when he felt it was necessary. Apparently, right now, it was necessary.

"Ford, I don't take to rich men who toy around with women." Leonard's jaw set mulishly.

"I would never insult Miss Thomas," Ford said calmly. "We aren't actually a couple. We met two days ago at Hillary's school fundraiser night." He laughed easily and I appreciated him defusing the situation with his natural charm.

Leonard pierced me with a look. "Is that true?"

"Yes," I replied, my shoulders relaxing. Another nervous giggle tried to work its way out. I'd always had a terrible habit of giggling when under pressure, and I hated how juvenile it could make me look. "And can I add that it's not 1850? You don't need to go around bullying men into treating me right." I meant the words seriously, but I loved him enough to also understand his intention behind it, so my lips lifted into a half smile.

"Hailey, say what you will, but I'll never stop making sure you're treated right." Satisfied, Leonard nodded once. "Besides, I have a good feeling about the two of you."

And that, according to Leonard Cox, was that.

Flustered and ridiculously uncomfortable, I turned to face Ford as Leonard walked away. "That was interesting."

"So, you know Leonard?"

"I do."

Ford nodded thoughtfully. His eyes focused on mine for the first time since I'd come up from the garage. Yes, he'd looked at me, but this was more. This was him trying to see inside of me. Those gray-blue eyes could make a brick give up its secrets . . .especially if that brick wanted nothing more than to snuggle in and spill her guts.

"Are you trying to decide if there's some kind of risk in him thinking we're dating material?" I dared to ask.

"Something like that."

I painted on my most practiced smile, honed over years of social functions with my parents. "For the record, I'm not looking to get set up on a date by your business partner."

A smirk bloomed at the reminder of words he'd slung my way a few days before. He raised the plate of cake he was still carrying as though making a toast.

"Please, call me Ford."

CHAPTER THREE

The soft leather soles of Meredith's slides scuffed across the carpet of my classroom as she paced back and forth in front of the small desks. She tucked her hands in her pockets, and then pulled them out to cross her arms before once again jamming them into her pockets. It would be a miracle if her black slacks didn't have holes in place of pockets by the time she was done.

"Maybe you should sit down," Lizzie said kindly from her perch on top of one of the desks where her short legs swung back and forth, not quite meeting the floor.

I nodded from my own desktop. "Lizzie's right."

"I don't know, I find it kind of soothing to watch her," Aryn observed. She was sitting down in one of the desks with her head propped sideways on her hand, making her long red hair brush the smooth desktop and waterfall over the side.

Ruby patted the desk near her, and Meredith sat on top of it with a huff. "I'm sitting . . . I'm sitting," she muttered, holding her hands up, palms out to ward off any more suggestions from us as her blue eyes flashed annoyance.

Meredith operated on a level of intensity that would exhaust any other person, but we all knew she loved us with that same fierceness, and it softened her in our eyes.

My friends had all been anxiously waiting for my post-party report, and as soon as the bell rang that afternoon, they'd all come straight to my classroom. The clicking of the large wall clock had been the only accompaniment to my story, and as I'd told them about Leonard's suggestion that Ford and I should be dating, Meredith had started pacing. Actually, plotting was probably a better description. Pace-plotting was a specialty of hers.

My weekends were usually a time of rejuvenation for me, but this past one had been shot as I'd vacillated about what to do. I'd gotten over the initial shock of meeting the literal man of my dreams and started to do a teensy, tiny bit of overanalyzing the possibilities. On the one hand, I wanted to spend more time with Ford, because what woman, when faced with the object of her most secret desires, is going to turn that down? All it would take is one phone call to Leonard and I could be having a romantic dinner with Real Ford. On the other hand, he'd made it quite clear that he wasn't interested in getting to know me, or any other woman, any better.

Rationally, I also understood that it wouldn't be healthy of me to spend time around him until I wrenched my make-believe life out of my heart and faced the facts. I may have pretended to know him, but the truth was that he was a stranger. Fake Ford would have ordered the lobster, but Real Ford might be allergic to shellfish.

In the short month I'd taught Hillary, I'd never had the chance to meet him, and the interviews of his I'd read were professional and high level, nothing personal that could actually give me a feel for who he was. This was a confusing and irritating predicament. The worst part was that I'd done it to myself by having internet stalked him in the first place. I'd given up my principles, and now I was going through the five stages of grief over a man who did not exist.

And it had gotten worse, oh so much worse. I still hadn't told my friends everything.

"So you went to Whittaker's birthday party," Meredith stated, raising one perfectly shaped, jet black brow.

I nodded, familiar with her habit of rehashing something until she fully understood it.

"It was really smart of you to wear that fantastic sequin wrap dress. I hope it had him immediately groveling at your feet," Ruby added.

After being badgered for an hour, I'd sent them a picture of me in the dress before leaving home. That had kicked off a text string that had kept going until I'd arrived at Ford's front door. There had been a lot of 'you've got this' from everyone but Meredith, who had sent me 'kill the beast' pictures, featuring cartoon characters. I'd laughed when I'd seen his castle-like home and sent a quick picture of it to the group. That tidbit had only encouraged Meredith

"There was no groveling," I responded.

"Well, there's no way he didn't notice your lady curves," Ruby pinched her lips. "He's not blind."

I shrugged, entertained by her irritation. "There was no conversation about any curves."

"Tell me again exactly what he said to you," Meredith chewed on her lip.

"He agreed with Hillary when she said I looked pretty and told me he was glad I could make it. Then he asked which flavor of cake we'd stolen. That was all before Leonard arrived."

"I'm such a fan of his mom," Aryn said with a smirk. "Stealing a birthday cake like that deserves my admiration."

"Cake, schmake. All he said was nothing. It was polite mumbo jumbo," Ruby moaned. "Where was the jaw hitting the floor? Where was him begging you for forgiveness and showering you with apology jewels? Where was the grabbing you and pulling you against his heaving chest while gazing into your eyes?"

"If he'd done that, she'd have had to punch him," Meredith replied.

"And then call 9-1-1," I added. "No chests should be heaving." Ruby pulled a face and I grinned. "He didn't need to apologize. He'd been right about Hillary's hopes."

"Well, even if what he said was true, he didn't have to be so rude about it." Lizzie's soft, easy voice entered the discussion. "He could have simply laughed and said, 'I think my kid wants us to date.' Why he even brought up marriage or accused you of being a schemer is beyond me."

Lizzie wasn't wrong, and my face threatened to warm again as I remembered those humiliating moments in the school cafeteria only last week. He definitely hadn't needed to go for the throat the way he had.

Meredith slapped her palms against her knees. "So the plan was a failure."

I shook my head, my mouth softening into a smile. "Not necessarily. I had a good time with Hillary and made her happy, which was the true plan all along," I reminded her.

"Hillary's so cute," Aryn inserted.

My toes wiggled in my shoes as I opened my mouth. "The thing is, there's more."

"More?" Meredith's eyes zeroed in.

I pursed my lips and tugged at the gold bracelet on my wrist. "Yeah, this has become like a boulder rolling down a mountain and collecting debris as it goes."

"What else happened? You did set Leonard straight, right?" Lizzie asked.

"Yes, but Leonard struck again at family dinner yesterday. He announced to my parents that I had met someone." I could still feel the horrified sting at his words, and I lightly gripped my hands together in my lap, staring down at my feet. "I stopped him on the way in and did my best to set the story straight one more time, but then he blabbed anyway. I was going to tell my parents the truth, but when I looked over at them, their faces were beaming with joy. Their baby had found someone. They hadn't wanted to pressure me, but they'd started to worry a little, and this was wonderful news. I was sunk."

I gazed around at those four familiar faces, expecting to see shock or sympathy or something that mirrored my own confusion and feeling of being trapped. Instead, I was met with bright, amused expressions and some soft chuckles, which I did not appreciate.

"This is a smirk-free zone," I stated. "What am I supposed to do? My parents are involved now." I pinched my lips. "They think I'm sort of dating Ford. I called you here to help me make an escape plan."

"You call him Ford?" Meredith asked in an innocent tone that was exceptionally fake. "I thought you were maintaining a proper distance."

"He told me to call him Ford after Leonard basically threatened him," I stated. "Plus, it's easier."

Double plus, I really liked his name and the way it sounded in my head. Fordham Whittaker. Sa-woon. Fordham and Hailey Whittaker. Ooh, boy, I needed to erase that thought.

Aryn nodded. "Makes sense. As co-victims of Leonard's giant assumptions, you should be on a first name basis."

"Seriously, what do I do?" I looked to Lizzie and Aryn, the only two that weren't either plotting a romance or a murder.

Neither of them had a chance to say anything before Ruby asked, "Didn't you say there was a fancy business dinner coming up?" I nodded. "I say you get yourself invited and then stage a breakup in front of Leonard."

No, nope, never. Ruby, an extrovert to the core, would think nothing of staging something. I, princess of the introverts, would rather fake my own death . . . and even that would be done quietly and without fanfare.

"I'm open to other ideas?" I looked to Lizzie once more.

"Just tell your parents what's going on," Lizzie replied in a completely logical tone. "They know Leonard well enough to be understanding about it."

I nodded. That much was true. Leonard was well known for plowing over people. Then I pictured their faces. Mom's so hopeful, Dad's so pleased and patient. "Yes, they would understand," I began. "But . . . would they really? They'd never told me they were worried about me finding a partner in life. I had no idea."

"That's a rough way to find out," Ruby agreed. "One time at a family reunion, I overheard my dad telling my uncle that he'd always wished I could shoot a gun. I felt so guilty."

We all blinked at Ruby for a moment before Meredith stated, "Rubes, this is hardly the same thing."

Ruby shrugged. "You don't understand my dad and guns."

"Hailey," Aryn drew us all back to my problem, "your parents are the evolved parents. They're really great at open and honest communication. If you don't want to let people assume you're together, talk to them about it. Maybe you could all sit down with Leonard and explain how unfair it is to both you and Ford."

Aryn had a point. My mom was a practicing psychiatrist, and Dad was a professor of psychology at the local university. I'd been raised in a home of open communication and ongoing efforts at improvement. Thankfully it had been done in a way that kept my family close, but we also functioned very differently than normal families. It had sometimes made me into an outsider, the girl on the playground always asking others 'how did that make you feel?' or 'have you tried some breathing exercises?' It wasn't until high school that I'd learned to blend in and shut off what other kids called the 'psycho babble.' I hated that phrase and found it very offensive, but I understood well that I couldn't control anyone but myself.

Still, there was one problem I was having a hard time overcoming. "Okay, I'm going to be really honest here," I said. They all sat up a little straighter and leaned in. It was highly unusual for us to be analyzing me. I knew they saw me as calm and cool, always supportive but rarely spilling my guts. They were delighted with the way I was opening up. "The thing is that because my parents are who they are, I didn't go through the parental disappointment thing like everyone else. They understood every phase of my mental and physical development and encouraged me at every turn. Our family dinners held discussions of healthy thought behavior. Emotions were worked through. When I felt grumpy, they accepted that. When I was nasty, they held firm but patient boundaries and never engaged with me. It was a very peaceful environment. So, this is kind of the first time I've ever heard them say they were worried. It's the equivalent of most parents saying, 'You've really let me down, and I cry myself to sleep every night over you.'" I sighed and deflated. "I'm not processing that feeling very well."

Ruby was sitting closest to me, and she reached out a hand to squeeze my shoulder. "You're not a disappointment at all."

"Thanks," I said, knowing in my mind she was right but fighting off the emotions.

"Man, that's rough," Meredith added. "My dad did not understand any of my phases, but I still wanted to please him."

"Okay." Lizzie hopped off her desk and said her two favorite words. "Let's brainstorm." She grabbed a white board marker and marched to the front of the room. "Pros and cons to the one big question. Does she go on a date with Ford or fess up to her parents? That decision will be the basis for everything else moving forward."

"How do you mean?" Ruby asked.

"I mean if she decides to play Leonard's matchmaking game, then she has to call him and listen to him gloat about it. If she doesn't want to date Ford, she has to call her parents and Leonard and get them to back off." Lizzie popped off the cap and pivoted, making her riotous curls swirl around her head. "Either way, she's facing down Leonard and possibly casting her comfort zone into the river."

"I'm not afraid of Leonard," I muttered. "Ford and my parents are the real issue."

"At the risk of stealing your joy, Lizzie, I'm not sure we need a full brainstorm over this. Hailey just has to make a choice," Aryn spoke up.

Lizzie looked over her shoulder and pulled a fake pouty face before turning back to the board and writing the words pro and con anyway.

A second wave of silence filtered through the room, and I realized Aryn was right. I had to be the one to answer that. "I'm probably overthinking it, yes. But it doesn't feel like a simple phone call, because now my parents' hopes and dreams are involved. Maybe. I don't know." I put my face in my hands, took a breath, and then dropped my hands back to my lap. I didn't dare mention that the idea of dining with Ford was straight out of my Fake Ford playbook. They had no idea he existed. "Is this what spiraling feels like?"

"This decision is harder because he's hot." Meredith stated with another smirk.

"No, the decision is harder because he doesn't want to date anyone," I replied, but they ignored me.

"He really is," Lizzie surprised me by giggling as she turned back to face the group. "I looked him up online."

"I saw him in person. His pictures online don't do him justice." Meredith said. "The man's a fox."

"Wait, I want to see him," Ruby pulled her phone out of her back pocket. "Where did you look him up?"

"Here," Lizzie walked over, her hand out for the phone. "I'll show you."

"You guys!" I cried. A scuffing sound announced that Aryn had scooted her desk over to see too. This was ridiculous. "His looks have nothing to do with this. I'm not that shallow."

Or maybe I was that shallow. If his looks hadn't captured me in those first online photos, would I have kept hunting down pictures and information about him and then formed this entire fantasy world with him as the star?

Oh boy. I was a disaster. My parents would have a heyday analyzing this traitorous part of my mind. Would I be eighty and still giggling over images of the cute guy at the bingo table, never having a fully matured brain?

"Oh," Ruby breathed when Lizzie handed her phone back. "Goodness."

Aryn leaned in, and her eyes grew large before she looked directly at me. "You should have him for dinner . . . and dessert."

That cracked everyone up, and even I had to let a giggle bubble up as they passed his picture around and compared him to a hot blond brownie with ice cream and caramel syrup on top.

"And hold the knife, waiter," Ruby hooted, "because that jawline can cut anything."

I playfully rolled my eyes even though my worries were lifting with their banter. "You guys are terrible, and we are too old for this."

"What, we don't have eyeballs?" Meredith stated. "We can't appreciate fine works of art?"

"Or hormones?" Ruby cracked. "We are women in our prime, and our biology will always encourage us to seek out the best specimen so we can . . . you know . . . propagate the species."

The amount of whistling and ogling that went on after that threw me back to high school and listening to other girls gush over boy bands and celebrities. I'd never understood the boy-crazy mentality; the girls who cried at concerts and wore t-shirts with handsome faces on them where alien to me. But I could understand the draw to a man who made your heart pound a little too hard.

Lizzie's hand landed lightly on my back as she whispered. "They were merciless when it was me and Jackson."

I had a flashback of sitting on our sleeping bags as darkness fell and razzing Lizzie about getting the nerve to kiss her man. The memory made me grin. "True. The only difference is you wanted Jackson and he wanted you, and it was an amazing fairy-tale adventure."

Lizzie shrugged. "So, like Meredith said, consider this Beauty and the Beast. You being Beauty, obviously. Save the beast instead of slaying him. Go live in his castle."

"She can slay his cold heart with her love," Ruby, having overheard, wiggled her eyebrows.

I bit my lip. "He's not a beast, exactly."

"Oh, I'll bet he's a beast when those gray eyes are focused on you . . ." Ruby puckered up her lips and dropped her tone, ". . .it's magic."

"This has completely gone off the rails," I sighed, although I was fighting a smile. I loved them so much for lightening the mood and reminding me that this situation wasn't nearly as life or death as I was making it out to be.

"Listen," Aryn said into the laughter, "From where I'm sitting there is no choice to be made. Hailey, you jump aboard this rollercoaster and enjoy the ride."

I turned to them and pulled a face. "People die on rollercoasters, you know."

Aryn made a kissy face. "But what a way to go."

Meredith waved her hands and forced the amusement off her face. "Okay, okay. Ford is good looking but looks aren't everything."

"Or even worth mentioning," I muttered. Hypocrite.

Meredith cocked her head. "Mmm . . . agree to disagree. His are mentionable. But, yeah, looks aren't everything."

"Thank you," I gestured to Meredith and gave the others a nod.

"Hey, Mer is the one who started this whole thing by saying how hot he is. In the interest of science, we had to test her hypothesis." Ruby defended. "Thornback women don't take people's word for it. They investigate."

That got us all laughing again, and it was another few seconds of talking about what pretty babies me and Ford would have, which had me blushing against my will because it was like they were reading a page out of my hallucination diary.

My heart sank, though, as I realized I simply could not go through with asking Leonard for the set up. Lying to my parents was worse than hurting their feelings with facts, and the truth does always have a way of sneaking out between the cracks of a lie. Plus, I was raised better than that. I'd been honest with them my entire life, so it seemed a little strange to suddenly go through a lying phase as an adult.

Even more importantly, Ford didn't want it. And no matter how I felt, I'd never force myself on a single, widowed man who had explicitly said no. And what about Hillary?

"I can't do it," I said, folding my arms. "It's not fair to anyone involved. He may be handsome and rich, but it's not enough reason to hurt people."

My friends, understanding that the conversation was basically over, graciously accepted my decision and filed out as they moved on to other topics. I stared after them, wishing helplessly that my heart didn't yearn so much for a shot with Ford, a real shot . . .

CHAPTER FOUR

Sweat dripped into my eyes before I had a chance to wipe it with my towel, and the burn made me hiss. Meredith had convinced me to attend her workout class after school, and my poor body was used to the calming practice of yoga, not pumping the pedals of a bicycle like my very life depended on it. About fifteen minutes in, my rear end had begged for relief, and sweat began pouring from places I didn't realize sweat could come from. Meredith, however, looked like she'd just returned from a battle where she'd pillaged and then convinced her victims to make her the new queen. She was glowing, her eyes bright, a big smile on her face. Spin class royalty.

"There's no other feeling on earth that comes close to this," she said, glancing at me in the locker room mirror we were both standing in front of.

Her hair was slicked back, which, being short, required copious amounts of bobby pins and a sweatband. Her blue eyes matched her exercise outfit perfectly. My pink exercise clothes also matched me, but it was the flushed cheeks and chest that really completed the whole 'I'm a strawberry' look. She was right. This was a special feeling. But there were a host of other feelings I'd enjoy more. At this moment those feelings would be more along the lines of falling back into pillows or dipping my face in ice water.

"Why isn't your face the color of a tomato?" I huffed.

She shrugged lightly as she pulled the sweatband from her forehead. "I was born for this."

"Born for spin class? Like, the heavens saved you for this very time in the history of the world so that you could rock the bike?" I teased.

She laughed and whipped the sweatband at my shoulder. "I'm going to take a shower. Are you heading home?"

"Yeah." I had zero desire to shower and get ready at the gym. I preferred my own bathroom and didn't enjoy hauling my products everywhere. "I want to soak in a tub."

"Wimp," she teased as she turned toward the lockers.

"Sadist," I shot back.

I was still smiling, wiping my small hand towel across my forehead and down my face as I left the locker room at the far side of the building when I ran into someone. Strong, warm hands closed over my bare upper arms as I attempted to rear back. Those hands kept me from slamming into a concrete wall. The mystery hands released me once I had my bearings, and I looked up to see none other than Ford Whittaker hovering over me.

It took a minute for my surprised brain to accept what I was seeing. I'd run into him around town before, which made sense because it was a small town, but had never entered his personal space. To be clear, I didn't follow him anywhere. It was happenstance, and we were never within twenty feet of each other. I made sure of that, because every time I saw him, a flush came over my skin and my heartbeat quickened visibly--things I had no desire for him to see considering they'd be odd reactions out of someone who was supposed to be a stranger.

"I've never seen you here before," he said, as he released his hold on me.

I glanced around and then back at him. At least at the gym, the flushing and heartrate could be easily ignored. I'd seen him here before but played it off.

"I'm not usually in this section of the building."

His eyebrows raised in amusement. "You're not usually in the exercise section?"

I was so busy cataloging his sweat-damp hair and slightly flushed face to answer very quickly. His shirt didn't have sleeves, and his arms were all lean and long muscle, not big and bulky, but well defined. I could feel the warmth radiating off his body and smell the scent of his soap--or maybe it was his deodorant--which meant I was standing way, way, way too close. I side shuffled a bit, using my towel once more to wipe at my forehead. With my light coloring I could only imagine how incredibly attractive I looked at the moment. Actually, I didn't have to imagine because I'd seen it in the mirror two minutes ago. Strawberries and cream. Then I remember that had been the birthday cake he'd requested, and a new blush rose.

"I do yoga," I replied with glittering wit, tearing my mind away from all strawberry related thoughts.

"Ah, I see. Not much use for weights and treadmills then." He nodded as though I'd said something profound. "I don't do yoga." An odd little nerve-giggle escaped against my will as he asked, "What brings you to this, the dark side of the building, where everyone just grunts and sweats?"

"Spin class."

He pulled a face and gestured to my sweaty towel. "I'm guessing it wasn't your idea?"

My shoulders tightened causing my posture to abruptly become straight. I wasn't sure if that was an insult or commiseration. "Why do you ask?"

"Sweaty towel, red face, general look of having survived something."

My genius reply was to blink at him a few times before nodding. He smiled, and I decided I should shove off before I embarrassed us both by taking another whiff of that delicious scent.

"Well, I need to get these sweaty clothes off and take a bath," I said.

The words hadn't even finished leaving my mouth, and I already wanted to slap my palm against my forehead and commence digging a humiliation hidey-hold to crawl into. I couldn't have just said goodbye? Maybe thrown in a casual 'have a nice day'? No, I had to mention sweaty clothing and nudity.

He clicked his tongue, probably also baffled by my choice of words. "Okay."

I kept my lips firmly together to avoid saying something else incredibly wonderful.

"Ford!" A deep voice called from the side. "My man." It belonged to a muscle-bound guy I'd seen before. He maybe lived at the gym based on the way he looked.

I used the distraction to slip away and hurry toward the front doors to make my escape. Once I'd reached the door, I pushed it open and found my feet didn't want to move outside. After a very short inner battle, I allowed myself one last glance. Ford was still standing where we'd spoken, facing my direction and talking to the muscle mountain guy. Maybe he sensed me looking, I don't know, but he glanced up, and we locked eyes for a brief moment before I ducked out into the cool evening air with toes that wanted to curl inside my shoes.

*****

"Okay, so you told him you were taking a bath?" Aryn said, holding up one side of the bulletin board trim I was stapling up. "What did he say?"

I shook my head and slapped my palm against the open side of the stapler. Aryn had popped by my classroom looking for my opinion on a lesson plan but had found me fighting with a long border that would not be contained. She'd immediately set down her notebook and come to help, clearly understanding that most people don't tell paper borders what a letdown they are, so I must be having some feelings that needed discussing.

I shifted closer to her and lined up the blue paper. "He only said 'okay.' He was probably too embarrassed to say anything else. It's not really an appropriate topic of conversation for virtual strangers."

"Baths are inappropriate?"

"Maybe not baths," I glanced at her. "But talking about stripping off my sweaty clothes? It's private time, and you're . . ." I lowered my voice, ". . . naked."

She bit down on her lips before they could finish tugging up. "And you're worried that he was involuntarily picturing you stripping and bathing and was too embarrassed to continue the conversation."

I slapped the stapler and scooted again. "Yes. Or else he's wondering what type of exhibitionist goes around telling people about her bathing plans for the day."

At this she did laugh. "Hailey, trust me, you didn't say anything scandalous. Awkward, maybe, but not inappropriate. What would you have thought if he'd said, 'Well, I'm off to shed these sweaty clothes and hit the showers?'"

I tucked a piece of hair behind my ears and let out a breath. "Nothing, really. People get sweaty at the gym."

"So you're saying it wouldn't have automatically thrown your mind into the gutter?" she prodded.

I'd reached the end of the border and motioned for her to let go so I could staple it in place. "I don't usually struggle with my mind going there." Admittedly, it came off a little haughty, and I hurried to backpedal. "I just mean . . ."

She put a hand on my shoulder as she grinned. "I know you, Hailey. I know you're not the type to entertain those kinds of . . ."

"But I am," I interrupted, my face dropping into my hands. Unfortunately, one of those hands was still holding a stapler, which cracked against my forehead.

It was silent for a second before Aryn reached over and took the stapler from me. Then she took my arm and guided me over to my desk before plopping me into the desk chair. We looked at each other for a few moments. Aryn, with her long, curly red hair, hands propped on her lean hips, head tilted to the side while her green eyes tried to pry into my soul. I ran my sweaty palms over my slacks, grateful they were dark today, before tugging down the hem of my blouse and then smoothing my hair down.

"Okay," she said. "You've now completely adjusted both clothing and hair. Something's up." She grabbed one of the tiny chairs from a desk and carried it over to sit in front of me. Aryn was tall enough that even sitting on the little chair, we were practically eye to eye. "Tell me everything, from the start."

I shook my head and wiggled my toes around in my shoes. "The thing is, this is really private and incredibly embarrassing, so you can't tell anyone else." She nodded. "I've been . . . um . . . thinking about Ford a lot." Aryn's face remained passive, and her open, curious expression eased me into spilling it all. "After I looked him up a few months ago, I sort of didn't stop looking him up."

Aryn patted my knee. "Don't sweat it, in this digital age everyone internet stalks other people. What do you think the point of social media is?"

I managed to get one side of my mouth to lift but shook my head. "If I'd kept it to internet stalking, it would be understandable. The problem is that he started popping up in my dreams."

When I hesitated, she smiled. "Again, not strange. The other night I was reading about different types of mental health therapies because a student of mine is struggling. All night I dreamed I was in therapy sessions. I didn't sleep well at all."

I took a deep breath. "But then I sort of let it morph into daydreams, and I started pretending we were dating." My voice dropped off at the end until it was barely a whisper.

Aryn watched me in the stillness, processing and doing a fine job of keeping her face completely expressionless. I ducked my head, prepared for her to tell me I was being super strange. Instead, she surprised me with a giggle.

"I've so done that."

My head popped up, my hair tickling at my jawline. "What?"

She nodded. "Totally. Remember a few years ago when that really cute, funny guy substituted for Lizzie while she was sick with strep for a week?"

I thought back, coming up with a fuzzy image of a blond man with big teeth. "I think so."

"After he left he starred in some pretty great daydreams of mine. We went snorkeling and hiking and had lots of snuggle time on the couch."

A smile tugged at my lips. "Oh yeah?"

"Sure. The thing is, Hailey, we're allowed to daydream a little. It's not wrong. You're not in a relationship daydreaming about another man. He's not in a relationship. You're a single woman daydreaming about a single guy. No biggie."

I relaxed back into my seat and let my head fall back. "You truly believe that this doesn't make me creepy?"

"Nah. Don't worry too much about it."

"At least the object of your fantasy life didn't suddenly appear," I moaned. "It's been so awkward. Like, I feel like I made up this entire story line in my head, and he should know it but in reality he has no idea that we're pretend in love with each other. And I'd given him a personality that has nothing to do with who he actually is, so my heart and head are totally confused when I'm around him. I'd decided to keep my distance, at his request, but now I'm running in to him everywhere, and I can't keep walking on by without him noticing me. I promised myself I'd stop thinking about him, but how can I when his perfectly healthy male body is so close to me and I can smell the . . ." My eyes grew large, and I slapped my hand over my mouth.

Aryn's own eyes were big but filled with laughter. "I'm not sure I've ever heard you say that much that quickly." She tilted her head. "So you like how he looks when he works out?"

I closed my eyes. "Oh my gosh. Aryn, this has grown out of control."

"You're one of the most properly behaved people I know, and I'm really excited to find out you're as human as the rest of us."

I moaned. "I'm not properly behaved; I'm shy, which keeps me from acting on the things that happen in my head. You have no idea how much goes on up here." I tapped my forehead with one fingertip.

"Apparently. But I'm kind of enjoying the tour of your twisted little mind."

I sat up, my mouth flopping open. "You really think it's twisted?"

She laughed loudly and leaned forward to grab my hands. "I don't. I'm trying to make a point here. It's normal to be attracted to a man and then think about him a lot. You've done nothing wrong. If it makes you feel better to stop thinking about him, then try to do it. Just stop beating yourself up about it."

"I didn't know I had it in me to be obsessed with someone," I stated. "I've dated, but I didn't think much about them when we weren't together."

Aryn nodded. "Not every guy is the right fit."

I released her hands and held up mine up, palms out. "Hey, I'm not saying Ford is the right fit."

"Your heart thinks otherwise."

"My heart can keep its thoughts to itself." I nodded once.

CHAPTER FIVE

The first hint of fall colors had appeared on the mountainsides, and I soaked them up on the drive from my condo on the valley floor to my parents' home in the foothills. Fall in Utah was strange in that whole 'if you blink you miss it' way, so I never took the views for granted over the short weeks when the trees were showing off. The temperatures were beginning to drop as the sun set earlier, and I'd thrown a knit cardigan onto the passenger seat next to the still-cooling cherry pie I was bringing for dessert. A carton of whipping cream bounced around next to it, and I couldn't wait to whip it up and let it swirl around my mouth against the sharpness of the cherries and the buttery crust.

I pulled into the circular drive and parked behind Leonard's luxury sedan. He and Connie had been to dinner last Sunday so I hadn't expected them this week, but it wasn't necessarily unusual for them to be there. And, thanks to Mom's southern upbringing, there was never a shortage of food. She always made so much that I'd started bringing my own set of reusable to-go containers in my big bag. Mom laughed every time I pulled them out, and I always thanked her for making me two meals instead of just one.

I was actually kind of glad Leonard would be there. It was the perfect time to have a little face-to-face about Ford and set the record straight. I'd spoken to my parents during the week, so at least I didn't need to tackle that this evening.

My parents' home was a large Tudor with triangle shapes for a roof line, red brick, and large white-trimmed windows that let in the sunlight. I'd always loved the light-filled den with shelves of books and a big rug where I'd sat in the sun like a cat, reading as I soaked up the rays. It had been a happy childhood, and home had been a comfortable place. Yes, there had been weekly mental health check-ins and goal-setting sessions. Truth be told, that's probably what Sunday dinner was still about. I had no illusions that my parents didn't do a full rundown of my behaviors and statements after I left. It didn't bother me because I could admit that their guidance and awareness of me had contributed greatly to my success as a person. Plus, they never crossed over into giving me unwarranted advice or feedback--which was exactly why finding out they were worried about my dating life had been so surprising. Normally, they would have already expressed that.

I pushed open the wooden front door and took in the scents of roast and rolls. Yum. My favorite dinner was the classic roast beef, potatoes, green beans, and rolls that Mom had long ago perfected. This probably explained the addition of Leonard and Connie, who were also fans. Add to that the pie I was carrying, and I could have floated down the hallway and into the kitchen.

Familiar voices that I'd known my entire life carried from the back of the house where it opened into the large kitchen and living space. My dad was calling out to Leonard about some Major League Baseball game that was coming up, and I could hear Mom and Leonard's wife Connie chatting comfortably as they set the table. The clink of cutlery and dinnerware sounding against the light classical music playing through hidden speakers all worked together to create a cozy atmosphere.

An atmosphere that I hoped to not destroy when I launched my truth bombs at Leonard.

I came out of the entrance hall into the warm room with a large smile on my face and held up my pie. "Hi everyo- . . ." My expression, and my body, froze midstep. The pie, however, was still hovering at chin level as my eyes took in a man, standing in the dining alcove, looking out over my dad's immaculate garden.

Ford Whittaker.

He turned to greet me with a friendly look, and my heart caught in my chest. Was I asleep? I blinked a few times as my fantasy world tried to overtake real life. Ford, standing in my parents' warm kitchen, smiling at me like he belonged there and had been waiting for me to arrive. I was stiff with confusion, knowing that something was wrong, so wrong. My heart was racing as my mind whirled. Why would he be here? Had things gone wrong at the business meal Leonard had mentioned, and he was hoping for a redo?

"Hailey," Mom called, setting down the napkins she'd been placing and coming to me with open arms. I had my mom's same light coloring, and she brushed her white-blonde bangs out of her eyes as she neared. Her blue eyes were watchful, but I saw a dangerous spark that reeked of hope. "That pie looks delicious. Cherry?" She typically hugged me in greeting, but a pie plate was firmly rooted between our two faces, my eyes still locked on Ford. So, she turned to Dad who was leaning against the back of the couch looking cool as a cucumber and incredibly amused. "Conrad, she made your favorite." Her voice was cheery, but her body language was off. She was nervous and fluttery as she reached back toward me. "Let me take that, sugar."

42

I pried my eyes away from the surprise guest, half thinking that when I looked back he'd have disappeared, and handed Mom the pie. I followed her to the island where she was staging the food until the table was ready. Dad pushed to standing and came to join us.

"You look beautiful, as always." He reached a hand around to my upper back and leaned in to kiss my cheek. "Leonard brought him, unannounced. Mom and I didn't know," he whispered against my ear, causing his gray beard to scratch against my skin. "But he seems intelligent, and he's certainly well groomed. I can see why Leonard thinks you'd be interested in him."

I looked into his eyes as he pulled back, and I knew he saw how horrified I felt. Although, he was still eating it up, as indicated by the way his brown eyes were practically shooting out beams of sunlight. If he wasn't careful, his glasses were going to crack. Leave it to Dad to find these situations hysterical.

I ran my tongue over my teeth before biting my lips. "It's fine. You and Mom know the truth, so . . ."

He straightened fully. "I look forward to getting to know him better." He tugged at the hem of his shirt, a habit I shared with him, and wandered off to finish his conversation with Leonard.

I hoped he enjoyed the time with his best friend, because even though I was going to do my best to be cool and calm, I was also plotting ways to get back at Leonard. The man had manipulated his last situation. I must have attracted the old meddler with my thoughts because he came to where I was standing. I braced my hands on the counter next to where Mom had set my pie and offered him a tight smile.

"Don't give me that look," Leonard teased. "I can't come up with a good excuse for why I invited Ford, so I'll just tell you that I hope you'll give him a chance."

My stomach clenched with worry. I wished I could attribute the invitation to their business but this stunk like old fish. "Is this a set up? At family dinner?"

He grinned like he'd brokered a deal that was entirely to his benefit. "If that's how you see it."

"I'm not the only one seeing it that way. Did you see Dad's face?" I wanted to hiss it out, but my words were measured and casual despite my forearms tensing. "And my mom? She's walking around like she doesn't know how to feel."

He nodded. "Conrad's enjoying it, but they both know not to get their hopes up."

"You do realize you've crossed a line here? I don't even know Ford."

"I know. Ford explained everything the other night at our dinner."

"So, again, why is he here?" I stood straight and grabbed the stack of clean glasses that were waiting to be moved from the island to everyone's place settings.

"The important thing is that he is here, isn't it?" he shrugged.

Ugh. That meant nothing. "You owe me for this." He grinned, which prompted me to say, "It'll be great to have all my fieldtrips funded this year." I moved to the dining alcove where Connie was primping the centerpiece.

Leonard laughed. "I'll consider it."

Too late I realized Ford was still hanging around in the dining area, his hands tucked into slacks, his eyes following me. He looked like a guy preparing for a photo shoot, relaxed and dressed well, hair attractively mussed, five o'clock shadow giving him an alluring edge. The light from the window near him showed slivers of gray in his beard growth, and it was a reminder of the fact that he was ten years my senior. Maybe if I thought of him as a friend of the Coxes, I could shake this melting feeling shivering down my spine.

I was not a person who made assumptions about the feelings of others. I took a person at face value, preferring to believe they meant what they said. So when Ford had said he wasn't looking to date, I'd never once thought he was merely playing hard to get. I wasn't about to chase a man who didn't want to be chased. Instead, I was doing my best to respect his words. Something I wished Leonard would do, too.

I took a deep breath and rose to the challenge of offering kind hospitality to someone who created a maelstrom of feelings inside of me. I wanted to run from them. My heart wanted to smile and flirt and bask in his closeness. My head screamed at me to be cautious and treat him like I would treat someone I'd never met.

While I couldn't understand how he was comfortable being here or what Leonard had said to get him to leave his children on a Sunday to have dinner at a stranger's home, I did understand that I could control how I acted. And I would. Just because he frightened me didn't mean I had to be rude.

"Hello, Mr. Whittaker," I said with as much calm as I could, struggling to meet his eyes. I purposely used his formal name, hoping to keep the four old schemers who were listening in from getting any ideas.

"Hi, Hailey," he replied in a very casual way. "How was the bath?"

Missile launched.

"The bath?" Mom asked with a squeak in her voice.

I shot a glance to my mom in time to see her offer Connie a little fist bump and a raised eyebrow, proving my theory that hope had bloomed. Ford may not have intended to elicit the reaction he got from that greeting, or maybe he knew exactly how it would go over. Either way, it made me look like a liar after the hour I'd spent only two days ago convincing my parents that Ford and I were barely acquaintances. Acquaintances were not aware of bath time. My entire 'don't get any ideas' speech was going up in wondrous flames.

I was surrounded by traitors.

I pressed my lips together in an unaffected smile and ignored the entire thing, especially the way the men were all trying to pretend they weren't laughing. They may as well have been giving Ford a high five for that preposterous statement of his and how it had made me visibly squirm. What had he hoped to accomplish there?

"Let's eat," Dad called, coming to the rescue as he strode to the kitchen and hefted the platter of roast.

The rest of us followed suit, grabbing food to bring to the table. Even Ford pitched in, carrying the mashed potatoes. Then, because even Connie was in on it, those four oldies moved faster than they had in years, leaving only one seat open for Ford. Yep, right next to me. It shouldn't have been a big deal, we could have pretended that that seat was always open, except that Connie gave a little giggle and gave Leonard's hand some sort of absurd celebratory hand squeeze, high five combo under the table.

This was bad. Connie--my only hope--had gone dark. A mixture of amusement and suspicion made a home in my chest. How was I supposed to manage their expectations when they were in the middle of some off-the-charts hustle right now.

From the head of the table, Dad thanked everyone for coming--a formality not normally seen around here--and suggested we hold hands to say grace over the food. I was a thirty-year-old woman merely trying to understand what kind of runaway train I was on, so it was with some shock that I felt Ford place his hand around mine. My hand had been resting on the table, and I hadn't moved it before he reached for me. The back of my hand was tucked into his palm. My other hand reached for my mom, but all I could focus on was Ford. His hand was surprisingly cool. My hand flexed involuntarily, which opened up space for two of his fingers to slide in between mine. While his hand remained relaxed, I could feel my skin heating where we touched, and I bit my lips in response as I closed my eyes.

Dad said grace, which was thankfully short, but I didn't hear a word of it. I simply felt every heartbeat as though it were filtered through the point of contact between Ford and me. I'd never experienced anything remotely like it, and I was terribly upset that it was happening. His hand against mine brought back silly images I'd created in my head. Images I wanted gone. The second the amens were said, I snatched my hands into my lap and looked across the table to be met by Connie's questioning expression.

Connie was as dark in coloring as my mother and I were light. She still kept her hair dyed the same black color it had always been and dressed in bright jewel tones. She was kind and warm, and something about the way she looked at me told me she understood my confusion even though she was fully supporting this disastrous plot. I ran my palms over my gray knit skirt and forced a relaxed smile as I tugged at the hemline of my white shirt. It was nothing more than a chemical reaction created by an attractive man and my discomfort. Anyone would heat up under those circumstances.

"The food looks great, Mom, as always," I said, proud of how perfectly serene I sounded.

"Yes, Dr. Thomas," Ford piped up. "I appreciate you allowing me to join you."

"Please, call me Sylvia," Mom said graciously. "We're always happy to meet a new friend."

A friend, yes. Even better, a friend of Leonard's. That's exactly how I should be thinking of him, I reminded myself. A corner of my mouth tugged up. I could do this one last, strange encounter, and then I'd cleanse him from my life and move forward. In fact, maybe I needed to get back into the dating world. It was clear that I was feeling lonely. Fulfilled people do not daydream about men the way I'd been doing. I needed to fill that space in my life with someone actually concrete. Someone open and looking for a partner. I'd give it some thought.

I handed my plate down to Dad, who was carving the roast on Ford's right-hand side. "I feel bad that you were pulled away from your children to be here," I said to our guest. "They must really miss you, with how busy you are."

Ford nodded. "It's a juggling act, that's for sure," he replied. "I find being a single parent comes with a lot of challenges, but we've been doing it for almost five years now, so we have a system set up that seems to be working . . . with the occasional adjustment, of course." He chuckled good-naturedly, united with the other parents at the table, and they all lapped it up.

I took my plate with a mumbled thanks when Ford passed it back to me and reached out for the green beans to start sending them around the table. While the others began a friendly dialogue, I found myself having a hard time joining in. With people I knew and trusted, conversation flowed. However, at this table it was as though words had dried up inside of me, and even though my thoughts were racing, my mouth had stopped working. It was probably for the best, I thought. At least this way I wouldn't actually say any of the embarrassing things racing around behind my stiff facade. Things like could you choose a less appealing aftershave, or maybe you need to buy baggier clothing because your arms are distracting me.

The four older adults at the table seemed relaxed, and I could see the way he was charming them. I wasn't the only person who found him to be magnetic. I was discovering that Ford was naturally sociable, easy going, and energetic. He was a man used to being the center of attention and liking it there. We were so completely different. I took a swallow of my drink and looked at him out of my peripheral vision, trying to soak him in without being obvious about it. Who knew if I'd ever have the chance again?

"What do you do for work, Ford?" Mom asked.

Without thinking I opened my mouth to answer, "Oh, Ford's . . ." I slammed my lips shut, shooting my eyes down to my plate. "It's obvious he's a dad first," I tacked on with a terrible giggle that made the entire room feel awkward.

I'd almost given myself up! What would everyone think if I was suddenly an expert on his business? Especially Ford himself? I took a big bite and did my best to look at him as though I hadn't read all about his company. Ignore me over here, I thought frantically, I have no clue what he does with his life.

I sent an apologetic smile around the table. "Sorry to interrupt. Bad joke."

Dad looked down at his plate with a grin. "Not at all, hon," he said to me. "Yes, Ford, what type of business are you in?"

One side of Ford's mouth tugged up, but he looked away at the rest of the table. "I own an essential oils and supplements company. I started it about ten years ago, and it's been quite an adventure."

"Have I heard of this company?" I asked, in for a penny, in for a pound.

"Possibly," he replied.

"Of course you have," Leonard burst in. "You take their vitamins every day."

Mom nodded. "Those Sun and Soil Essential Vitamins I got you. You said you loved them."

"I do," I said sincerely, doing a fantastic job of reeling my near catastrophe back in. "I've been using the oils diffuser in my classroom, too. It's really great when you have twenty-five kids with assorted levels of cleanliness."

The others laughed. "I'm glad to hear they're working," Ford replied.

"So how did you and Leonard meet?" Mom asked.

This was something I hadn't found much info on, so I was glad she'd asked. I was genuinely curious about this one, too.

"Actually, we met up at an open house last year. You remember that sixtieth birthday open house for Jay Miller?" Leonard boomed, his voice always louder than necessary. "Ford was there with his two children, and their little faces were covered in chocolate cake. Connie and I wandered over to introduce ourselves, and pretty soon, we made the business connection. Ford was looking to take Sun and Soil to an international level, and as you know, I'm in international pharmaceuticals. Seemed to us that together we could do some good work."

"It's taken a year?" Dad asked.

"Yes," Ford replied. "We had to develop a product that met all international guidelines, and Leonard had to network his contacts and find sellers to line up. Now it looks like things are set, so we've signed together on a new parent corporation that we'll co-own, and . . ." He trailed off with a self-deprecating chuckle. "I won't bore you all with the details. Let's say it should be final this week."

"What about that dinner on Friday?" I couldn't help but ask, looking to Leonard instead of Ford. "I thought that was about finalizing plans."

"Oh, that meal was a celebration," Connie said, her voice soft. "The papers were signed earlier that morning."

"Ah," I replied softly as the wheels turned. "So, it really wasn't a big deal that I bowed out, after all," I mumbled.

"Bowed out?" Mom asked. "You were invited?"

"It doesn't matter," I gestured wildly, wanting Mom to save her questions for later.

Unfortunately, my wild gesture had the unintended consequence of knocking over my glass of sparkling red juice. The glass crashed onto my plate where it created a tsunami that gathered up mashed potatoes, some gravy, and bits of green beans before splashing over the edge, hitting me in the stomach, and running down to my lap. I was covered in a mess, and there was no way my white shirt was hiding any of it.

Mom leaned as close as she could to try to help, but she couldn't make any difference. Ford, to my right, snagged my glass so it would stop spilling more juice and offered me his napkin at the same time. Obviously, his parenting skills paid off in his reflex time when it came to spills, because he was on it. I snatched the napkin and scooted back my chair, thanking him while excusing myself to slip away and see if I could do some damage control. Dad followed, saying he'd take care of what had landed on the floor.

"Hailey, you're not yourself tonight," Dad said under his breath as we reached the short hallway off the kitchen that housed a cleaning closet and a half bath. "It's totally understandable. You were caught off guard by him being here. Maybe you could take a minute to do some deep breathing or mindfulness exercises while you're in the bathroom to help you feel calmer."

I'd thought I was playing it cool, but apparently I was coming off as tense and bewildered as I felt. "I'll sure try," I replied, stepping into the bathroom.

"One last thing," he said, leaning his head inside. "Ford seems like a nice man. Try not to punish him for Leonard's behavior."

"He could have turned down the invitation tonight," I replied.

"We don't know that for sure."

Dad's retort rang in my ears as he bustled away. He was right. I still had no idea why Ford was here or what Leonard had said to him. Maybe Ford was as upset about it as I was, only he was able to keep conversation flowing while I was locked up tight.

I turned on the sink and wetted the napkin. While I did so I took a look at myself in the mirror. What I saw looking back was a total stranger. My normally smooth bob looked like I'd rubbed a balloon on it and gotten some static going. My cheeks were rosy; my eyes looked like I was fighting back tears. This was not who I was used to seeing. This was not who I was used to being. Dad was right, I was in an emotional state of some sort.

I practiced some deep breathing exercises while I scrubbed at the spill on my shirt and skirt. I knew that the stains most likely wouldn't come out, but I had long ago stopped leaving clothes at my parents' house so my only hope was to at least get the chunks wiped off. I also reminded myself of a few key things, which I whispered aloud:

" One: I am thirty years old. I am not thirteen. I should react appropriately. Two: I am a school teacher. I have seen some stuff, and I have handled it. Melting down is below my skill level. Three: I am a strong, independent, and loved daughter and friend. I do not need to prove myself. Four: Just because my meddling honorary uncle is trying to set me up, doesn't mean . . ."

"Well," Ford's face popped into the mirror behind me, and I squealed, dropping the napkin and gripping the sink edges. I saw him smirk. "Sorry."

"Did you need the bathroom?" I asked.

"No," he replied, leaning back against the door jamb. "They've sent me here to check on you."

All the deep breathing and list making flew out the window. "That's incredibly humiliating," I said under my breath as I reached back into the sink for the wet rag and started scrubbing again.

"I'm sure they'll be relieved to hear that you're taking the time to list out important facts. That always helps me to calm down."

Oh geez, he'd heard. Double blush coming on. "I don't need calming."

"Sure." He moved from the door jamb, stepping closer to my side, and I caught a whiff of the same laundry detergent I used, mixed with the spicy scent I'd noticed at the gym. It was really, really nice. Not that I cared about that. "You're going to work a hole into that shirt," he stated.

"It's already ruined," I replied, loosening my grip on the rag. I forced a deep breath in through my nose and let it out slowly as I closed my eyes and formed my mouth into an O shape. "You can report back to that gray-haired bunch of ne're-do-wells that I am fine and will return shortly."

"You know, Hillary used to tell me last year that the thing she liked most about you was how you never got mad."

My face immediately set on fire as a blush raced up from my chest to spread over my cheeks and forehead. I wasn't sure what to say. Men usually didn't bait me like he did. They didn't push up against my natural reserve. I had no idea what to do with this.

Grasping uselessly for any sense of strength and pride I could muster I said, "It's true, I'm usually very calm."

He nodded sagely. "I can tell."

I bit my lips and sucked another breath in through my nose, fiercely enough to make a really unattractive sound. I took a step back so that I was pressed against the wall as far from him as I could get and held up my hands, palms out. "Okay, so I'm having a hard time processing all these developments."

"What sort of developments? I thought we were just having dinner."

I scoffed, a sound so rare that it actually hurt my throat. "Don't insult me by pretending you don't know." His eyebrows raised, and his shoulders shifted. "You asked about my bath." I had to push the words out.

His face loosened into a smile. "I was trying to get you breathing again. You saw me and totally froze up."

"I'm not in the habit of discussing my bathing habits with strangers, much less announcing it to my parents."

He stepped closer, looking down into my eyes in that intense way of his. "It embarrassed you." The words were a whisper, and I nodded sharply. His gaze was keen, as though the thought of me being embarrassed fascinated him. "I didn't realize."

I looked down at our feet, closer together than they had any business being. "You and I, well, the moment we met you made it clear that you weren't interested in getting to know me. So why are you here? It can't be to meet my parents. They have nothing to do with your line of work. And it can't be to see me. So why?"

"Leonard invited me to dinner, and not many people would pass up the offer of a dinner like your mom makes."

"How would you have any idea what kind of dinner my mom makes?"

"Leonard sang her praises. And a home-cooked meal that I didn't have to make sounded really nice. I like Leonard and Connie, and I enjoy meeting new people."

I dared to meet his eyes again and crossed my arms in a show of strength, but it was really because my hands were trembling so hard. This was the first argument I'd had in . . . well . . . forever I suppose. I had enough confidence to stand my ground, but it was terrifying to do it outside of my head rather than imagining I had after the fact.

"As simple as that, huh?"

He crossed his too. "Yes. I didn't think it would be a problem."

"Uh-huh."

"Why are you so upset about it?"

"Leonard told my parents last week that I'd met someone . . ."

I shook my head, jaw clenching, as I uncrossed my arms enough to gesture at him. I was unwilling to tell him that I was wondering what my parents were thinking right now. Or that I was worried I'd somehow imagined him into reality, as though the universe had heard my lonely cries and delivered him right to my doorstep and then said 'no touchie.'

"When is the last time you dated?" he asked.

My mouth opened and shut. It was none of his business that it had been at least five years since I'd truly dated anyone consistently. "Why?"

"I'm thinking that someone who dates regularly is more comfortable around men. I'm trying to decide if it's me you're upset about or if any man would have gotten under your skin this way."

Of all the arrogant assumptions. "I'm plenty comfortable with men."

He nodded. "Fair enough. I'm sorry I said anything."

I moved sideways in the tiny space, wanting away from this conversational nightmare. I fully intended to escape at all costs, even if it meant bumping him into the vanity as I made my way out. Fortunately--because really, I would have felt bad later--he swung sideways, and my shoulder brushed his chest as I passed by.

51

"Cherry pie is my favorite," he said a millisecond before I rounded the corner into the kitchen where the others were.

"How disappointing," I replied over my shoulder.

He had the audacity to laugh.

CHAPTER SIX

My forehead was pressed tightly to the faculty lunch table as I let out a moan, having barely finished telling my best friends about the fiasco that was Sunday dinner the night before. Ruby placed a comforting hand on my back and rubbed in light circles.

"It sounds awful," she soothed.

I shook my head, making a squeaking sound as my skin scraped back and forth. "It was me and only me." I looked up at their sympathetic faces, knowing I had a red mark on my forehead and not caring. "I turned into some sort of Mr. Hyde monster, completely transforming into a horrible version of myself that I did not know existed."

"It's true that I've never seen you act that way. I'm kind of having a hard time picturing it," Aryn soothed.

"Some men will drive you to it," Meredith said, the tone of experience behind her words. "I'm perfectly lovely until Brooks VanOrman . . ." We all groaned, having heard much about him over the past several months. Poor Brooks VanOrman--who we only ever called by his full name--had gotten on Meredith's bad side from almost the first moment he'd been elected into his position as her HOA president. "What?"

"We get it, Brooks VanOrman is your nemesis. I wish you'd kiss him already and be done with it," Aryn said, mouth pinched.

"Kissing does have a way of helping people find middle ground," Lizzie nodded wisely.

Meredith's mouth dropped open. "Kiss him? We are not here to give me unsolicited advice. We're here to support Hailey. I'm simply saying, I understand what she's going through. I'm not myself around Brooks VanOrman." She huffed and picked up her drink, sitting back in her chair to take a sip. "Let's get back to Hailey."

With kind-hearted mutual agreement everyone refocused on me, and I sat up straight again.

"What did your parents think about it all?" Lizzie asked, twirling a tight curl around her forefinger as she spoke.

"I don't really know," I replied.

"I'm still in shock that you left the bathroom, grabbed your things, and stalked out of there," Aryn said in an awed tone. "Welcome to the world of drama."

"Without even one bite of what was probably an amazing pie," Ruby commiserated.

I shook my head, humiliation washing over me once more, taking all the volume from my voice. "I've never done anything like that before. I didn't know I was capable of it." What must Ford think? I moaned to myself.

Aryn patted my arm. "We're all capable of dramatic episodes." Her hand on my arm squeezed lightly, reminding me that she truly understood the depth of my inner battle.

"Although you're usually our classy cucumber," Lizzie observed.

"Classy cucumber?" I questioned, feeling a tug of mirth.

"It's not a bad description," Ruby joined in. "You are usually so cool and unflappable."

I nodded with an eye roll. "Well, consider me flapped, then." I sighed loudly. "I actually feel physically ill today. I was mean. Can you get a meanness hangover?"

All eyes swung to Meredith, who threw up her hands. "Why are you asking me?"

We all laughed, which had a relaxing effect, and my shoulders loosened. "All of you just need to pray that I never have to see Ford Whittaker again, and all will be well."

"Why would you have to?" Meredith asked as she started packing up her lunch wrappings in preparation to get back to class. "Where else would you possibly find yourselves together?"

"Exactly," Aryn said. "Leonard knows to stop pulling strings, and now you can relax."

"Plus, you've both lived here for years and never met until now. So, it's obvious you don't frequent the same places." Lizzie supplied helpfully.

If only that were true. I'd seen him all over the place, but I'd never talked about it. I pushed down the image of him standing near me at the gym and nodded.

"You're totally right. I'm going to let all this angst slide off my back and get back to normal."

"Huzzah!" Ruby cheered.

Huzzah was right.

CLASS ACT

*****

It was Meredith's fault. If she hadn't thrown down the gauntlet to the universe by asking why I would ever need to see Ford again, then things would have quietly died down. Instead, not long after lamenting to my friends about what a nasty person I'd been, a cheerful voice rang through my classroom.

"Miss Thomas!" Hillary entered; her cheeks rosy from having been playing outside. "I have to hurry back to class 'cause the bell rang, but I wanted to give you this." She stopped in front of my desk and handed me a pink envelope before skipping back out the door. "See ya," she called.

I was not exactly excited about opening the envelope. I had a bad feeling about this. (In the interest of full honesty, I also had maybe a 10% butterfly launch. This invitation could possibly get me some more Ford time. Glutton for punishment, that's me.)

That envelope taunted me from my desk throughout reading time, spelling time, and all the way until the last backpack was slung over small shoulders. I walked my students in their haphazard line out to the front door to release them and offered cheery farewells, still wondering what new circumstance awaited me.

I held the envelope to my chest as I made my way to Ruby's health office near the front of the building. My friends and I typically gathered there for ten minutes at the end of the school day, where we laughed about daily adventures and cleared our minds before heading back to lesson plans and prep time. We called it Recap and Recoup. But I was haunted by the pink envelope, so I sat quietly on the little exam table, waiting for the others to join us.

"What's that?" Ruby asked, nodding toward the envelope.

"It's from Hillary Whittaker, and I'm afraid to know what's inside," I replied.

She raised an eyebrow. "Fear and excitement both feel the same in our bodies."

I just blinked, and she left it alone, knowing I was waiting until everyone was there. I leaned over and sat it on top of her desk. She eyed it and then my face before looking out the doorway to see if the others were coming.

There it sat, waiting. Maybe it was nothing more than a thank you card or a pretty picture she'd drawn for me. I was being silly, imagining the upheaval it contained. I even forced a laugh out to prove that I was being ridiculous. It fell flat.

"Are you okay?" Aryn asked as she entered, followed closely by Meredith and Lizzie. "Because that was not an actual laugh. It was . . . odd."

"She has an envelope," Ruby replied, motioning toward the pink problem.

Lizzie scooted around to see. "Where did you get it?"

"From Hillary," I stated.

"I'm closing the door," Meredith said, and the door clicked closed.

"She's just been staring at it, hardly said two words," Ruby said to the others.

"Hey, maybe it's a drawing or something cute like that," Meredith came to sit next to me on the table. "Nothing to get worked up about."

Honestly, the fact that Meredith was trying to comfort me only skyrocketed the worry. So, I abruptly snagged it off Ruby's desk and tore it open. My heart sank as I read the words 'You're Invited' at the top. I quickly scanned the pastel paper, hoping Hillary was taking me up on my offer to paint nails in my classroom and inviting me to a spa party or something. But I was out of luck. She'd invited me to her dance recital in three days. At the bottom of the formal invite was a hand scrawled 'please come' in her third-grade penmanship.

If it wasn't Leonard, it was going to be Hillary.

And Ford didn't want me. Well, Ford didn't want anyone.

I put the envelope down and leaned my head against the wall in defeat. "She's invited me to her dance recital," I moaned.

"Let me see that." Meredith snatched it out of my hands and read it out loud to the others.

I really liked Hillary, and I could see that she wanted a relationship with me. However, encouraging that meant the risk of hurting her exponentially when she finally realized that I was not a contender for stepmother status. Her dad and I . . . well . . . the point was that the poor thing did not need another hurt in her life.

"The plot thickens," Lizzie said when Meredith finished.

Aryn added a breathless, "Oh boy."

"Yeah." I agreed.

"What are you going to do?" Ruby asked.

I stood and moved around the tight space, forcing Meredith to tuck her legs up and the others to press against the walls. "I'm not sure. I feel bad not supporting Hillary when it's so obvious that she's looking for something. Yet, her dad brings out the worst in me, and I'm committed to avoiding him." I shook my head. "Why is he everywhere all of a sudden?"

"It seems to me like once you've noticed a person out in the world, you tend to see them a lot." Lizzie shrugged. "It's the law of attraction."

"Not quite," Meredith said. "The law of attraction is a philosophy suggesting that positive thoughts bring positive results into a person's life while negative thoughts bring negative outcomes. It's not the same as meeting someone new and then suddenly running into them everywhere."

"Well, that explains it then," I said while pulling a face. "I've been thinking a lot of thoughts about Ford, and it keeps attracting him into my life."

The others chuckled.

"What kind of thoughts?" Lizzie asked.

I looked at their faces and threw caution to the wind. "Warm thoughts."

"How warm?" Ruby asked.

"Embarrassingly warm. But he doesn't want anything to do with dating, and I doubt he's looking for a friend either. So . . ."

"What are you going to do?" Ruby asked for the second time.

"Not sure. Seems like my options are all lose-lose." I responded. I moved back over to Ruby's desk and leaned a hip against it. "I don't want to hurt Hillary. If I say no to the recital, she's hurt. If I say yes, she's hurt later when nothing happens between Ford and me."

Aryn nodded before saying, "I feel bad for her. She's looking for some connection."

"I know," I said sadly. "And I'm actually really flattered that she's found something in me that she's comfortable with. Trust me, if I didn't think she was also trying to make me into her new mommy, I'd be more open, but I'm afraid she's set her heart on her dad and I falling in love."

"Maybe we're overreacting here," Lizzie said thoughtfully. "Maybe we're putting thoughts into that little head that aren't actually there. What if she's legitimately looking for a friend, nothing more, and thinks you fit the bill."

One of my mom's favorite phrases popped into my head. Be curious. I tried to see it from a different angle. Maybe she was innocent in her desires to spend time with me. Maybe I was overreacting because of my violent attraction to her father and it had never occurred to her to try to replace her mom.

"What about the way she acted at her dad's party? Trying to build me up to him?" I hedged. "She mentioned that her and her brother's names start with an H, and so does mine. Just like her mom's did." I emphasized the last part, and their eyes grew large.

"Oof," Meredith shook her head. "That's not good."

"She said I'd fit right in because of it," I added, deflating even more.

"Poor little thing," Aryn said quietly.

"And she keeps listing all my good qualities to her dad every chance she gets. 'Isn't Miss Thomas pretty? Miss Thomas has good manners.' It's adorable but awkward, too." I crossed my arms.

"Again, I'd argue that kids do that all the time when telling their parents about their friends. My nephew was telling me about his friend the other day, all the awesome things he does and toys he has. It could be innocent." She shrugged.

"If we chase Lizzie's theory, sometimes kids get attached to an idea, and it's all they can think about for a few weeks, but then the next shiny thing comes along, and they forget," Meredith said.

Lizzie's face brightened. "It's true. After that high school orchestra came to visit last spring, one of my students was determined to be a flute player. It's all she talked about for two weeks until suddenly she discovered jump ropes at recess, and then she wanted to be a jump rope champ."

I tilted my head. "So, you think I might only be the shiny thing of the month and that Hillary will move on soon?"

"The theory seems sound to me," Aryn stated. "And a lot more comfortable to deal with than her trying to get you to date her dad."

I smiled. "Maybe you're right." And maybe I could see Ford without seeing Ford.

"In the meantime, there's no reason to hurt her feelings. I cheerfully talked to my student about the flute, never once saying how hard it would be to learn or how expensive they are. And when she moved on to jump ropes, I did the same. I think you should go to Hillary's recital. Give her some warm fuzzies while you're in her sights. When she moves on, she'll have nothing but happy memories of how kind you were." Lizzie's eyes sparkled with excitement as she laid it out, and the feeling was contagious.

"Besides," Ruby added, "we all had a teacher growing up that we especially liked. It's natural to feel that way."

"You're right," I stood straight and nodded. "I'm totally overreacting. I can ease the loneliness of a little girl. And I do enjoy watching people dance." And Ford, I could be near him one more time.

"It's settled," Meredith grinned. "Off to the recital you go." She turned to leave the room but paused at the doorway. "You know, if it's Ford you're worried about, nobody said you have to sit with him at the recital. You can sit anywhere and then go say hi to her when it's over." She offered a little wave and disappeared.

"She's right," Aryn said, following her out.

"She is right," I whispered to myself and gave Lizzie a little wave as she left the room, too. I was a pro, after all, at soaking him up from afar.

Ruby smiled at me as I followed the others out. "Good luck."

I walked down the hall feeling much lighter having spoken to my friends. I'd be Hillary's flavor-of-the-month, give her support, and help her feel happy, all while keeping Ford's wishes for distance intact and enjoying a little eye candy for myself. No more lose-lose, things were looking up.

CHAPTER SEVEN

The scribbling of pencils was the only sound as I walked slowly around the desks in my classroom, watching my students work and helping where I was needed. I'd finished reading them Frog and Toad Are Friends, and they were writing a very short story about friendship. For once they were all on task, and I was pleased, although I didn't go so far as to pat myself on the back. I'd learned in my first years of teaching that celebrating a victory like this moment was asking for total chaos to erupt.

"Teacher?" Joel asked, raising his hand and looking up at me. "How do you spell toad?"

I walked closer to him and spelled it out. "T-O-A-D. What are you writing about?"

"I toad my friend we should play soccer at recess."

I stifled a snort of amusement. "It would be, I told my friend. That's spelled T-O-L-D."

He giggled at his mistake and erased the letter A to replace it with L.

I moved back through the classroom and was stopped by another student with a raised hand. "Yes, Zeke?" I asked.

"How do you know if a girl is a kid or a mom?" he asked.

"Easy," Kelsey piped up before I could. "She carries a purse. If she's carrying a purse, then she's done growing up."

Zeke took it in thoughtfully. "Thanks."

I loved teaching for these moments. Kids were so open to discussion and willing to share without fear of judgment. I loved how they wanted to know things and asked so many questions. I also truly appreciated them still thinking that the teacher was cool. It's why I'd chosen to focus on the younger grades, and I had no regrets about it. I wished my parents could spend a day or two with me here. They'd been mostly supportive of my career choice, but I didn't believe they totally understood it. My parents weren't really 'kid' people. They loved me, but they didn't seek out children in general. I, however, was the opposite. I'd always sought out children and interacted with them. They were easier than adults, in my opinion. I was in middle school when I'd decided I wanted to teach, and I was so grateful to have a classroom full of kids to shower my affection on.

After a few more minutes of writing their stories, it was time to pack up for the day and head home, and before I knew it I was sitting in Ruby's office with my friends laughing over some of the happenings of the day during Recap and Recoup. I started the ball rolling with my stories, but theirs were just as funny if not better. The kids had really been on one today.

"I asked my class why freshwater fish can't live in saltwater," Meredith chuckled. "One of the kids replied that it would be dangerous for them because salt causes high blood pressure."

"We're working on the clock right now, and the problem was 'If Mira goes to the library at 6:15 and leaves at 6:30, how long was she there?' Luke's answer was 'Not long, teacher.'" Lizzie had us rolling with that one.

Aryn held up both hands, her smile beaming. "I think I win today," she called. "I asked the class to list five good things Abraham Lincoln had done. My favorite answer was 'When the war was over, he celebrated by taking his wife to a show.'" She barely made it through without cracking up. "Another kid yelled out, 'Yeah, and he died at that show, so I guess it wasn't really good choice.'"

I pressed my hands against my stomach as I joined in the amusement of my friend group. "What about you, Ruby?" I asked. "Any adventures from your day?"

"Two barf buckets and one rash. It was awesome."

I wrinkled my nose. "I don't know how you do it."

"Well, I hate to break it to you, but if you plan on being a mom someday, you'll have to do it, too."

I shook my head, feeling green at the thought. "My husband will take care of those kinds of things."

"Uh-huh." Lizzie laughed. "Last time Jackson and his daughter Sally were in town, Sally got carsick driving up the canyon to Tony Grove. Guess who helped mop it up?"

I made a face. "No more, please. I should never have asked."

"Pets aren't any better," Meredith stated. "My cat coughed up something atrocious the other day, like straight out of a horror film, and I had to dispose of it and sanitize the house. I thought about calling in an exorcist."

"I don't know how you stand that cat," I said. It was no secret that I wasn't a pet person. Hair and messes everywhere did not appeal to me. "Isn't she like eighty years old now?"

Meredith rolled her eyes. "She's ten. She probably has another ten good years in her considering she's very spry and incredibly intelligent."

"She's coughing up her insides, one hairy ball at a time," Lizzie wrinkled her nose. "That doesn't seem intelligent."

"Betty will do what Betty will do," Meredith stated. "It's best to stay out of her way and let her live her life."

"Like pet, like owner," Ruby said under her breath, and we snickered at the face Meredith made.

"The things people do for their pets," I teased.

"The things we do for our students," Lizzie sighed.

"The things we do for their parents," Meredith added.

"Parents are harder than kids, every day of the week," Aryn agreed.

"Try calling one and telling them their kid is sick," Ruby inserted. "No parent likes getting a call from me. Half of them freak out and think their child caught leprosy and the other half can't be bothered and say to keep them in my office until the school day is over."

"Man, right now, I am the perfect parent," Lizzie said in such a nonchalant way that it took us a second to register her teasing.

"Me, too," I laughed when I realized what she'd meant.

"My kids are totally perfect," Aryn added. "No one ever complains about them."

"I'm nailing this parenting gig," Meredith agreed. "Betty the cat is well adjusted and independent."

"She's not from planet earth," Lizzie replied.

"Neither are half the people in this building," Meredith quipped.

With that we broke up, chatting lightly as we made our way back to work.

*****

I entered the auditorium of the local high school holding a bouquet of bright pink dahlias as a shield against my chest. It was warm and noisy with family members and friends greeting each other while others posed on the stage for pictures. The houselights were on, but it still felt dim as I looked carefully to see if I could spot the Whittaker family, and then sit on the opposite side of the room. Over the past few days, I'd done a fabulous job of cutting Ford out of my thoughts. I was feeling more in control and had even confided in Aryn that I was open to being set up on dates. She'd clapped her hands and sworn that she wouldn't tell the others just yet, but she was getting to work immediately on my first date.

For tonight, the plan was to greet Hillary when the recital was over, give her the flowers, and then hightail it out of there without any mental drooling over her dad. I figured with a few more of these low-key interactions, I'd be able to greet Ford around town when we were in the same places and my fantasies would be a distant memory. If I could manage it, it would be practically like they'd never happened. Easy peasy. After tonight, I'd slip away and go back to my role as her former teacher. Ford and I would be friendly associates and nothing more.

My heart lurched at the thought of giving Ford up, but I sternly practiced the mental mantra I'd created for such a moment.

I heard the familiar squeal before I saw the face behind it. I turned in time to have a fluffy teal ball of flying hair and bows slam into my side at the same time that two tiny arms wrapped around my waist. It caused me to take a step back, but I was able to catch myself with a laugh.

"You're here," Hillary cried.

I patted her back with my free hand, the motion causing my purse to fall off my shoulder and swing from my wrist. "I'm here," I said warmly. I certainly couldn't complain about being greeted this way. It felt nice.

She pulled away and grabbed my hand. "I had Daddy save you a seat."

Some of the warm feelings dissipated as I followed, grateful that she didn't need a response, because she was already gabbing about how long it had taken her nanny, Ellie, to get her hair and makeup done and how hard it had been to wear a seatbelt in the car without squishing the costume she was wearing for her performance. I was thankful for her enthusiasm, because it gave me time to get my bearings as we moved through the crowds of people.

Plan A had been dashed. That's okay. I'd had plans dashed before, and I was capable of regrouping. Sitting by her family wasn't the end of the world. I was hoping upon hope that I wasn't the only guest. Maybe her Grams was still in town, or her nanny was there too, and I could put some distance between Ford and I. So, Plan B was born. Space. That was the entire plan.

No, distance is bad . . . my sneaky brain thought. I swallowed hard, promising myself that either way, I'd be totally unaffected, very pleasant, and keep all emotions and strange zinging reactions to myself. Scratch that, there would be zero zinging because that stuff was out of my system thanks to the power of the mind, which power I had been exercising more often lately than I'd like to admit.

"Here's Daddy." Hillary stopped so suddenly that I almost plowed her down.

As it was, I came to a stop as the bouquet was about to come to rest on top of her head. I lifted the flowers in the air and forced my body into backwards motion, steadying myself in the process. The stop-and-start way she moved made me want to crack up, and amusement tugged at my lips as I looked up to see where she was pointing. Ford was standing up in greeting. We made eye contact, me with my face amused and warm before I could pull it back to polite. He took me in as he always did, his own expression brightening a little.

Hillary saved me from figuring out how to greet him by spouting off some more excited gibberish that I barely understood. The main message seemed to be that she was supposed to be with her class, and she'd see me after. She looked up with glowing gray eyes, waiting for a response.

"Sounds good," I said with a smile for her, hoping it was what I was supposed to say.

It was enough, and she spun around, braids flying, before making her way to the stage. I followed her zig-zagging blur of teal fluff until she disappeared through a side door. Sadly, that took only a few moments, and then I was forced to face Ford again. The last time I'd seen him had been at my parents' house, a memory I wouldn't exactly be scrapbooking. I took quick note of the fact that it was just him and Henry, and Henry was on Ford's opposite side. I did not take note of how handsome he looked in a blue sweater and casual jeans, because I did not care, at all.

Looks aren't everything. Sure, they can suck a girl in and make her dream of sailing the Mediterranean together, but they're not the real seal-the-deal kind of stuff.

"Pretty flowers." Ford gestured.

I looked down at them and back up, sensing immediately that I wasn't nearly as committed to giving him space as I'd hoped to be at this point in my efforts. Plan B cracked under my eager heartbeats.

"Dahlias are my favorite. I thought Hillary would like them too."

"Pink is always appropriate with Hillary," he added.

I noticed an open seat on the other side of Henry, shining like a lighthouse in a storm. I was going to duct tape Plan B together if it killed me.

"I'm happy to take that seat near Henry and leave this open for others, it being near the aisle and all." I beautifully phrased it like I was being thoughtful. "If you'll let me slip past you."

Ford shook his head, amusement lighting his eyes. "If you'd prefer not to sit next to me, I can have Henry trade, but that seat is actually saved by the family next to us. Sorry."

I purposely flashed my dimples and pasted on an innocent expression like I wasn't at all ruffled by him being on to what I really thought. "I'm not trying to avoid sitting next to you." Another lie for the universe to lap up and use against me later.

"Great." He gestured to the seat next to him and waited for me to arrange myself, my purse, and the flowers before he took his seat. "Hillary has talked non-stop about you coming tonight. Thank you for being here."

It was the final nail in the coffin. All plans had failed. There would be no more making plans. I was a pawn in this whole situation.

"She's a sweet girl. I'm happy to support her." I mustered up some genuine good cheer.

My purse slipped off my lap and I reached for it at the same time Ford did. We both bent down, and our hands tangled, sending that same shiver I'd experienced at my parents' house snaking its way up my arm. I immediately let go, and Ford picked it up, handing it to me.

"Thanks," I said, trying to sound calm but coming off unnerved.

"Do other students invite you to their recitals and performances?" Ford asked, settling back into his chair.

His wide shoulder brushed mine in the narrow space as he placed his right ankle on his left knee and folded his hands against his stomach. I shifted away, ruffled over the fact that I'd let a few zings through the gate.

"Um, not often," I replied, opening my purse to get out a piece of mint gum, hoping the chewing would help with my agitation. I was not supposed to be reacting to him in any way. He was nothing more than a friend of Leonard's, the parent of a former student, a member of my community . . .

"She really likes you. I tried to get her to invite her current teacher, Mrs. Slater, but she insisted it had to be you."

I was halfway through unwrapping the gum, but his statement had me pausing to look his way. "You tried to talk her out of inviting me?"

The dimples were gone, and my eyebrows dropped. Offended and grateful is a strange mixture, I'll tell you what. Knowing it would be for the best but still taking it personally isn't a good feeling.

"It sounds bad when you say it that way."

"I'm saying it exactly how you said it," I replied, popping the gum in my mouth while looking straight ahead at the stage. "I suppose it's a good thing, then, that I'm only a blip in her life."

"What does that mean?"

"It means that a lot of kids have something they're into for a short amount of time before they move on. Hillary will move on from me soon enough. You don't need to worry."

"You're assuming I'm worried in the first place."

Had the man not just finished saying he'd tried to talk her out of inviting me? It may not have been worry, but at the very least it was discomfort with me being around. More proof that he'd meant those harsh words in the cafeteria. He was not interested.

I bit my lip and did a round of deep breathing through my nose, wanting to tell him that he should be worried because people were trying to match us up and he'd straight up told me he wasn't getting remarried. This was a . . . no . . . time to engage my thinking brain rather than my caveman brain. Time to take a pause.

"This is the second time you've done that breathing routine around me," he interrupted my healing thought process.

I did another deep breathing cycle before saying, "It helps."

His eyes crinkled up, but he graciously moved on. "So, you were saying something about being a blip?"

I slipped into teacher mode, a place I felt a little more in control. "I'm simply saying that children her age tend to find something interesting for short bursts of time. Right now, I'm that something. I'm a novelty, and I'll wear off. In the meantime, I'm doing my best to leave her with happy memories and help her feel loved."

"So, you're temporary."

"I'll be out of your life soon." I glanced at him with a wicked little smile that I didn't even know I was capable of. "And then, you can enjoy these things with the wonderful Mrs. Slater."

He laughed. He actually laughed. The sound of it was so carefree that I immediately understood his popularity. His gray eyes crinkled up and his teeth flashed white with pure enjoyment. I felt that sound down to the soles of my feet, and it made me feel restless and unsure. I didn't want to like the sound of his laughter. I didn't want to like how he looked with his face open and happy like that. I didn't want to think up ways I could make it happen again.

I faced forward and was beyond thrilled when the stage curtains opened and a woman dressed in a sparkling black dress walked out to call us to order and welcome everyone. I clapped much louder than necessary, something Ford seemed to find humorous. She spoke for a few minutes, thanking people and applauding the dancers for their hard work. During her talk I relaxed each muscle in my body and settled my mind until I was in a good place, ready to cheerfully take in the performances and support my very young friend.

"Mrs. Slater is old, you know," Ford said, leaning to whisper in my ear, his shoulder brushing against me again. "I don't see Hillary picking her as a new friend."

And, sadly, I missed the entire first number trying to calm the goosebumps that had risen when I felt his warm breath on my neck.

*****

"You did such a great job!" I cheered as Hillary found me in the foyer after the recital was over.

Families had left the auditorium to congregate in the larger space, greeting each other and taking pictures. It was a festive spirit, but I was still tied up in knots over the way I could sense Ford standing slightly behind me. He was taller than me by at least half a foot, and it didn't escape my traitorous mind that I could tuck myself in against him. I was completely uncomfortable with my state of mind around him, and the odd feelings that he gave rise to. All my mental preparation had been thrown to the wind after sitting with his shoulder lightly touching mine for the past hour. It had been a lot, and I wanted to jet.

"Did you see how I got to be in front for part of it?" she asked, joy radiating from her small face.

"I did. You were beautiful." I handed the flowers to her. "Even more beautiful than these flowers I brought for you."

Her eyes grew large, and her mouth grew to match. "I've never had flowers before," she said.

I glanced over my shoulder at Ford who had moved closer to hear the conversation over the commotion. "Are you new to this dance thing?" I asked in a hushed tone. He nodded. "Flowers are tradition. You need to bring her some for each recital."

He nodded again before moving around me to bend down and kiss Hillary's cheek. "You were perfect," he said, and she giggled. "Miss Thomas is right, you did a great job."

"Thanks," she giggled. "Did Henry watch?"

Henry, who had been leaning against a pillar playing with a handheld gaming device glanced up when he heard his name. "You did good," he said.

Hillary beamed. "Thanks." She turned back to her dad. "Where are we going to dinner, and can Miss Hailey come?"

Oh, so she'd dropped the Thomas and was calling me by my first name. I scrambled to answer, needing to keep some boundaries in place. Public recital = okay. Private family dinner = not okay. Not even my daydreams had landed me in the family storyline. I knew it was a danger zone.

"I'm sorry, but I have other plans," I said kindly.

Ford backed me up by saying, "Miss Thomas is busy. It was so nice of her to take time to come tonight."

Hillary's face fell a little, but she did her best to keep her voice bright. "Okay. Thanks for coming," she said to me.

I nodded at her. "Thanks for inviting me. I love watching dance."

"You do? Have you seen a ballet?"

"I have. I go with my parents every year to the Nutcracker and sometimes to other performances too," I replied, happy at the memories of the times with my parents.

"Daddy sometimes goes to . . ." Hillary began.

Ford interrupted. "Come on, guys. We can walk out with Miss Thomas and then go get some dinner."

Hillary slipped her arms into the jacket that her father was holding and then immediately grabbed my hand, thrilled to be walking out together. For my part, I was grateful that Ford had interrupted what was most likely another attempt on her part to get him and me spending time together. She chatted happily while we walked along, Ford and Henry following behind us having a softer conversation of their own. I couldn't hear what they were saying, but it felt oddly familial, and I shivered. It was dark when we left the building, and I blamed my chills on the light breeze cutting through my shirt. I'd left my jacket in the car, and now I couldn't wait to get it on.

Ford seemed to notice. "Let's say goodbye now," he said from behind us when we reached the parking lot. "It's cold, and Miss Thomas forgot a jacket."

I didn't bother correcting him but instead bent slightly to Hillary's level. "You did great tonight. I'll see you at school, okay?" She grinned, nodded. I turned to her brother. "Hey Henry, have a good night." He smiled at me, ever the quiet one, and followed Hillary who had started skipping away.

Ford paused for a moment, watching them. "She's always planning something."

I kept my mouth shut, not knowing for sure what he'd meant, and not interested in asking.

"Goodnight, Hailey," was all he said as he lifted a hand to wave and turned to follow his children.

With any luck, that wave was the final goodbye. The last thing I needed was more time around a man who made my skin spark and my entire logical mind become a teeming mass of glittering hearts.

CHAPTER EIGHT

The way I see it," Lizzie said the next night around a bite of warm chocolate chip cookie, "I very rarely hit my head on anything, my legs never hang off the end of a bed, and all blankets are long enough to cover me completely. Being short is best."

"I disagree," Aryn said from her cross-legged seat on the floor, back leaning against my couch. "I can reach cupboards without a stool. I can see over people in a crowd. I'm easy to spot when you're looking for me."

"Is that because you're tall or because you're loud?" Ruby asked and then squealed when Aryn threw a pillow at her.

"I can see over the steering wheel," Aryn went on. "Pants don't have to be hemmed when I buy them."

"I have news for you, those pants you're buying should go to your ankles," Ruby tossed the pillow back. "They're not supposed to be capris."

"You should've tossed that pillow to Lizzie," Aryn heckled. "She may need to sit on it to see over the dash."

"Hailey, you need to end our debate. Tall or short? Which is easier?" Lizzie asked me.

I smiled, ready with the same neutral answer I always gave when this came up. "The average American woman is five foot four inches."

"I'm closer to perfect than you are," Lizzie laughed and wiggled her finger at Aryn. "Look at me, the ideal woman."

"One who carries a step stool everywhere?" Aryn chuckled and popped a grape into her mouth.

"Hailey's the lucky one," Ruby sighed. "Not tall, not short."

"Average," I joked.

"If I could have picked my height, I'd have been five foot six like you," Ruby responded.

"You're only two inches taller," I soothed, picking at my own cookie. "That's roughly the height of a golf tee. It doesn't buy you much."

"Should I be offended that you wouldn't have picked to be nearly six feet like me?" Aryn asked.

Ruby grabbed another cookie from the pile. "What I'd take from you is your lean limbs."

"Don't sell yourself short, Ruby. Your curves are great." Aryn replied.

"My curves would be better if they were stretched out over your frame."

I stood and walked into my kitchen as the timer I'd set on my phone rang. "No one is entirely happy with their body, you know," I called as I grabbed a hot pad. "But that doesn't mean there's actually anything wrong with any of us. I think we're all beautiful."

I pulled a homemade lasagna out of the oven and took a deep breath, letting its scent rush over me along with the steam. The smell of bubbling cheese, savory sausage, and tangy marinara filled the air with happiness. It was going to be delicious.

"Do you think we did it out of order, baking cookies first?" Ruby asked as she came to grab the salad fixings out of my fridge.

"Keep those nasty thoughts to yourself, Ruby," Aryn giggled. "We're old enough to have dessert first."

"And afterward, too," I reminded them with a dimpled grin.

We settled in to light chit chat as Aryn put her breadsticks on a serving plate and Ruby mixed up a green salad. These were my favorite kind of weekend nights, with my friends in my kitchen making good food and talking about whatever. Lizzie had provided the cookies, so she stayed on the couch watching us move about in familiar patterns. We were only missing Meredith, who was attending an HOA meeting at her condo complex, where I was sure she was taking on her mortal enemy. I couldn't wait for the wild tales she'd have for us next week.

"What's the movie choice?" Aryn asked as we filled our plates and moved to my living room where I'd set up TV trays.

"*He's Just Not That Into You,*" I responded as I set my food down.

"Ben Affleck is delicious in that movie." Ruby took her seat. "Maybe even more so than this lasagna, although it looks amazing, Hailey."

"Thanks."

"I wonder if Ford Whittaker is a lasagna guy," Lizzie tossed out.

I paused with my finger over the play button on my remote and gave her a look. "This is a Ford-free zone."

She held up her hands and laughed. "Fine. Sorry."

I glanced at Aryn as I hit play, and she gave me a sympathetic look. Only she knew how hard I'd been working to leave thoughts of him behind. I went through the motions of chewing my food and watching the movie, but Lizzie's little comment kept my mind chugging along through all the ups and downs of love on the screen. Did Ford like lasagna? What would my friends think of him? Why did his gray eye color have to be so appealing? And the little flecks of silver I'd seen in his end-of-the-day facial scruff . . .

"What's the sweetest thing a guy has ever done for you?" Lizzie asked when we paused the movie for a food reload. "Like, how did you really know if a guy was into you or not?"

"That's tough," Ruby answered first. "I dated a guy for a couple of months who was really good at hunting and skinning. He brought my family a lot of venison."

The rest of us stopped what we were doing and looked at her. For a second she was oblivious, reloading her plate with gooey lasagna, but she paused with a string of cheese dangling off the serving spoon.

"Ruby, my friend, your life is full of odd stories, and I am here for it," Aryn broke the silence with a belly laugh. "Did that feel like true love to you?"

Ruby cracked up. "No. I think he was in love with what my mother could do with the venison, because she always invited him for dinner. Sweet and sour venison, venison dumplings, venison low mein."

"How many deer did he bring you?" I asked.

"Probably four before my dad scared him off. Said his wife wasn't going to be wooed away from him with superb cuts of game." Now Ruby was busting up, too.

"That's the funniest thing I've ever heard." I sputtered.

"Well, you asked what the nicest thing was, and that's it." She dried her eyes. "I never thought he actually loved me, but it was nice to have some attention for awhile."

I sighed as she handed me the serving spoon. "I have nothing to compare to that, Rubes. What about you Aryn?" I scooped my helping and passed her the spoon, moving on to the salad.

Aryn wrinkled up her face as she dove into the lasagna. "I haven't had much luck in the love department, which should be obvious considering I'm still single at age thirty-two. But there was this guy in high school who sometimes left little notes of encouragement in my locker. He did it anonymously, but I knew it was him. It was sweet."

"That is sweet," I said with a soft smile.

"Why didn't he fess up?" Ruby asked. "Or ask you out?"

Aryn blushed, which forced Ruby and I to pause on our way back to the living room. Lizzie, hearing the silence, stopped herself before sitting back on the couch and bounced back up to face the kitchen.

"Is there a scandal we should know about?" Lizzie asked.

Aryn shook her head. "He was kind of dating someone, so . . ."

Ruby's eyes grew large. "Way to be a tempting vixen."

"It wasn't a big deal. We were friends, and it was nice of him."

I felt like there was more to that story, but I could tell Aryn was uncomfortable, so I redirected as I led the way back to the living area.

"I'm glad I've never had anything really terrible happen to me, dating-wise," I said. "There are a lot of people who get hurt."

"You know," Ruby said thoughtfully as she plopped down into an armchair. "Even though we're getting older and we're still single, I think we have a lot to be happy about. I always wanted sisters, and now I have four. I'm extra lucky to have a job I love."

"We get to eat Hailey's cooking," Aryn added.

"Don't forget Lizzie's famous enchiladas," I said, mentioning those cheesy delights that had been considered a total prize in the past.

"It's good to remember that we're luckier than we think we are," Ruby stated. "Sure, sometimes it can get lonely, and occasionally I can feel my mom mourning the passing of my birthing years, but I think we're fine."

Yes, we were lucky. But you could be lucky and lonely all at the same time. I kept the thought to myself, however. Last May when Lizzie had begged us to go on an adventure and said she needed a change, I hadn't related but I'd been supportive. I was newly thirty at the time and wasn't feeling the tug quite as hard as she had been. However, I could feel the yearning sneaking in, and it was unwelcome. Sandy blond hair, intense eyes, and a perfectly formed face flashed in my mind, and I shook my head.

"We *are* fine," I said, more intensely than I'd meant to. Their eyes flew to my face, and I felt my cheeks warm. "Sorry," I mumbled.

Aryn grinned. "No, really, you're right. Ruby is right. We have a good life."

I ate a bite of the lasagna and hit play on the movie again. Life was better than good. It was great. So, so great.

*****

My phone dinged at 7:15 the next morning, and I rolled to my side to see who was messaging me.

Meredith: I need to do yoga today. I'll pick you up in 15.

Me: You hate yoga

Meredith: I know. So do our other friends. See you in 14.

I jumped out of bed, knowing that chatting with her was wasting time. When Meredith Atwood said she was on her way, she was most likely already pulling up to your house. My body felt sluggish after the loads of pasta and cookies consumed last night, so I wasn't too upset about her wanting to exercise. I needed it.

Meredith: We're going to the park

I paused in pulling on my yoga pants and frowned. Why? The gym had a perfectly good yoga area.

Me: It's 40 degrees outside

Meredith: It's the opposite of hot yoga. Hot yoga sounds like torture. This is chilly yoga.

Me: I'm not sure you can stretch well in those temperatures.

Meredith: Dress warm. 10 minutes.

I shook my head and finished dressing. Dressing warm meant layers. I put on a long-sleeved shirt and pulled a sweatshirt over it. My thickest yoga pants, warm socks, and tennis shoes would have to complete the ensemble even though bare feet were the norm. I told myself I'd warm up when we got going and decided not to fight the wishes of my blustery friend. I freshened up in the bathroom, ate a banana, and grabbed a water bottle with minutes to spare.

I opened the blinds in my living room and closed my eyes as I felt the rising sun warm my face through the glass. It had been a couple of days since I'd taken the time for my regular yoga practice, and there was some strain in my muscles as I began to lightly move them into stretches, tugging my feet up to my bottom, reaching over my head and attempting to prepare myself. Two minutes later I saw her pull up outside my condo, and I grabbed my things and hustled out to meet her.

Meredith's blue eyes were frosty this morning, and I felt the chill of her mood as I sat down in the passenger seat and buckled up. The car was still cold, something that seemed to match the vibes inside the vehicle.

"What happened last night at the HOA meeting?" I asked, hugging my mat to my chest and shivering at the icy leather seat against my legs.

"Other than finally having proof that I'm living in a tyrannical regime? Not much." Her voice was clipped.

I wasn't sure what to say, so I sat back against the seat and tried not to cry out at the way she was taking corners and gunning it off stoplights. Her driving fit her mood this morning. It only took a few minutes to get to a park that she deemed worthy, which most likely meant empty. This wasn't something hard to come by at 7:30 a.m. on a Saturday in cold temperatures. She cut the engine and shoved open her door, so I followed suit. Maybe she'd talk to me during the exercise portion of our morning adventure.

"What's that?" I asked her when she stood from getting her things out of the backseat. "It looks like a foam mattress camping pad."

She held up the three-inch-thick piece of yellow foam and gave me a look. "It's what I had."

I bit my lip to keep from laughing. "It's not really going to be useful for yoga."

Her own lips pinched. "It'll be a lot more comfortable than that towel you've got."

I looked down at my plastic mat and then back to her. "What kind of towels are you using at your house? Mine are a little less plastic."

"Shut up and follow me."

She started walking, creating a hilarious picture as she schlepped a six-foot-tall foam pad across the dewy grass towards a pavilion that housed two picnic tables. It was then that I noticed more fully what she was wearing--a knit cap, puffy coat, mittens and sweatpants with boots. What on earth was she going for here? This was not yoga, but it was going to be entertaining.

She entered the pavilion and leaned her gigantic pad up against one pillar while going to shove the picnic tables to the side. "Come help me," she grunted.

I set my nicely rolled mat next to her mattress and went to help. "When is the last time you did yoga?"

"In college," she replied as she shoved the table. It squealed in protest, but we were able to get it moving.

"That's quite a while ago."

"That's because I don't like yoga."

Yep. I knew that. In fact, I'd mentioned that earlier, but, yeah. "I think we have enough space now."

She put her hands on her hips and nodded. "Good. Shall we?" She moved to where her mattress was and hefted it to the now open space. "You're going to have to lead, and I'll do what you do."

I nodded and situated my much smaller, much more plastic pad next to hers. "We'll start with a simple warm up."

"Nope. Let's get right to it. I want to sweat out all this negativity."

I guided her through a few simple moves, and she did her best to keep up, but she kept falling off balance on account of her mattress not supporting her without giving way. Her boots were too heavy to hold her legs in the right position, and her knit cap kept falling over her eyes. Before too long I was the only one doing yoga, and she was lying on her mattress, looking at the ceiling of the pavilion while I exercised.

"I never thought I'd turn into a shrew," she said thoughtfully, clasping her gloved hands against her stomach. "I don't actually like being seen as evil."

"I don't think anyone sees you as evil," I replied, holding a pose.

"Mm-hmm."

"Maybe a little fierce."

"Brooks VanOrman called me 'bitter' last night and accused me of attending the HOA meetings with no other purpose than to antagonize him and slow down the democratic process." Her voice was tight, and I was able to hear what she wasn't saying. The words had hurt. "All I did was ask why they were voting on a rule that would require people to carry their pets when in the common areas. Carry their pets. No walking your dog or letting your cat meander around if you're in a public space."

I blinked a few times and transitioned into another pose. Once I was centered in it, I asked for clarification. "I don't understand. You can't let your pets walk on grass?"

"Yeah. In the parks or common areas, like the community clubhouse lawn or playground areas. If someone has a pet, they have to lift them off the ground and carry them until they're off the grass."

"Why?"

"To, and I quote, 'preserve the integrity of the grounds.'" She scoffed. "It's insane."

"And Brooks VanOrman agreed with this policy?"

I glanced her way when she didn't answer and saw her shrug. "I don't know where he stands on it. I simply know that he called for a vote, and when I objected he accused me of being a stumbling block in the process."

"What did you say when you objected?"

"That I know for a fact some older people in the neighborhood have big dogs and won't be able to carry them and that I think it infringes on peoples' rights to take their pets on walks. I also said that as a school teacher, I can promise people do more damage to grassy areas than the few pets passing through. These people pay their HOA fees. They should be allowed to use the common areas."

I took a deep breath and let it out as I shifted again. "That doesn't sound shrewish to me."

"In fairness to Brooks VanOrman, I'd also objected to paying fees for overnight guests and having a dress code for garage sales."

This time my pose faltered, and I flopped down onto my bottom. "What?"

"You heard me right. You'd have to pay $10 a night for overnight guests, and if you want to host a garage sale, you could do it in April or October, but to designate yourself as the seller you have to wear a blue polo shirt and khaki pants."

A shocked laugh burst out of me. "Those rules are absurd. Are they actual rules or do people bring these to the meetings to vote on?"

"Right now they're not rules, or at least they won't be this month thanks to my strident work. But, yeah, people show up to the meetings wanting to implement these wacky rules, and then the board votes on them. Only I've started attending and shooting them down."

"And Brooks VanOrman, HOA president, got tired of you doing that? I don't understand why he'd be upset with you rather than commending you for your common sense."

She sighed. "He's tired of me just like I'm tired of him. It's been a few long months of battle. The things is, I'd back off if the guy grew a backbone. I have no idea how he even got elected."

I leaned over and patted her arm. "Maybe they realized they'd never get anything past you and so they went for the soft guy."

"Brooks? Soft? Hardly. The man has a big beard that would make a lumberjack jealous and a tattoo peeking out from the sleeve of his wrinkled button-down shirts. He looks like a guy who knows how to handle things, you know?"

I'd never seen him, but I did know he was a worthy opponent for my friend. The same friend who had moments before dropped his last name and only called him Brooks. It was more telling than she realized, considering for the past year we'd never called him only by his first name. He was getting to her.

"Plus," she continued, "he didn't even run for the position. They found out he's a lawyer, and so they asked him. I was begging for the job, and they sought out this random dude that wanted nothing to do with it."

"Ouch."

"Yeah." Her head sank further into the mattress. "If I play my cards right, he'll quit."

"Is that what you really want?" I kept my tone soft in the face of her uncharacteristic vulnerability.

"I don't know." She turned her head to face me. "He confuses me."

I smiled. "Welcome to my life."

"Does Ford confuse you?" she asked, and I nodded. "In a good way?" she asked.

I shrugged. "I'm not sure, and I'm trying really hard not to think about him at all."

She reached out and took my hand. "I think I'll try that plan for myself. Thanks for doing yoga with me this morning."

I squeezed back. "You mean watching you snooze on your big comfy bed while offering my services as a therapist?"

"Yeah, that." She grinned, and I was relieved to see regular Meredith in her eyes. "Any time."

CHAPTER NINE

I needed this night, so much. It was exactly the perfect way to finish the purification of my thoughts and emotions. It was one of my happy places, and it had never let me down before. I'd meant what I said to Meredith about trying to let go of thoughts that weren't serving me, and the theater was the ideal place to reorder my disjointed mind. Was I putting undue pressure on the opera to pull me out of my funk and get me back on my feet again? Probably. But the mind is a powerful tool, and the opera could only enhance its gifts, as far as I was concerned. I was going to immerse myself in the magic and come away renewed.

Dressed in an elegant black dress and strappy silver heels with my cashmere shawl around my shoulders, I was upbeat and excited--the very image of a class act. I'd managed to pull my hair into a short updo, and I'd taken extra time with my makeup, all culminating in me feeling pampered and ready for a wonderful evening. I entered the theater with my hand through Dad's arm and Mom on his other side, all of us talking happily as we discussed the upcoming performance. We were season ticket holders to the opera and loved attending together, soaking in the music and reconnecting with other friends who attended.

I couldn't wait to lose myself to the intricate theater with its whites, golds, and reds; lovingly restored murals; and divine music. I hadn't told my parents about Hillary's dance recital or my ongoing emotional reactions to Ford, and I was glad I hadn't. It meant nothing would need to be discussed tonight. They probably assumed the last time I'd seen him was at their house a while ago--an assumption I was happy to support.

I let go of Dad's arm and dropped back to follow him and Mom up the stairs to our balcony seats. We loved the bird's-eye view, and as a relatively introverted person, I also enjoyed sitting inconspicuously off to the side where I could feel most comfortable. I never could relax when I felt like people were watching me or there was even the slightest chance I'd be pulled up on stage or spoken to by the performers. A bubble of excitement rose as we walked into the main auditorium and could hear the orchestra warming up over the hum of the audience gathering.

"I love Carmen," Mom said over her shoulder to me. "I've been looking forward to this all week."

"Me, too," I replied.

Dad slid in first, leaving Mom and I to sit together, which we were happy about. The seat on the end next to me remained empty, as we'd agreed to have a night just the three of us, even though we had four tickets for occasions when I couldn't come, allowing another couple to attend with my parents. Mom and I spoke in soft undertones, me telling her about my classroom and her updating me on the convention she'd be attending the next week. She was taking a full week away from in-person patient work to travel to Boston and meet with other psychiatrists about the latest innovations and new practices. Mom was passionate about her work, and it showed in the way her eyes danced as she told me about meetings and discussion forums she'd be participating in.

"I wish you could come," she said to me. "My evenings are free, and Dad can't get away. Although I'm not sure how hard he tried. He's a terrible homebody. But Boston is beautiful in the fall, and it would be wonderful for you and me to have some time together."

I leaned against her and nodded. "I agree. Too bad that getting subs and prepping a week's worth of lesson plans isn't easy on short notice. Next time?"

She patted my knee. "Okay. I'll do better about giving you a heads up."

We settled back into our chairs as the lights dimmed in preparation for the beginning of the opera. I tugged my wrap off and rested it across my lap, my eager eyes focusing on the stage. Chills started at the top of my head and washed over me as the beauty of the music filled the space. It had always been like this for me: the music calling to me in a powerful way. The familiar melodies wrapped around me as the acoustics of the auditorium were put to the test, and when the singing started, I was spellbound. For nearly two hours I was so still I hardly breathed, and when the last notes faded and the lights came up signaling intermission, I had to blink a few times and suck in a breath.

"Wonderful," Dad said as he stood, clapping enthusiastically. "Simply wonderful."

"The cast this year is incredible," Mom agreed, also standing.

I stood too, my heart in my throat, and wiggled my shoulders to get some blood moving again as I clapped alongside them.

"How is it intermission already?" I smiled when the sound died down. "I was so engrossed in it that the time absolutely flew."

Mom squeezed my arm. "That's how you know it was a truly remarkable performance."

"We have twenty minutes. Would anyone like to walk around for a minute?" Dad asked.

I nodded. "It would be good to get my circulation going again."

"Wait." Mom grabbed my forearm, stopping me from turning. "Isn't that Leonard's friend, Ford Whittaker?" she asked.

I froze, scanning the area, but didn't see him below us. "Where?"

"Over there, on the opposite balcony."

I looked up and was surprised to find him looking back at me from across the way. It was straight out of my dreams, and my chest felt suddenly tight and warm. Regardless of all my pretending, I'd never have suspected he was actually an opera guy. This new knowledge tugged at something deep inside of me, something frightening that stirred a desire for . . . more.

How would it feel to sit next to him in the darkness while beautiful music floated around us? The image made my mouth suddenly dry.

His expression was calm as his eyes locked on to mine. He stood with one hand in his pants pocket, his suit jacket pushed back, and the other hand braced against the balcony railing. If the theater company had wanted a model for promotional material, they could have snapped his picture in that moment and had the ladies flocking to buy tickets. It was unfair how good he always looked.

I'd typically shied away from beautiful men and the way that they made me feel unaccountably tongue-tied. It was a struggle without explanation. It was how my mind worked, and I'd never had much reason to question it. I simply ran the opposite direction.

Tonight, this strung out, electric moment only confirmed that quirk of mine. He looked capable of hurting me in a way I couldn't make sense of. I shivered under the questioning intensity of his gaze and looked away, grabbing my wrap off the chair to sling around my shoulders.

Who was he really?

I had to shut the questions down, and it had to happen now. I lightly pulled away from my mom, ducking my head and swallowing hard as I turned to leave our row.

"That's him, yes," I mumbled. "Shall we?"

I snapped my shawl tightly around me and led the way out of our row and down the staircase to the foyer. Dad followed, but Mom stayed in her seat, begging off and saying she'd spotted a neighbor she was hoping to catch up with. Dad and I reached the foyer in record time, and I guided us toward the long hallway that would lead us outside. Dad fell into step beside me, his feet nearly soundless on the long gold and black rug as I walked quickly, trying to escape my rapid heartrate that had everything to do with seeing him, here. What was he doing in my happy place?

"Some fresh air might be nice," I said, explaining my rush to the front doors.

What I didn't say was that I wasn't interested in running into Ford in the foyer.

"You really dislike him, huh?" Dad commented as he held the entrance door open for me.

I hugged my shawl closer against the outside air and turned right, setting a slow pace. "Who?"

Dad chuckled. "Ford Whittaker."

"Oh. I don't dislike him," I replied as casually as I could.

"How do you feel when you're around him, then?"

Knowing my dad would accept nothing less than complete honesty and that he was a safe place for me, I unloaded it all. "Confused, annoyed, scared, unsure. Curious and worried. He's arrogant but then surprisingly charming. Our first meeting was not good. He assumed I was scheming with his daughter to marry him, which is absurd, considering we'd never met, and what kind of adult uses an eight-year-old to get dates?"

"He thought that?"

"Well, he said it out loud and made the accusation, so he believed it to some degree. And then, like a fool, I went to his birthday party, anyway, where Leonard pulled a scheme of his own."

Dad chuckled. "No wonder you weren't happy about seeing him at Sunday dinner."

"Yeah, and now I'm seeing him everywhere, and his daughter keeps inviting me to things, even though that might be a phase she's going through. I don't trust the way I act and feel around him, either."

Dad listened as we strolled, not asking questions or interrupting, letting me get it all out. I unloaded it all, telling him about each and every interaction we'd had, and when I was done, he let silence fall until we turned at the end of the block to slowly walk back. I didn't rush a response from him; I knew he was processing it all.

"That's a lot to take in, especially for someone like you who leads a pretty quiet life," he said thoughtfully.

"Yeah."

"So because of all those feelings, you're off balance?" he asked.

"You saw me at that Sunday dinner," I muttered.

"True." He sounded amused. "And the other times you've seen him, is it like that between you all the time?"

"Pretty much. Somehow, it's always me, too. He's calm and cheerful while I make a fool of myself."

"Hmm. That's not like you."

"I know. Thanks to you and mom I cut my teeth on emotional intelligence and proper manners. I know better, which is why I entirely blame myself for this mess."

"Is it a mess, then?"

I glanced to him and blinked. "Of course it's a mess. It's a disaster."

Dad took my hand and wove it through his arm. "Next question. Why do you blame yourself for this alleged disaster?"

This was it, the big moment where I confessed to my dad all about my completely inappropriate mind-romance with Ford. My words were halting, as I weighed out how I wanted to present this story to him. When I was finished telling him about it, he simply squeezed my hand against his side and chuckled.

"Hailey, my profession is dealing with the human mind, and I can completely guarantee that you're not a monster."

"It's a breach of privacy."

He shook his head. "Remember when you were little and your friends all wanted posters of their favorite bands hung in their rooms?" I nodded. "That entire industry--the poster making, the t-shirts for sale, the action figures--that's all because people like to imagine they're part of the lives of their favorite celebrities. It's normal to fantasize to a certain degree. It's using your imagination to picture something you want. Often, we fantasize about someone because we want to feel the way they make us feel in these daydreams. We want that special someone. We crave that connection." He tugged me to a stop and turned so that we were facing each other directly. "I have to say, though, the problem with this type of thing is that you're creating a fictional character. You're romanticizing them, glorifying them, and putting them on a pedestal. So, while it may seem harmless because it's not interfering with your work or taking over your real life, and you aren't following him around, it can still become a problem."

I bit my lips and nodded as my stomach clenched unpleasantly. "I know. I felt safe doing it because I didn't think we'd ever be in the same circles. Then we met, and it's been really strange to try to separate the pretend version from who he really is. I'm such a wreck."

Dad pulled me in for a light hug. "You're not a total wreck. You might be searching for something, and daydreaming about Ford soothed some of those feelings in a way that felt safe because, like you said, you never thought you'd actually meet." We started walking again. "I'm not trying to make you feel bad. Just be aware that those emotional needs for connection can be better fulfilled in other ways with real people who love you." We arrived back at the theater, and Dad held the door for me to enter. "This was pretty heavy stuff for intermission," he chuckled once we were inside. "You okay?"

I shivered a bit as my body adjusted from the cool outside air to the warm, crowded heat of the theater. Rather than walk all the way in, I stopped by the entrance and looked up at my dad. He was as tall and lean as he'd ever been, but his hair was almost entirely gray now and his goatee matched. His frameless glasses stood on the same indents along his nose as they always had. His dark eyes were as open and loving as they'd always been, and I had such an urge to throw my arms around him and have him make it all better.

I sighed, feeling deflated but ready to face the facts, no matter how painful it was to admit. "You're right. I've been doing my best to curb it ever since we met, but just when I think it's all behind me, there he is again, bringing along that feeling tornado. I'm trying to roll with it and separate the fact from fiction, but it's hard work when there's so much emotion involved."

"What's the verdict so far? As you get to know him, how different is he from what you'd imagined?"

I twisted my lips in thought. "Well, he's much more outgoing than I'd imagined, but he's mostly kind. Seeing him here is a punch to the gut."

Dad nodded. "I'm surprised that he's gotten under your skin so thoroughly. Most guys don't."

"This is a first for me."

"Only time will tell, but I'm not sure the reaction he's getting out of you is all bad. Some of those irrational feelings can be good . . ."

I started walking, throwing up a hand to stop him. "I swear, if you start telling me about the mating habits of animals and all the fighting that goes on there, I will disown you."

He caught up to me easily, taking my upraised hand and tucking it through his arm. His suit jacket was cold against my palm, a temperature which I appreciated at the moment.

"Okay, I won't tease you. It's okay to be confused by him. Be patient. It will settle and, pretty soon, you'll know where the reality lies," he soothed as we started climbing the stairs. "For what it's worth, I hope you give him a run for his money. Every man could use that now and again."

"Dad!" I squeezed his arm. "That's terrible advice. He's not interested in spending time with me, you know."

"If you say so."

"I do. Plus, I am not going to play games with Ford Whittaker or any other man. What would your students and colleagues say?"

"They'd say that we can pretend to be evolved, but at our core we're still a little bit caveman."

I laughed out loud, my dimples sinking into my cheeks as we passed through the doorway to the balcony seats where Mom was waiting. She was standing facing us, talking to a man whose back was turned our direction. My eyes darted across the room to see that Ford's seat was empty, and I knew, I knew, that somehow Mom had gotten him over here, and he'd be sitting in our spare seat. I cursed that extra seat, even as I promised myself to not let this throw me for a loop. Especially after the conversation I'd just had with Dad.

My amusement died as heat crawled up my spine. Ford, hearing us, turned around with that same charming smile he always wore.

"Conrad," he greeted my father kindly with an outstretched hand. "Sylvia was telling me about her trip to Boston and we were exchanging restaurant recommendations."

Dad took his hand and shook it firmly. "I hope it was all seafood, because I hate the stuff and encourage her to get her fill when she's back east."

Ford chuckled, and his eyes moved to me. As usual, they quickly took me in from my slipping smile to my silver heels. He zoned in and that feeling tornado launched in my chest as he gave a short nod.

"Hailey."

I returned the greeting exactly. "Ford."

"I've invited Ford to watch the second half with us," Mom said happily. "He was alone tonight, and we have the extra seat."

I was surprised that he would come to the opera alone. I imagined him as always having people around him. I glanced at Dad as he slipped into his seat, and his expression reminded me that he didn't see Ford as dangerous or me as a monster, which helped me loosen my stiff spine as I sat next to my mom. Of course, this left Ford on my right-hand side with only me to talk to unless he leaned around me. I reached up to pull off my wrap, suddenly much too warm for it, and he unexpectedly helped me. His fingertips lightly brushed my bare shoulder as he slid it off and into my lap in a fluid motion.

"Thank you." I managed over a sea of sensations.

"I didn't know you are an opera fan," he said conversationally.

His tone was relaxed and curious, and I was a little jealous of his ease as I sat facing forward, not allowing my eyes to drift his way.

I could say the same about you, I thought, but I replied with, "I love it."

"I come any chance I get. An occasional night off from work and parenting goes a long way."

That was probably the most personal thing he'd ever told me about himself. Too bad I wouldn't be responding in kind, even if I wanted to know even more about how his thoughts worked and who he was. I was not here to open any doors between us. Keeping it light, keeping it professional . . . that was my goal.

"Are you familiar with Carmen, then?" I glanced toward the orchestra pit where the musicians were taking their seats.

"It's the first opera I saw. After that, I was addicted."

He kept his voice low, speaking under the noise of the crowd even though I was facing partially away. Turning had been a mistake, because it meant that his voice came straight to my ear, creating this unwanted feeling that we were sharing a secret. I closed my eyes, shoving down the wave of . . . something . . . and took a breath.

"More deep breathing, huh?" he teased.

I ignored him and kept my eyes focused on the stage. "Does your family enjoy opera?" I asked. "Did you go with your wife before she passed?"

I couldn't believe I'd dared to bring her up. So much for avoiding the personal stuff. But it was a desperate attempt to keep me from feeling things. Things with a capital T. Things that might not be real. I folded my hands in my lap and squeezed my fingers together.

"Heather wasn't a big fan, but initially she came because I liked it." His response was halting, as though he was dragging the words out against his will. "Eventually, she said she couldn't get into it, and it was something I could do on my own."

I dared a glance back at him. He had a far-off look in his eye as he spoke, not really focusing on anything. "Her name was Heather?" I asked, like I didn't already know.

"Yes. Like Hillary said, it started with an H."

"Which is fair because they all had your last name," I repeated Hillary's words.

One side of his mouth raised in a sad sort of half smile. "Makes sense, right?"

I wasn't sure if it did or not, but it wasn't my place to dissect that situation. "Only if it didn't hurt your feelings."

He blinked, and his expression transformed back to the easy one I was used to seeing. "It didn't."

I kept any further thoughts to myself as the lights dimmed. I was happy to lean closer to my mom and watch the stage as the music picked back up. Even sitting next to Ford couldn't distract me from Carmen. The music swelled, and my heartbeat picked up, matching it beat for beat. I loved the second half of the opera, the music and acting, all of it. My hands gripped the arms of my chair and moisture filled my eyes after a particularly beautiful song. When it was over I leaned more fully against the back of my chair and reached up to dab under my eyes.

A white tissue appeared as Ford said, "That was incredible."

The low, gentle, and intimate tone unraveled all my best plans to keep him at bay.

I took the tissue and dabbed away the wetness before balling it up in my fist and refocusing on the stage. Only, I couldn't focus anymore. Knowing he was sitting there, loving opera as much as I did, knowing he too felt the power behind the music, well, it was a distraction.

His soft breathing stole my thoughts, and every shift of his leg brushing against the skirt of my dress was a jolt to my system. His shoulder bumped mine, leaving confusion when he didn't pull away. For the last twenty minutes we were touching, shoulder to shoulder and knee to knee. I wanted to pull away, but more than that I wanted to snuggle in closer to the strength and warmth coming off him.

When the last note was sung and the audience sprang to their feet with applause, I was more than happy to join them. I stood so quickly that I wobbled on my heels, but Ford reached out and steadied me before I could tip over. Once I was standing firm again, he let go and joined in the clapping. I didn't dare look at him or say one word. I kept my eyes down as we gathered our things and left. When it was my turn to say goodbye to him, I said it to his nose, too scared to look into his eyes and let him see the vulnerability and longing in mine.

Even more scared of seeing something else entirely in his.

CHAPTER TEN

It took me almost a week to admit it, but after some time spent separating fact from fiction, I fully accepted that I was lonely. I was lonely enough that I'd created a pretend world in my mind where I got all the benefits of love without any of the risks involved in dating. Once I'd accepted that, I was ready to do something about it.

I'd given Aryn the official green light, and midway through the week she had approached me with the name of a guy who she thought would be a great fit for me. Although my heart had beat hard in my chest with nerves as Aryn gave me the rundown on him, I'd accepted, and tonight I'd be going on my first blind date ever. I was only a little panicky about it.

His name was Shane, and he was a friend of Ayrn's brother. Shane had been divorced almost two years ago and was ready to get back into the dating scene. I didn't have anything against a divorced person. I was realistic in understanding that dating at my age often meant dating men who had experienced some things. However, I did wonder if his heart was still broken and what we'd have in common. I was trusting that Aryn knew me well and would be selective in who she set me up with.

We had agreed to meet at a local restaurant for a light dinner and then he said he had an after-activity planned and to dress in layers. Layers meant cold, which didn't exactly leave me with an excited feeling. I was kind of a fair-weather person and made it through the northern Utah winters with a lot of wool socks and hot tea. Still, I was keeping an open mind, so I dressed in jeans, a blue sweater that did amazing things for my eyes, and my best pair of leather boots. I shoved mittens and a scarf in my purse before heading out with my coat draped over my arm.

When I entered the warm lobby of the Thai restaurant he'd chosen, my eyes immediately started scanning the people around me for anyone meeting the description Aryn had given me of a tall man with black hair and a mustache. It was a busy Friday night, the lobby filled with a mix of college kids and middle-aged parents out for a free night. He saw me before I saw him, and a tap on my shoulder had me turning around. I had to stifle a giggle. Aryn had said tall, but she'd meant gargantuan. I wasn't short at five foot six, but Shane was probably at least six foot five, and my eyes had to climb forever before landing first on his mustache and then up to his eyes. His shoulders were broad, and he blocked some light as he leaned toward me.

"White hair, dressed nice? You must be Hailey," he said in a gruff, low voice.

I smiled up at him, amused at the description of me. It was lucky he hadn't tried to pick up a ninety-year-old. "Hi Shane, nice to meet you."

He offered me a huge hand that fully enveloped mine as we shook. "I was already seated. Our table's over here."

I followed him through to the back of the dining area where there was a small two-person table pushed up against the windows. His large coat was hanging off the back of the chair, tickling the ground, and I thought about Aryn and her extra tall brothers. She probably thought Shane was a normal height.

"So you teach school with Aryn?" Shane asked, sitting down.

I nodded as I took my seat. "I do. I teach second grade. What do you do?"

"I'm an accountant for the university," he replied, picking up his menu.

A sudden image of a floor full of cubicles with his head and shoulders popping out of the top made me want to grin again. "Do you like it?"

He glanced at me and pursed his lips in thought. "I'm not sure if it matters. A job is a job. Pays the bills, and I don't dread going to work."

Okay. Fair enough. I picked up my own menu and looked over it even though I already knew what I wanted. The Massaman Curry here was to die for. I wanted to ask Shane more about his thoughts on not needing to like work. It was an interesting concept, to not be seeking for his passion but to only see it as a job that paid the bills. So many people put work first and wanted it to be their identity. Did it mean he wasn't driven to find more, or did it mean that he was content and laid back? It was probably a healthy mindset in some ways.

The waiter came before we spoke again, and we both gave our orders. He took our menus and then there was nothing between us except a vase with a tea candle inside.

"I understand you've never been married," he said.

Oh. I hadn't seen that as the first line of discussion, but I quickly recovered. "I haven't. Aryn tells me you're divorced?"

He nodded. "Yeah. She's living down in Salt Lake. We didn't have kids. Do you have kids?"

I shook my head. "I don't."

"That's good. They could complicate things. I think it's easier to start fresh, you know."

I picked up my glass and took a sip of water while deciding how to reply. His eyes were dark and intense, watching and waiting for me to answer. In a flash I thought of Ford who also occasionally watched me intently, and I realized with a start there was a difference. Ford's intensity was curious while Shane's seemed heavy, as though he was giving me a test of some sort. I tried to think of a diplomatic answer as I took another swallow. Sure, I understood that melding children into a new marriage could be difficult, but I didn't see them as a 'complication' that would be distasteful.

Redirection seemed like my only tactful option. I wasn't looking for truly serious conversation at this point, anyhow. We were just meeting.

"What kinds of things do you do outside of work?" I asked.

His expression held mine for a moment longer before he leaned back in his chair. "I like to hike and play sports. I play with Aryn's brother, Sean, in a basketball league."

When I realized he wasn't going to ask me the same question, I volunteered the information. "I really like to cook and do yoga."

"Hmm. Do you play any sports?"

I shook my head, allowing a self-deprecating smile to raise my lips. "I'm not very athletic that way."

"That's too bad. Aryn tells me you really like kids."

Aaand . . . we were back to the topic of children. "I do. I couldn't enjoy my job as a teacher if I didn't."

"Do you want kids yourself? Like, to be a mother?" he asked, and I nodded. "What was your mom like?"

"She's warm and understanding. I had a wonderful childhood," I answered, feeling less relaxed and more like I was seriously being interviewed.

"What about your dad?"

"He's funny and kind."

"What's their marriage like?"

"Good. Healthy. Loving." I didn't feel like he was interested in embellishments.

"Great, great," he muttered as the waiter sat his plate in front of him.

I was so flabbergasted by his interview-style questioning that I ate my food slowly. However, I must have said a few things right because after a few bites of his own food he became a totally different person. He had me laughing with some stories about his youth, time spent with Aryn's brother, and even some accounting humor. He asked me more about myself and seemed interested in me. Eventually I was able to give full sentences as answers. I was beginning to see why Aryn thought we'd suit and wondered what that initial questioning blitz had been about. He must have been deeply hurt in the breakup of his marriage. I could understand him being wary of not suiting with someone new.

By the time we were done eating, I was willing to continue the date and see what he had planned. I had second thoughts when he told me to follow him to the ice skating rink in North Logan. Seemed like my entire 'I'm not athletic' speech had gone in one ear and out the other. But I gamely painted on a smile and followed him as instructed.

I was quiet while we rented skates and changed into them. When the skates were on, I stood, wobbling slightly, and Shane offered me one of his hands to hold while using his other to help me into my coat. I wrapped my scarf around my neck and tugged on my mittens before nodding at him. He kept hold of my hand as we made it out to the ice, and I appreciated him not teasing me about how uncoordinated I actually was. I tried to not notice the complete lack of any reaction to holding his hand, unlike Ford who only had to brush past me to set off dancing ponies in my stomach.

I'd been ice skating a time or two, so it wasn't like I had no idea what I was doing. It was more that this wasn't an activity I'd choose to do, so I hadn't put much effort into improving at it. With my hand still in Shane's, I managed to stay upright. He was confident and graceful on the ice, and it helped me to relax enough to let him tug me along. In fact, letting him pull me made it easier because then all I had to do was balance.

He kept up the conversation, vacillating between funny and intelligent, and paranoid and angry, open and kind, and reserved and cynical. My mind was going around in the same circles as we were. I couldn't decide if I liked him or not. The dichotomy between his two personality types kept me from joining in much.

"I need to use the restroom," he said fifteen minutes later as we neared the entrance to the rink. "I'll just be a minute."

I nodded and released his hand, watching him skate off and exit the arena. I'd been feeling more confident, so I thought I'd skate alone for a bit and see if I could get comfortable skating without holding on to him. I was halfway around the rink when something--or some*one*--barreled into my side, knocking me flat onto my back. I was looking up at the ceiling, feeling the cold seep into the seat of my jeans, when Hillary's bright eyes popped into view.

"Miss Hailey," she chirped. "I'm sorry. I didn't mean to make you fall. I wanted to surprise you."

Ford's amused voice entered a second before his head showed above hers. "Are you okay?"

He reached out a gloved hand, and I took it without thinking, letting him pull me to standing. The motion was faster than I expected, coupled with the fact I was on ice, and I tumbled up against him, ending with my nose pressed against his chest. His arms came around me quickly, somehow holding me up and keeping us both from falling as my legs slipped and slid beneath me. For me, the moment froze. Even through all the layers of my clothing, I could feel the muscles in his arms and the firmness of his chest. His breath puffed against my forehead as he laughed, and I felt as though I were in a dream, when my own arms launched around his neck to hold on tight . . . which kind of, accidentally, sort of turned into hugging him closer as the motion had my feet skidding forward to bracket his.

"I've got you; you won't fall," he soothed, amusement still lacing his tone.

I freed my face from his squashed position and nodded, my mouth unable to form words as I soaked in a feeling better than any of the daydreams I'd given up on. He smelled good, he felt good, his voice wove its way into me, calming and soothing. It took extreme willpower not to turn my head to press my cheek against his shoulder and beg him to let me stay.

"Who was that you were holding hands with?" Hillary asked.

Her voice and her question were the equivalent of slapping my face with an ice-cold rag. I quickly released Ford and skated a step, reaching up to smooth down my hair before tugging at the bottom of my coat.

"He's . . ."

"He's her date," Ford stated, those gray eyes smiling at my obvious discomfort.

"It's such a surprise seeing you here," I said, looking down at Hillary, where it was safe.

I hadn't noticed quiet Henry joining us, but he stood solemnly next to his sister, watching everything.

"Sorry again that I knocked you over." Hillary pulled a face. "I thought it would be funny to sneak up on you, but Daddy said to leave you alone while you were with that man. Who is he?"

"His name is Shane."

"Are you in love with him?" she asked.

I shook my head. "I only met him tonight. We're on a blind date."

"But I thought holding hands was for being in love." She tilted her head sideways with a questioning look.

"Sometimes it's for keeping me from falling down. Did you have to hold your dad's hand when you were learning?" She nodded, and I looked back at Ford, feeling a pressing need to make him understand. "I tried to tell him I'm not very athletic, but he'd already bought tickets to skate tonight."

"It's not a bad move, bringing a girl somewhere where she's forced to cling to you all night," he replied with a grin.

His nonchalant answer was a pinprick reminder that he'd have no reason to care that I was on a date. His stance was clear, and he hadn't asked for or needed an explanation from me. I used the dull throb of sadness to firm up my resolve. After a silent, deep breath I got back into the zone and laughed at his comment. Sure, the laugh was a little late, and his expression said it was ill-timed, too, so I doubled down by rolling my eyes.

During my eye roll--which may have been a little excessive--I caught sight of Shane skating toward us. I gestured to him. "Looks like he's back. It was fun to see you, Hillary."

I turned to move back toward Shane, who was almost upon us. I wasn't sure about the protocol for introducing blind dates to former figments of your imagination, but it seemed like something to avoid. So I threw a wave behind me and met him several yards away. He held out his hand and I took it, even though I knew I was being watched. My face heated as I realized I could still feel the warmth of Ford pressed against me.

"Who was that?" Shane asked as we got moving again.

"A girl I taught last year," I did my best to smile up at him.

We resumed circling the rink, and I forced myself to engage more with him during this second half of our skating adventure. I laughed quite a bit, and I did my level best to be the most delightful person he'd ever met. I refused to make eye contact with the Whittakers or to compare and contrast Ford and Shane. Ford, all golden and charming. Shane, all dark and sort of damaged, somehow. I must have managed to give off the performance of a lifetime, because suddenly Shane tugged me to a stop and turned me to face him.

His eyes searched mine, and before I could read the look in them, his lips were headed toward mine. His hands had moved to grasp my shoulders, but with the height difference and the fact I was neither expecting nor wanting his kiss, I lurched backwards while he was still bending.

The end result was that no lips made contact, but I slammed to the ground with his full weight landing on top of me. My head cracked against the ice, followed by his chin slamming against my forehead, and then I felt a sharp pain in my left wrist. I'd involuntarily reached back to stop our fall, and now my wrist was bent at a strange angle beneath the two of us. Pain shot up to my elbow, and I let out a muffled exclamation. Shane seemed stunned. At least that was the explanation I came up with based on the way he kept laying there making no move to get up. My wrist was going to snap if I couldn't get this weight off of it, so I shoved at him with my right hand.

"Get off!" I cried.

My voice woke him from whatever stupor of idiocy he was caught in, and he put his hands on either side of my head before pushing off and rolling to his back. I rolled to my right side and freed my wrist, hugging it to my chest and taking huge gulping breaths of air. The man was a behemoth. My head throbbed, my wrist throbbed, and when skates popped into view followed by Ford's handsome face bending down, I felt tears gather at the corner of my eyes.

"You okay?" he asked, his head tilted sideways.

I rolled onto my back and shook my head as my throat grew thick. I was hurt, embarrassed, and a little angry that Shane had tried to kiss attack me. I turned my head to look at Shane. He'd sat up and was rubbing at his chin. Oh, yeah, that's right, he'd chin-butted me on landing. It was all I could do not to glare up at him when he finally looked down.

"You okay?" he asked. At least he sounded sincerely concerned, which helped me feel less steamed.

"Yeah," I replied.

"She's hugging her wrist," Hillary volunteered, and I smothered a groan. "I think she hurt it."

"She hit her head pretty hard," Henry added as he joined the fray. "I thought maybe the ice would crack."

Freaking fantastic. The entire Whittaker clan was here to witness this debacle. I closed my eyes against a wave of emotion and pushed it down, knowing I could cry in my bathtub later. For now I wanted off this ice and to go home with what little dignity and class I still had.

"Let's get you up," Shane said, and my eyes opened as I felt him reach for my arm.

"Careful," Ford inserted. "She hit her head pretty hard, and she's not saying much."

"She hasn't had anything to say all night." Shane shrugged, dropping his hand to his side.

The jab was annoying, considering I'd been feeling pretty good about how well I'd held up my end of the conversation. But the sting was gone when I saw Ford's face split into a grin as our eyes met.

"Really?" he said, and I immediately knew he was thinking about all the things I'd had to say to him.

Hillary sat next to me and patted my shoulder. "I'll sit here with you until you feel good enough to get up."

I smiled at her in thanks. I simply needed my head to settle down, and I'd be good to go. After a few minutes of silence, I used my good hand to push to sitting. When that didn't cause any dizziness, I reached up my right hand for a little assistance. Shane got to it before Ford could, and he hauled me up. Unlike Ford he didn't wait to see if I was balanced but stepped back a hair. I wobbled, but Hillary's little arm wrapped around me from the side, and she steadied me. It was so incredibly sweet that I wanted to hug her.

"I guess we're done here, then?" Shane asked. I knew he meant more than just the skating.

"Yeah, I think so. Thanks for dinner and everything." I gave him the kindest look I could through the pounding in my head . . . oh, and the fact I wanted to deck him for the entire stupid idea of kissing me like that. "I'll tell Aryn."

"Can I help you get home? Are you okay to drive?" he asked.

I took a deep breath, analyzed, and then lied. "I'm fine. Don't worry about it."

"If you're sure?" He asked once more, and I softened again.

The poor oaf hadn't meant for it to end this way, but he was as anxious to ditch this awkwardness as I was. It couldn't have felt great on his end to have so severely misread a situation and then injured your date.

"Yeah." I replied.

"You should probably get your head and wrist looked at."

"I will."

He nodded once and skated away quickly, leaving me standing with my aching wrist held against my chest. I looked to Ford and Henry, who were watching with identical expressions of reproach as Shane skated away. It was enough to break the cloud that had formed in my mind and make me genuinely grin at the sight of little Henry shooting daggers.

"We'll take you home, won't we Daddy?" Hillary, who was still hugging me, said to Ford.

"No, thanks. My car is here," I argued when he looked to me.

"I'm not sure you should drive," he replied. "Are you okay leaving it here for now?"

"Please, Miss Hailey," Henry joined in, surprising me. "We can help you."

Any fight I had was gone with his plea, so I nodded, and Ford skated closer. He reached his hand through my right elbow, allowing me to still support my hurt wrist and giving me some stability as we made our way out of the rink. I'd come with one man, and I was leaving with another. My life was definitely in unfamiliar territory.

CHAPTER ELEVEN

ord kept one arm threaded through mine as we made our way into the darkened parking lot. Night had fully fallen, and I shivered even though it was no chillier out here than it had been inside the rink. He led the way to a large white SUV and helped me into the passenger side. The big seat formed comfortably to me as he laid it slightly back and leaned across me to turn on the seat warmer before buckling me in. These were all things I was totally capable of doing, but I silently let him perform the little tasks, loving any chance to be close to him.

I was quiet on the ride, worried about my wrist, worried about how to get my car to my house, worried about the way Ford kept glancing my way without trying to get me to talk. I sat with my head leaned back against the headrest, watching our progress through slitted eyes while Hillary and Henry chatted about who knows what in the back seat. They spoke fast, occasionally giggling, and I didn't try to keep up with their words. I was still bundled up in my coat, my floral print scarf and pink woven mittens sitting on my lap. Hillary had gotten my purse, and she was holding it safely in the back seat.

I insisted that Ford take me to my condo rather than the doctor's office. There had been a moment there where I could feel the argument coming from him and knew that he could probably convince me to go to Urgent Care if he used his strong personality and natural talent for persuading, but he had backed off and done as I asked. As we neared my condo, I gave Ford directions in a soft voice. I was in more pain than I wanted to admit.

Ford parked in my driveway and grabbed my purse from Hillary before instructing the two kids to wait for him in the car. Hillary protested, saying she wanted to help make me a comfy bed on the couch, but Ford saw my pale face and teary eyes and firmly told her to stay put. His hand lightly touched my back as we walked to my front door. With my permission he dug my keys out of my purse and pushed the door open for me to enter, reaching to find a light switch.

"Let me help you with your coat," he said, his tone soft and soothing.

I imagined it was the same voice he'd use with his children to sooth scraped knees and hurt feelings. It was nice.

I tugged my zipper down and he eased it off my right arm before we worked together to get it around my sore, swollen wrist without bumping it. I hissed as the tight sleeve slid off, the pain causing my eyes to tear up once more, but kept from saying anything else as he hung it in my coat closet.

"Is there any way I can ask you to reconsider the doctor visit?" he said, scanning my face and taking in my expression. "I can drop my kids at home with Ellie and come back to get you."

A flash of wanting made me feel light-headed. To let him care for me that way was incredibly tempting, but I blinked it away and shook my head.

"You've done enough. I'll call Ruby. She's a nurse, you know." And then, suddenly, as though Ford and I were longtime friends and this was totally normal, I started blabbing. "That was the strangest date ever. First off, did you see how big he was? I've never dated a guy that big. He kept asking me rapid fire questions, and I barely got out a one-word answer before he'd shoot off the next one. I felt like I was at a job interview." My brows dropped. "I don't think I'm getting the job."

His eyes crinkled. "His loss."

I moved on without really internalizing what he'd said. "But then all of a sudden, he'd be funny and relaxed. At one point I remember thinking I liked him and could see why Aryn set us up."

"Aryn? She's one of your friends?"

"We teach at the same school. She's a teacher friend. No, not just a teacher friend, a bosom friend." At his questioning look I added, "You know, like Anne of Green Gables? A kindred spirit?"

He smacked his lips together. "Must have missed that one."

"Hmm. Well, Shane kept me on my toes, I suppose."

"Until it ended with you falling flat on your back."

I smiled and then remembered he'd not asked to stand there and dissect my blind date. I blushed and said, "Thank you for the ride home and for not bullying me into seeing a doctor."

His brows dropped into a V shape. "I'd never bully you into anything."

Warmth, sweet and gooey, blossomed in my chest. "Okay."

We watched each other for a heartbeat, me wondering what was keeping him from leaving, before he reached out a hand and wrapped it lightly around my upper right arm. He leaned toward me and pressed an airy, unexpected kiss to my forehead. I stayed still, closing my eyes and taking in the sound of his breathing and the smell I now associated with him.

"For the record, Shane really knows how to mess up a first date," he said millimeters from my skin. I could feel as his mouth pulled into a smile and my own mouth answered in kind. He released me. "I know you won't take me up on it, but I'm around this weekend if you need something." I nodded, and he left, closing the front door behind him.

What did that all mean? Was he rethinking his aversion to getting to know me better? Maybe he did need a friend. I could be a friend.

Sigh. No. Being a friend would feel terrible when it came to Ford. I collapsed on my couch and let the tears come. My wrist hurt terribly, and my head was beyond pounding. I picked up my phone and called Ruby. She answered after a few rings, and I quickly explained the situation. She promised to come straight over. She arrived fifteen minutes later with Lizzie in tow. They'd been playing a rousing game of chess--a game I had no idea either of them played--and of course Lizzie wasn't about to be left out of the excitement.

"Oh my gosh, Hailey. Are you okay?" Lizzie asked, coming straight to my couch to stand in front of me.

I blinked and sucked in a breath to steady myself, which somehow made the throbbing in my wrist worse. "It's okay," I managed. "I'm not too hurt."

"You're hugging your wrist, and you're super pale." She lightly touched my head, wiping strands of my hair from my eyes. "It's good you called Ruby."

"Convenient," I replied, "having a nurse for your friend."

"So how hard did you hit your head?" Ruby asked.

"Hard. It was on ice, and I was chin-butted, too. So both sides. It hurts, although not as much as my wrist."

"Chin-butted?" Lizzie asked.

"Chin to forehead," I replied with a grimace.

Ruby gently lifted my right hand off where I'd been holding my left wrist steady. "You're really lucky you didn't get knocked out." She spoke soothingly while she probed at my arm.

When she hit a certain point on the outer edge, I gasped. "That's the place."

She sat my wrist back down and helped me sit up. "Do you feel dizzy at all?"

"Not anymore."

"Good."

"Is her arm broken?" Lizzie asked, and then looked to me. "If so I'm cooking you dinner every night until you're out of a cast."

Her face was worried, her hands clasped, and I offered her a smile, hoping to help her relax. "Maybe not every night, but I'll take one or two dinners."

She brightened, happy to feel useful.

"I'm not sure if it's broken or sprained," Ruby said as she pulled an ace bandage out of her kit. "But you definitely need to head up to Urgent Care for an x-ray."

I sighed. "That's what Ford said, but I just wanted to get home."

"Ford?" Ruby asked as she took my left wrist in her soft hands again and wrapped it securely in a fancy way that immobilized it. Then, she got another ace bandage and looped it around my neck and shoulder, effectively making a sling for me. "I thought you said you were on a blind date."

"I was. But the Whittakers were there ice skating, too, and they stepped in when I got hurt. They brought me home."

"How romantic," Lizzie said.

I had to admit that the way Ford had cared about me and gotten me home had been pretty dreamy, but I wanted to keep it to myself for now.

"Wow, Rubes, you're a professional," I complemented when my arm was wrapped up tight.

She quirked a grin. "That's why they pay me the big bucks. Let's check out this head stuff now."

"Okay."

Ruby ran through a series of questions, testing my sensitivity to light and asking about dizziness or nausea. She asked me a few questions and examined my head with light fingers. "I think that since you have to go to Urgent Care anyhow, we'd better get a second opinion. I'm not overly concerned right now. Might be best, though, if I slept over tonight."

"First step, let's get you some pain meds and head to the doctor's office," Lizzie said.

She went to my medicine cabinet and got me a few ibuprofen and a glass of water. Once I'd taken the pills, Lizzie and Ruby each took me under an arm and hoisted me to my feet. Ruby kept her hand on my back, making sure I hadn't lied about being dizzy, but I was fine, and once I stretched my stiff back out a little, I went to the coat closet to get the coat Ford had recently hung there. Lizzie held it while I fed my right arm through the sleeve and then draped the empty left arm over my shoulder.

"Ruby, you take her to Urgent Care. I'm going to get some things ready for when she comes home," Lizzie said.

"Liz," I teased her on our way out, "you're more upset about this than I am."

"How would you feel if roles were reversed?" she asked.

I sighed. "The same."

"I'm taking care of you tonight," she insisted.

I hadn't had a lot of times where I needed the help of others, but tonight I felt extra grateful for the care of my friends. "Okay. I accept. Thank you."

My wrist throbbed all the way to the Urgent Care building across town, and I started to worry that I really had broken it. I did my best to find the silver lining in the fact that it was my left wrist and I was right-handed, but I knew it would be a pain to be down one arm regardless.

After a thorough exam--why do they always poke the sore spot?--and an x-ray, I was relieved to learn it had been sprained but not broken. The doctor recommended keeping it wrapped and rested for forty-eight hours, along with pain killers and ice, and that I should use it lightly for the next couple of weeks until it had fully healed. They also felt like I had a mild concussion and should use the same forty-eight hours to rest my body. My weekend was shot, but I was so grateful to not need a cast for six weeks that I happily took his advice and went home.

When we got there, Lizzie was sitting on my couch, and the house smelled amazing. She'd made quick work of cooking, and I sighed happily as I sank into a recliner.

"You really didn't need to do this," I said to her.

"It's not every day I get to play nurse to my friend," she replied with a cheeky grin.

"Well, it smells good, so I'm not going to argue too much."

"I made soup that we can reheat tomorrow and cookies for tonight. I know it's pretty late, so we can skip it and get you settled in bed if you want."

Ruby had already slipped into my room to turn down the covers and lay out pajamas. "She needs to rest," she stated in a truly firm, non-Ruby way. She was fully in nurse mode, and both Lizzie and I were quick to give her control. "Let's get you settled and then Lizzie and I can figure out our own sleeping arrangements."

I had no energy or desire to argue, so I followed Ruby into my room where she helped me change into pajamas. I washed my face and brushed my teeth while she leaned against the bathroom doorway, and then she tucked me in like a child. I kind of loved it. As a person who had always been fairly self-sufficient, it felt a little bit decadent to allow others to care for me.

"I'll be in the next room if you need me. Any nausea or dizziness, come tell me. If you feel confused, come find me."

"If I'm confused, how will I know to find you?" I teased.

She stuck out her tongue. "Worst patient ever."

"I'm not confused at all, Rubes. I love you. Good night."

She ran a light, comforting hand over my forehead, the same spot Ford had kissed, and said. "Love you back."

CHAPTER TWELVE

The next morning, I awoke achy and sore and made my way out to the kitchen and living area. Lizzie and Ruby were sitting at my small table talking softly, and they looked up with a matching set of smiles as I came into the room feeling rough.

"Can I ask you a question?" Lizzie asked me.

"Sure."

"Do you actually live here, or do you keep it as a facade and live somewhere else?"

I rolled my eyes and laughed, knowing where she was going with this. "I live here."

She pulled a face. "Do you only sleep here but never use your main living area?"

"Lizzie, I'm tidy. You know this."

"Yes, but I liked to think that maybe you always tidied up when we were coming over. Now I'm thinking this might be every day around here. I'm worried about people who keep their books at such tight ninety-degree angles on the coffee table or who fold their throw blankets or whose couch pillows are actually on the couch."

"Just like I worry about people who leave their things flung everywhere," I teased.

"I'm working on it," she giggled. "In fact, when Jackson and I were registering for wedding gifts, I told him not to bother with pillows and throws because they'll just be on the floor all the time."

"How did you sleep?" Ruby asked, standing and stretching her arms high above her head. "Any issues? How's your pain level?"

I gave her a rundown of my aches and pains, and she went to the cabinet to get me some more pain pills while Lizzie served me up pancakes that she'd kept warming in the oven.

"You two are my favorite," I said, stifling a yawn.

They exchanged a look and seemed to play some kind of rock, paper, scissors game before Ruby looked to me. "We tried to go get your car this morning, but it was gone."

"What do you mean gone?" I asked, suddenly very alert.

"Gone. As in not parked at the ice rink anymore," Lizzie said, setting the plate of fluffy yumminess in front of me.

I looked down at the syrup-soaked pancakes as though they'd have the answers. "But that doesn't make sense. I left it there."

"Any chance it could have been towed?" Ruby asked.

I shrugged. "Maybe. I guess I'll call the ice rink and ask them."

"Sorry," Lizzie said softly. "We feel really bad springing that news on you first thing."

"It's okay." I offered them a smile and dug into the pancakes. "Isn't Jackson coming to town this weekend to take announcement photos?" I asked Lizzie, referring to her long-distance fiancé.

"Oh, no." Her face fell a little. "Sally got an ear infection, so he had to stay with her while his ex works. I'll video call them later."

Sally was Jackson's six-year-old daughter, and Lizzie had grown close to her over the past several months, which was a good thing, considering Jackson had proposed and they were planning a Christmas wedding.

"So all that waxing and plucking goes wasted?" Ruby teased.

Lizzie chuckled. "I'm making Jackson pick up the bill for the next round."

I'd never seen Lizzie happier. She'd gotten a second chance with the one that got away, and she'd proved that sometimes it just took a little while to find the right guy. I'd loved watching them reconnect on our river adventure trip over the summer, and while I hadn't said much out loud to anyone, it had made me want what they had. So far, though, I hadn't had much luck, and the misadventure with Shane wasn't helping my confidence.

"I'm sorry, you must really miss him," I said. "It must be hard to plan a wedding and live five hours apart."

Lizzie pursed her lips and then shook her head. "It's not too bad. This is his second wedding, so we're keeping it pretty low-key. Telephones are the ticket to making it happen. Don't think for a minute he doesn't come with me on all my errands," she laughed. "He just does it on a tiny screen while sitting on his couch."

"Too bad they don't have scent-o-vision yet. I'm thinking I'd miss the smell of my guy being next to me," Ruby sighed.

"Smell is important," Lizzie agreed kindly while winking at me. "So, subject change. Because our dear Hailey is on restricted movement, I brought something for us to watch."

Oh no. Lizzie was known for her love of Halloween and all things horror. In fact, our friend group jokingly called Halloween 'Lizzie Christmas' in honor of her deep and abiding love affair. Every October she tried to get us to let her come decorate our homes, but so far Meredith was the only one who had caved, and I strongly suspected it was because she knew her HOA president would be appalled.

"Uh, what is it?" I hid my wary expression by looking down at the pancake I was cutting.

Ruby noticed my response and smothered a laugh.

"*What Lies Beneath* with Harrison Ford and Michelle Pfeiffer. It's a classic, but it's fallen out of popularity recently. I'm starting a movement to resurrect it."

Lizzie cheerfully dug a copy of the movie out of her purse and showed me the cover. It did indeed have the two big stars on the cover, although it did nothing to make me more excited about watching it. She set it down on the coffee table and came back to the kitchen to start loading dishes in my dishwasher.

"Liz, don't be offended, but horror isn't really my genre," I said as I took my last bite of breakfast

"I know. That's fine, because I usually talk through movies, so it's not like you have to watch it that closely."

I knew this. Ruby had the same problem, and friend movie nights didn't always involve watching the movie. While I didn't really like people talking through movies, I knew this about my friends and never set my heart on actually seeing a movie with them. I'd watch it on my own later if it was one I wanted to see. In this case, however, their chatter would be welcome as it would keep me distracted from whatever happened on the screen. I didn't understand the draw to horror, at all. Halloween was not my holiday.

"Is Jackson okay with your movie talking?" Ruby asked. "Most of the guys I've dated haven't liked it."

Lizzie's eyes sparkled. "He's got no choice." Then she cackled evilly, and we all busted up.

"Go sit on the couch; we'll be over in a minute," Ruby said and I obeyed, gratefully letting them clean my kitchen.

Lizzie spread a throw blanket over my lap in the same moment that my cell rang. She was quick to grab it for me, and I gave her a silent thanks as I answered the call.

"Hi, Hailey?" asked a man's voice.

"Yes."

"This is Shane. From last night."

Surprise had my mouth dropping open. "Uh, hi."

"Look, I know we're not going to go out again, or anything, but I wanted to make sure you're okay. That fall was pretty hard, and I had a headache myself. So . . . yeah . . ."

Another surprise had me blinking. That was, actually, really kind of him. "It's nice of you to call. My wrist is sprained, and I have a mild concussion, but my nurse friend is here caring for me, and I should be back in top shape very soon."

He cleared his throat. "Good. Glad to hear it."

We exchanged the normal farewells, and when my two eavesdropping friends joined me in the living room, they made me give them a play-by-play of the entire evening prior, something I'd been in too much pain to do before.

"Too bad it wasn't the beginning of something wonderful," Ruby sighed. "But it was nice of him to check on you."

"And it was good for Ford to see he has competition," Lizzie said knowingly with raised eyebrows and big eyes.

"Stop that face," I said to her. "Ford doesn't want to date me or anyone else. You two know this already." Lizzie and Ruby exchanged a look, and I chose to ignore them. "What's this movie about?" I asked instead.

"So in this movie there's a couple, and the wife starts getting haunted by a female spirit," Lizzie said as she settled into her seat. "The wife thinks it's the next-door neighbor lady because she hasn't seen her for awhile. But it turns out that it's the spirit of a girl who had been having an affair with her husband, you follow?" I nodded, realizing that the more I let her say the more she'd spoil and the less tense I'd have to feel while watching it play out on screen. "Anyhow, he was cheating on her, which is, you know, the worst. Could you imagine?"

"Nope. Seems like a pretty big violation of trust."

Lizzie poked her finger in the air. "Exactly. I totally trust Jackson, and if I found out he'd been cheating on me because I started being haunted by the ghost of his lover, I don't know what I'd do."

"I'm assuming it was a ghost because the husband killed her to keep the affair secret?" Ruby asked, smothering a yawn.

I looked at her face and realized she'd probably sat up most of the night listening for me. I hoped there would come a time when I could repay her for the kindness.

Lizzie giggled. "Yes. Exactly. It was so tragic. He threw her in a lake, but then the couple ends up in that same lake." Lizzie paused to look at me. "Well, I don't want to give too much away."

I bit down a smile. She'd given away about 99% of it already. "Do you believe in spirits haunting the wife of the guy who killed them?"

She shook her head. "Not really. But if it did happen, I'd kill the guy, and they could travel the spiritual void together."

Ruby and I laughed. "Something we can agree on," I said.

"Ford doesn't seem like the type to cheat," Ruby stated.

I choked on my own spit and had to cough a couple of times. "Why are we back to him again?" I rasped out.

She shrugged. "He brought you home last night. That was a solid move."

I gave them both a look. "You've never even met the man."

Ruby gave me a look back. "I'm good at reading people."

"Uh-huh." I folded my arms.

"And I'm telling you, he's legit."

Lizzie made a noise of agreement. "He was out ice skating with his kids on a Friday night. That's not the way a disreputable man spends his weekend nights."

I waved a hand. "It doesn't really matter if Ford is the cheating type or not because I am not dating him. His weekend activities are none of my concern."

"But you are open to dating him, right?" Ruby asked.

"No," I said. "I'm not. I ruled him out weeks ago."

"Because of the mean things he said?" Lizzie asked.

"Yes," I cried. "I believed those words. Can we please watch our movie?" My voice was climbing, and Ruby sat up to watch me closely. I took a breath, knowing she was worried that a change in behavior could signal a worsening concussion. "I'm fine, Ruby. Just . . . tired of Ford this and Ford that. He's a friend of Leonard's. That's all. A good Samaritan who happened to be in the right place last night."

"If you say so," Lizzie said in a placating tone.

"I do." I tugged the throw blanket up under my chin and nodded toward the screen. "Now let's watch this movie before one of you ends up in the spiritual void."

Not five minutes later my phone rang once more, and Lizzie paused the movie while I answered. Her eyes took on a glow that told me she'd seen Ford's name flash at the top of the screen, and I ducked my head as Lizzie mouthed 'It's Ford' to Ruby and pointed at the phone in my hands.

"Hello?" I answered, my voice sounding strained.

"I wanted to check on the local ice-skating champ and see how she's holding up after last night's performance," he said, his voice different from other times we'd spoken. More friendly, more open. Chummy, maybe?

"Hardy har har," I replied, somewhat sarcastically, which only made him laugh and Lizzie's eyes nearly pop out of her head. Admittedly, it wasn't the way I typically spoke to people.

"How are you feeling?"

I gave him a very brief, very fact-based rundown on the night while my two friends soaked up every facial expression and tone of voice they could. I sounded almost robotic in my efforts to not give away how elated I was that he'd called.

"So, your friends are still there?" he asked.

"Yeah. Lizzie is making me watch a horror movie."

"Hmm. Seems like that might spark a relapse."

I cracked up and then had to squeeze my eyes tight when it caused a pain to shoot along my forehead. "I'm telling her that."

"Telling who what?" Lizzie mouthed.

I shook my head. "It was nice of you to call."

It was a dismissal, one I didn't really mean, and he picked it up quickly, hopefully understanding it was about my eavesdropper friends and not my lack of desire to talk to him. Then again, I didn't want him to think I wanted to talk to him, right? Ugh.

"No problem. Hey, I also wanted to let you know that I had your car towed. It was supposed to be delivered to your house, but the company messed up and sent it to mine. I only noticed it when I went out for a run this morning. Sorry about that. I hope you weren't worried. I'll make arrangements to get it to your place."

"No, don't," I blurted without thinking. "I . . . " Why had I blurted that? "You've already done more than enough. When I'm cleared to drive, I'll come get it. Unless it's in the way? I could send up my friends to pick it up."

"No, not at all. It's fine where it is."

"Okay."

A pause, and I swore I could feel him smiling through the phone. Ruby's comment about wanting scent-o-vision suddenly didn't seem so silly. I could almost smell a hint of Ford as though he were here.

"Hailey?"

"Yeah."

"I'm glad you're okay."

"Thanks."

We hung up, me with butterflies wanting to shoot out of my earholes, and I put the phone in my lap.

"Well," Ruby said, "how very interesting."

"He has my car," I stated.

"I don't think that's the only thing of yours he has," Ruby mumbled.

Lizzie patted my hand and hit play on the movie, kindly leaving me to my own thoughts . . . as jumbled as they were.

CHAPTER THIRTEEN

I was lying on the couch Sunday around lunchtime, watching mindless TV, when a loud, rapid knock on the door caused me to nearly jump out of my seat. Ruby and Lizzie had gone back home, and I wasn't expecting anyone. My mom had spent the night last night, still concerned about my head injury, but she'd been appeased by that morning and had left with a promise to call me later in the day. The rest of my friend group had already checked in and, well, I didn't get many visitors. I stood and walked to the door, not caring that I was in leggings and an oversized Aggies sweatshirt, about as comfy as I ever got. My hair was a little rough, seeing as I'd done it one-handed and then laid on a couch all morning. I wiped at my eyes, remembering I hadn't done my makeup yet.

Hillary's tear-streaked face greeted me, and I looked behind her to see a slightly less upset but still worried Henry. He was holding his bike upright, but her little bike was lying next to my porch alongside a smashed bag. My eyes flew back to her, and her entire face crumpled.

"I told Daddy I wanted to bring you cookies, but he was busy and said I could bring some to school on Monday. So I got Henry to bring me. It was so far, and I got so scared."

I looked back to Henry, and his lip quivered as his face turned red, but he bravely held his chin higher. "I'm not scared."

My jaw fell open as I mentally mapped the route they must have taken to come down the foothills from their father's estate to my condo. My stomach clenched at the thought of the main roads they'd crossed and the danger they'd been in.

"How did you know how to get here?" I asked, shocked.

"We have a spare phone at home to use for emergencies," Henry answered while Hillary sniffled. "I know how to use the maps."

I was completely confused about how he'd have gotten my address, but now wasn't the time to be asking too many questions. I crouched down and took Hillary in my arms, careful not to bump my hurt wrist, and patted her little back as she sobbed against my shoulder. I wanted to lecture them on the big mistake they'd made, but I quickly realized that the terror she was feeling was punishment enough. As for Henry, I didn't believe for a minute that he hadn't been a little frightened when he'd realized how far from home they'd come and that his little sister was melting down. I didn't see either of them repeating this misadventure. The next order of business was to get them home, immediately.

"Does your dad know you're gone?" I asked as I set Hillary slightly away from me, keeping my good hand on her shoulder.

"No. Daddy will be so mad," she wept.

"He might. It's because he loves you. He's probably so worried."

Hiccups sounded as she sniffled. "I know. I was so scared. That was a long ride."

"Why didn't you turn around when you saw the big roads?" I asked, brushing at the hair that was stuck to her face with tears. I looked to Henry, who shrugged.

"I don't know," she replied shakily, answering for them both.

"Okay. Well, I'll call your dad."

This was a terrible time to not have my car. I'd planned to have one of my parents take me up to Ford's tonight, but that didn't solve anything right now.

"I dropped your cookies three times." Hillary pointed at the bag next to her bike. "Now they're crumbs." Big tears spilled again, and I patted her back.

"I love cookie crumbs."

"You do?"

"Sure. They're really good on ice cream."

She wiped her nose on her sleeve. "Really?"

"Definitely. Come on inside, you two."

We left the bag of cookie crumbs outside as I ushered them in and found my phone. I was scrolling through my phone, looking for the number I needed, when my own phone rang, and I jumped to answer it before looking at the caller ID. Maybe Ford had realized they were missing and was calling me to see if I knew where they were.

"Hello?"

"Hey, when did you want to go grab your car?" My dad asked. "I'm driving past your street now on my way home, if it's a good time."

"Yes!" I practically yelled it. "That's perfect. I need a ride immediately."

"Um, okay." He sounded confused, which was zero surprise. "Everything okay?"

"Ford's kids are here, he doesn't know it, and I need to get them home."

"I'll look forward to hearing that story later," Dad replied, unruffled as ever. "I'm two minutes out."

I hung up and smiled at the two blonde adventurers. "My dad is coming right now. He'll give us a ride to your house."

Hillary teared up again. "It was a long ride."

"I know, honey," I soothed, rubbing her upper back in light circles.

"Now two dads will be mad at us," Henry mumbled.

I shook my head and moved my hand from Hillary to him. "That's not true. My dad won't be angry. He's happy to help you. Let's wait outside for him, okay?"

I put on shoes and grabbed my purse so I could lock up the condo. We gathered up their bikes, and as we did so a headache began to form behind my eyes. I was technically supposed to be resting through the remainder of this day, but Hillary and Henry were far more important than my stupid head trauma. I kept thinking that even after Dad arrived it was still going to take us ten minutes to get there by car thanks to traffic and stoplights. I couldn't imagine how long it had taken their little legs to pedal the distance.

I kept conversation light as we waited, and a rush of relief flowed through me when my dad turned onto my street. He made fast work of loading their bikes into the bed of his truck, and then we were moving through the neighborhoods and up into the foothills.

I hurried and shot off a text to Ford, nearly slapping myself for not having done it the moment they arrived at my house.

Me: I have your kids. I'm bringing them home now.

His response was an immediate ringing of my phone.

"Hello?"

"They're with you?" he said intensely.

"Yes, I have them here. They're safe."

"Thank goodness." He paused, and I heard him take a deep breath. "You don't have a car."

"My dad happened to be here, and we're on our way." It was a slight fib, but I didn't want him to worry that I'd inconvenienced my dad over this.

"Thank you so much, Hailey."

My stomach dropped at the sound of my name and his genuine gratitude. "Of course. We'll see you soon."

We said goodbye, and I tried hard not to notice exactly how busy the streets were that these two kids had ridden their bikes across. I needed to be cool. I rubbed at my forehead and asked what they were going to be for Halloween, and we talked about how Hillary had been wanting a kitten, but her dad was allergic. My dad shared a few funny stories about kittens from his childhood, and by the time we pulled up to the Whittaker property, Hillary was her usual, bubbly self. Henry, however, had become more and more quiet. I was guessing it was nerves over what type of reception they were going to receive. I, myself, was a ball of nerves and had a full-blown migraine forming.

"Hailey, you're looking pale. Why don't you wait in the car, and I'll walk them inside," Dad said, putting a hand on my arm when I was slow to open my door. "The doctor said you were supposed to rest, and this stress is probably making it worse."

My wrist ached where I'd accidentally bumped it when loading Hillary one-handed into the back seat. My stomach was clenched as I pictured Ford rushing outside to blame me for the entire incident. And I suddenly realized that I looked about as 'Saturday morning' as possible. But, even with all of that, it needed to be me who walked in with them. I owed it to Ford, and more importantly, I knew the kids needed an ally at the moment.

"I'm okay," I said. "I'll take them in. Thank you so much for bringing us up here. No need to wait. I can get home myself." I gestured to where my car sat parked off to the side.

Dad's eyes were still concerned. "Don't stay long. I can see by how your eyes are pinched that you're in pain again."

I nodded, knowing better than to full-out lie to him. "I'll be fast. I want to get back to that couch, too."

We all climbed out and worked together to get the bikes out of the truck bed. By the time they were unloaded, Ford was walking down the large stone stairs toward us with purposeful strides. Hillary became subdued, matching her brother for mood as my dad nodded to him. Ford's hand was outstretched as he approached, a smile on his face that didn't reach his eyes.

"Conrad, thank you so much for bringing my children home."

Dad took his hand, his expression relaxed and kind. "Not a problem at all. Kids are going to throw you for a loop here and there." Dad looked to me, and I nodded, letting him know I'd take it from here. "See you later," he said to Hillary and Henry, who showed almost no reaction to his words other than looking his way as he climbed back into his truck and drove away.

Ford had eyes only for his children, as it should be. I could see the way his chest rose and fell, his eyes flashing a mixture of anger and relief. Hillary and Henry shuffled their feet, still holding their bikes upright at their sides. Hillary sniffled, salty paths still on her rounded cheeks. I felt so bad for them and so bad for Ford and honestly a little bad for myself, because I hated being the reason they'd done something so dangerous.

"Hi Daddy," Henry said in a glum voice.

"What were you thinking?" he asked tensely. "I've called all the neighbors, all your friends, and I had no less than ten people out searching for you before Hailey called."

"We took cookies to Miss Hailey," Hillary said.

He glanced toward me, and a thunder cloud passed through him. I felt it clear to my toes.

"Ford," I began in a calm tone, intending to help ease the tension, but he held up a hand and shook his head.

"Why did you go to Miss Thomas's house after I told you no?" he questioned his daughter.

She ducked her head. "Because I wanted to help her feel better."

"And you went with her?" his eyes swung to Henry.

"I couldn't let her go alone."

His face tightened, and I could imagine he was running those streets in his mind the same way I'd done. One hand rested on his hip while the other jutted through his hair. "My gosh, you're lucky you weren't hurt or killed or . . . " He trailed off, and my own heart swooped with fear over what could have been.

My good hand tugged at the hem of my oversize sweatshirt, and I cleared my throat. "The good news is that they're home, and they're okay. A little shaken up, but okay," I offered with a cheer I did not feel.

"Did you know they were coming to see you?" His gray eyes pierced mine, and I shook my tender head, wincing at the movement.

"No. I'd have never allowed it. Especially alone on bikes."

"All that way." He turned his back to us and looked up at the house.

I could tell he was trying to calm himself, and I appreciated how terrified he must have been. I was only the teacher--former teacher--and I'd had heart palpations over it. As their father, wow, he was probably cycling through a huge range of emotions.

"Daddy," Hillary's voice was as small as her frame, "Miss Thomas says if you're mad it's only 'cause you love us so much."

Ford turned to face her and nodded. "She's right. But it doesn't mean there won't be some sort of consequence for this." He looked to Henry. "At ten, you know better."

"I know." Henry's cheeks turned red. "I'm sorry."

"You should probably take my bike for a month and never let me eat cookies until Christmas time." Hillary nodded sagely.

Some of Ford's turbulent feelings calmed, and I watched his throat work as he swallowed. "We'll talk about it soon. Right now you need to put your bikes away and go to your rooms. I need to speak with Miss Thomas alone."

They both nodded as my own limbs tensed. I had not come here to talk to Ford alone. I'd come to make sure his sweet babies got home safely. As far as I was concerned, my time here was done. But I stayed in place as they walked past me with a sad wave and headed toward the garage.

"Thanks again for bringing them home," he said after a beat of silence.

Something about the way he stood there, watching his children walk away, his shoulders drooping and his hair sticking out, made me want to wrap him up and hold him tight. How many times had Ford faced these scary parental moments alone? How hard it must have been to be solely responsible for their love and care along with their worldly needs.

"Of course. It was a total shock when I opened the door and they were standing there. Even more when I realized what they'd done." I breathed out a sigh, hoping to convey that we were on the same side here.

My fingers itched to wrap around his, and I formed my hands into fists to keep from giving in to the feeling.

"You don't seem to be a phase," he said as he looked to me and tucked his hands down in his pockets. "In fact, she still talks about you all the time."

I so badly wanted to reach up and smooth down my hair and then have a magic mascara appear, because the way he was looking at me told me he was cataloging the differences from how I usually looked. Or maybe he was aware of the strain in my face and the way I felt a little woozy standing there.

"I feel terrible about it," I said. "I thought she'd moved on."

"She hasn't."

A throb shot up my arm from my hurt wrist, and I unconsciously hugged it to my chest with my good arm. "Maybe Hillary had forgotten about me. I was out of sight, out of mind, you know. But then the ice skating thing happened, and suddenly I'm the shiny new object again."

"So, you're saying this is simply phase two of Hillary's laser focus, and in time it will wear off. Again." It was not a question but a sarcastic statement.

I didn't rise to the bait because I understood it came from a place of fear. "That's what I'm saying." It was time to get going. "Anyhow, I need to head back home."

"How are you feeling?"

"Kind of crummy," I said honestly. "I'm supposed to be resting through the weekend."

"What are we going to do about Hillary?" he asked.

White spots started to dance around the edges of my vision, and I couldn't filter my thoughts. "We? She's your daughter and I . . . " A piercing pain cut me off, and I put my hand on my forehead. "I'm not . . . I can't . . . "

"Come with me," Ford said.

I shook my head. "I'm going home. How much do I owe you for the tow?"

"Nothing."

I frowned at him. "I don't want you paying for my responsibilities."

"I'm the one who had it towed." He sighed. "Hailey, come inside and sit down, please. You're obviously in pain."

Challenge rose up in me, confusing and yet thrilling at the same time. Was this what an out-of-body experience felt like? I'd heard people talk about it, but I hadn't understood before. It was like I was watching from a distance, words coming out that I had no control over as my head throbbed.

"Why should I?" I asked.

"Are you safe to drive?"

"Absolutely." I swayed a little, and he was immediately there, his hands wrapping around my upper arms. "I had peaceful days before meeting you Whittakers," I said in a near whisper.

I was aware of him stepping to the side and putting an arm around my shoulders, gently pushing me forward toward the stairs. Away from my car, away from home.

"Yes, but it was boring, admit it," he responded.

I looked at him with a sweet look. "Never underestimate the draw of boring."

We reached the bottom of the stairs, and I took hold of the railing without any real thought about it. I slowly took the stairs, mumbling senseless things about ice skating and horror movies and how much I loved a good cup of hot cocoa. As I babbled along my hand slipped on the railing I was using for support, and I found myself falling up the stairs, dizziness making me unable to accommodate the sudden shift in my weight. I made to grab for the railing with the other hand, but when a giant current of pain ran down my arm, I yelped and pulled it back. The momentum threw me backwards, straight into Ford's chest.

"I suppose you're going to blame your fall up the stairs on us Whittakers too?" Ford asked calmly as he wrapped a steadying arm around my middle.

It took me a minute to realize that my back was pressed up against him, his arm banded around me, and when I did my blush could have melted the hand railing. I sank into it for a heartbeat, soaking up the feeling of being safe, before sheer force of will had me moving forward out of his embrace.

"It's tempting to blame you for a lot of things," I grumbled.

He came around to the front of me and reached out a hand. I froze, wondering what to do next in this little back-and-forth of ours. I'd never engaged in this type of playful fighting before him. So, I stared at it and then back up at him.

"What am I supposed to do with that?" I asked, nodding toward his hand.

"Take it." He stated with pinched lips.

I tugged down my sweatshirt and took his hand. It was like the first time we'd touched, and while I'd prefer to blame railing burn for the heat I felt on my palm, there was a chance it was the result of his hand in mine. His strong fingers wrapped around mine, and he held me firmly until I'd made it up to the step he was on. Then he turned and tugged my hand through his elbow until it was resting securely there. If I'd wanted to, I could have taken a little visit to bicep land to see what it had to offer, but I chose to avoid that particular minefield.

What I really wanted to do was lean my head against his shoulder and let him boss me around. It wasn't a concept I'd typically find appealing, but in the moment it sounded utterly delicious to allow his strength to carry me along.

"I'm not trying to boss you around here," he said, and I giggled at him basically reading my mind, "but you really need to lie down." His voice was kind and soft, the same soothing tone he'd used the night I'd been hurt. "Just until you aren't so dizzy." Worn out and tired, I followed placidly as he slowly helped guide me up the stairs. "Is there anything I can do to thank you for bringing my kids back?" he asked as we walked into his home and made our way to his family room.

"No. I'm so glad they're safe."

"I could spring for a new sweatshirt. Did you buy that when you were in college a decade ago?"

I glared up at him. "Yes, I did. It's comfy and cozy, and I don't usually wear it out of the house."

"It should be made into rags," he teased.

"That's mean." I tugged my good hand out of his arm and walked myself to a big, inviting couch. "I happen to love this old rag. I don't want you to spring for anything. In fact, I'm probably the only woman in the world who doesn't want a thing from you. Not even the smallest, littlest, tiniest thing." All propriety was cast out as I made myself a bed on that couch and tugged a blanket over me. I closed my eyes.

"Oh yeah?" I could hear the amusement in his tone.

"Yeah. And another thing, go easy on Hillary and Henry. I think that bike ride cured them of all devious plans."

"Maybe not all of their devious plans," he said, still sounding entertained. His hand was light on my cheek as he brushed some hair away from my face. "I'll bring you some pain medicine, okay? Or does that count as me giving you something?"

"Thanks. Just put it on my tab," I replied and he chuckled.

I slitted my eyes and watched as he walked out of the room, my stomach in knots as the feeling of his fingertips lingered on my skin. I'd lied to him just now. I didn't want anything from him . . . I wanted everything.

CHAPTER FOURTEEN

I woke up hours later and glanced around, confused and worried, not knowing where I was. The room was familiar, but it took me a few minutes to realize I was at Ford's house, napping on his couch. The sound of voices came from a TV in front of me, and I blinked a few times, bringing the cartoon characters into focus.

"You're awake," Hillary said, patting my leg. I glanced her way to see that she'd settled at the foot of the couch and had my feet on her little lap. My shoes were gone. She grinned at me. "You slept for a long time."

"How long?" I asked, pulling my legs toward me and moving into a sitting position.

The blanket that had been covering me fell to the floor, and I reached down for it, needing something to focus on while I got my bearings.

"Long enough that Daddy says he's not mad anymore."

I smiled and ran my hand through my hair. "That's good."

"Want some food? Daddy's making spaghetti."

I shook my head. I didn't want anything other than to get myself out of whatever this was. Napping on their couch with my feet on Hillary's lap? It was far too domestic and cozy. It was the sliver of a dream. The force of my longing surprised me, and I immediately wanted to retreat to my safe space. My hands clenched in the blanket.

"Daddy!" Hillary's cry startled me. "She's awake!"

I blinked and was happy to note that the headache seemed to have passed. Sleep and pain meds had done their work. I felt much better: good enough to hit the road, that's for sure.

"My mom loved spaghetti," Henry said.

I gasped, startled, having not noticed him in the recliner next to the couch. I took a breath and pressed my hand to my chest to settle my heart rate.

"Oh yeah?" I managed. "I like it, too."

"Dad's a good cook. You should eat some. Mommy said his spaghetti could make anything better."

"I . . . that's sweet," I replied, happy that he had that kind of memory of his mom.

"Hey," Ford's voice entered the picture. "How do you feel?" His long legs made short work of crossing the room, and when he got to the couch, he crouched to be eye level with me. "Your eyes look better. Did the headache pass?"

I blushed at his direct gaze and busied myself folding the blanket in my lap. What bizarre universe had I fallen into when everyone was acting like having me here was an everyday occurrence? Like him checking on me was totally routine? My stomach tightened, and I knew I had to leave. I couldn't do this. Playing house was dangerous.

"I'm sorry," I said.

"For what?" he asked, still watching me from the crouched position.

I shook my head and waved my hands. "Sleeping here for what must have been hours."

Hillary slid across the couch and leaned up against my side, her head pressing against my upper arm. "I like having you here."

At this I did finally meet Ford's eyes. He'd asked me earlier what to do about Hillary's attachment to me, and this could not be helping. My eyes widened, hoping to convey that very thought to him, but instead he stood.

"I'm bringing you some dinner," he stated.

And then he walked out. Like this was nothing. This cozy, homey, ludicrous situation should have had him running, but instead he was going to the kitchen to plate me up some dinner. I did not understand this man or his children. Hadn't he accused me of scheming to be in exactly the place I was right now? How was he suddenly okay with it?

I abruptly stood, smiling down at Hillary as my motion caused her to fall on her side. I couldn't let down my wall if he was going to put his back up anytime soon.

"I'm so sorry, but I have to get home," I said to them.

And I darted out of the room as fast as my feet could carry me. I was aiming for the front hallway, but somehow, I ended up in the kitchen where Ford was loading a plate with spaghetti and salad. He looked up when I came in, and he must have seen the freak-out on my face, because he put the plate down and walked slowly toward me.

"You okay?"

No, I'm not okay. I'm not okay at all because this is like a dream come true, I screamed in my head. For him, though, I only nodded.

"I can't stay to eat." My voice was unsure when it should have been strong.
His answer was calm, quiet. "You can."

What did that mean? I can what? If he suddenly opened a door between us then I was going to full on lose my heart to him, and that terrified me as much as it made me want to leap through the door and hang on for dear life. There's nothing as painful as a one-sided love affair, and it was getting harder and harder as he blurred the lines between fantasy and reality.

"I can't."

He reached for my hurt hand and gently lifted my arm, tracing a finger around my wrist. "How's this feeling?"

I gulped as starlight raced up my arm. "It's okay."

"Any particular reason you're turning down what I'd consider the best spaghetti in town?" he asked. "If you're feeling awkward or embarrassed, you don't need to be."

Oh, Ford . . . there were so many, many reasons. Number one was that I could not cast aside his words regardless of what his actions were telling me. I needed to process this development. I needed to be able to take a full breath again.

"I just can't . . . tonight." I tacked on the last word, hoping it would sound less like a rejection, for what reason I couldn't have said.

He smiled and released my arm. "Okay. I'll walk you out to your car."

He was easy, breezy, acting like whatever I decided to do was no skin off his back. I appreciated that, because one of us needed to be reasonable about all of this, and it was becoming quite clear that would never be me.

*****

Having my mind chugging over Ford did not help anything for the next couple of days. I kept messing up lesson plans, or finding typos in the email updates I sent to parents. It all culminated when my computer died five minutes before parent teacher conferences were scheduled to start—obviously. It went blue and then black and then, puff, nothing. I dropped my head into my hands and moaned. Why me? Why now? Why did computers rule our world but always let us down? I unplugged it from the wall because computer tech always asked if you'd powered it off and back on, counted to thirty like my dad always said I should, and plugged it back in. I was rewarded with a black screen and a circling icon that hovered there for the entire three minutes I watched it. Now my first student-parent duo was due in two minutes, and I hadn't printed off his reports because I'd gotten stuck in Recap and Recoup telling my friends about The Whittakers' Great Escape, as I was now calling it.

The part about sleeping on his couch had taken a very, very long time to discuss. And when I'd told them how he'd held my wrist and run his finger across it, they'd all playfully fanned themselves and launched into a war room style discussion.

Suffice it to say that my friends were as freaked out as I was but for different reasons.

They thought I should go for it, push through any barriers, and enjoy life in a castle. I was still doing my best to respect his wishes to stay free from relationship entanglements.

The main thing tickling my mind today was how could Ford say he wasn't interested in a relationship and then keep doing unexpectedly kind things? Was this how he treated everyone? Did he realize how bone-meltingly flirty his actions came off? Were other women in need of his spaghetti? Was I reading too much into it? Maybe he went around town performing heroic acts and caressing wrists daily.

Okay, so there was more than one thing I was trying to make sense of. Real Ford was giving Fake Ford a run for his money. And neither Ford was up for grabs.

I picked up the phone on my desk and buzzed number 818, computer tech support, hoping Wesley was still in the building, even though he also did tech support for another elementary school and switched days.

"Hello?" he answered.

"Oh, wonderful. Wesley, this is Hailey Thomas. My computer is totally dead. Do you have a minute to come down to room eight?"

"I'll be right there."

I hung up, feeling at least a smidgen of hope that he could figure it out before the next wave of students and parents came. I had this first conference and then a free hour before everyone else had signed up. Sure enough, Wesley arrived quickly as promised. His glasses reflected the blank screen as he slid into my chair. Before I could tell him what had happened, my student walked in.

Wesley's typing and talking to himself at my computer was a little distracting, but I was able to get through the conference with the information I could access on my phone. When the fifteen-minute meeting was up, I bid Joel and his mother goodbye before scooting over to where Wesley was sitting. I stood behind the chair and looked at my screen. It was no longer black, but nothing looked how it was supposed to look either. Icons were all over the place, and my pretty wallpaper was missing.

"What happened, and did I do it?" I asked him.

His eyes stayed trained on the screen. "Not sure."

"How long until it's working again?'

"Not sure."

"A man of many words," I teased. "Thanks for the hope."

At that he did look up over his shoulder and grinned. "I know how to keep the customers happy."

I giggled as I noticed three blond heads enter the doorway. It was the Whittaker clan, and warm bubbles rose in my chest. It had only been two days since I'd woken up on their couch and scooted on out of there. That awkward feeling did its best to attach itself once again as I smoothed down my shirt front and walked around my computer to greet them.

"Miss Hailey!" Hillary called. "You look better today."

I grinned. "I hope so. Thanks for taking good care of me Sunday. What brings you guys here?"

"We're here for our conferences," Hillary said. "Daddy said since we were all done, we could stop and say hi to you before we leave."

"Oh." I raised my eyebrows at Ford. "That was nice of you."

Ford's eyes crinkled, but it was Henry who spoke. "It was Hillary's idea; she wanted to make sure you weren't dead."

"Henry," Ford said firmly, covering up a laugh. "Be polite."

"I see. I hope I look alive enough today." I laid it on thick, spinning in a circle and looking myself over.

"Daddy said you were probably fine, but I wanted to see myself." Hillary shot her brother a dark look.

"Fine is what I am." I smiled, my dimples flashing.

"What did you do to your computer?" Ford asked, gesturing to where Wesley was sitting totally focused on my monitor.

"Why do you assume anything is wrong? This is my good friend Wesley, and he comes in here all the time to share funny jokes and things with me. That's what we were doing when you came in," I said. At that Wesley's head popped around the screen and then darted back, but his expression said I was lying. I continued. "Didn't you hear me laughing?"

"I did," Hillary said while nodding.

"That's because Wes is such a crack-up." Yes, I shortened his name to make it seem like we were buddies. Maybe he hated being called Wes; I didn't know. I was so asking for bad karma from this. "How were your conferences?"

"Good," Henry answered and then went to check out the aquarium of tadpoles I'd recently brought in. "Cool," he said as he walked toward them.

"I'm doing okay," Hillary said a tad mournfully. "Mrs. Slater is hard."

"School gets harder every year; that's part of growing up," Ford said in response.

Her eyes grew uncertain, and I hurried to alleviate her worries. "It's still early in the year, and sometimes it takes a little bit to adjust to a new grade and new teacher. You're such a smart girl and I'm sure you'll have it all figured out soon."

"Hill, come see these tadpoles," Henry called, waving her over.

"You don't have to coddle my kids," Ford stated when they were out of hearing.

I warred within myself over what to say and ended up engaged in my first-ever stare down. I had no siblings, I'd lived at home during college, I'd lived alone after college, I'd only ever dated soft-spoken and sweet men, and I rarely felt enough emotion to have a confrontation. My heart rate increased as though I was about to plunge down the first hill of a roller coaster ride. Ford's eyes drew me in, and all thought drained away as I watched him for any hint of what he was thinking. Did he feel this too? This push and pull, wonder and worry? Was his heart pounding as hard as mine? I could feel it in my fingertips and the backs of my knees.

I began to feel fidgety, so I blurted out what had been on the tip of my tongue. "You don't have to scare them out of wanting to grow up and attend school. A little empathy goes a long way."

He took a step closer to me, his voice dropping to a near whisper. "You have a lot of opinions," he muttered.

My head jerked back, and I blinked rapidly. A sarcastic burst of laughter tried to escape. The fact was that most people wondered if I had opinions. If my family and friends could see me now, they'd be buying bags of popcorn to eat with the show. Ford's eyes were coasting over my face, watching the shifting of my expressions as I tried to decide what to say next.

"Ask anyone, I'm the most agreeable person they know," I finally sputtered out, my own voice as low and intimate as his.

One side of his mouth tugged up slightly, as though he were already amused by the words he was about to say. "When is the last time someone kissed you?"

My jaw fell slack, and I swallowed hard. "What?"

"Just curious," he said. Then he took a step back and glanced around me to Wesley. "Is it true that Hailey is agreeable most of the time?"

Wesley leaned over again to look at Ford past the monitor. "I'm not really sure. She seems nice. I'm only here to fix her computer."

Ford's expression was smug when he looked back to me. "Really? So not sharing jokes then. What did you do to your computer?"

I rolled my eyes and crossed my arms. "I told it you were coming, and it died on the spot."

Ford laughed, and Wesley cleared his throat to cover a spot of amusement that I was very pleased to have caused.

"It's not every day I scare a computer to death," Ford said with a grin.

His expression lit me up inside, and I wanted to keep sassing and goading him. It was thrilling somehow, an element I'd never experienced with a man before.

"Hillary was right; you look good," he said.

Oh. I was suddenly breathless.

"Daddy." Hillary was back by my side, and I stepped back, lengthening the distance between Ford and me. "Some of the tadpoles are growing legs."

Ford walked with her to take a look, and I watched them go, noticing once again how nice he was to look at. And he never did what I expected him to do--which was exhilarating but also so, so scary. I was constantly off balance around him.

When the family of three returned to my side of the room, Hillary and Henry said quick goodbyes and took off. Ford, however, paused at the doorway and shot me a full smile that had my fingertips tingling.

"Until next time?"

It seemed silly to pretend we'd never see each other again, and a little ill-behaved piece of me was happy that whatever this was, it wasn't over yet. He'd asked me about kissing. If that wasn't an opening in the armor, I didn't know what was.

I nodded and replied, "I'll be ready."

So, so ready.

CHAPTER FIFTEEN

y friends and I were seated around what we considered our round table in a back corner of our favorite Mexican restaurant a few days later. Back here the music wasn't quite as loud, and we could stick around for a while. The smell of peppers and seared meat floated to us from the open kitchen, and I reached for the chips and salsa when I was sure everyone else had taken some. We always came straight from school in the late afternoon. The beauty of being in our thirties is that we'd stop caring about appearing "old" and openly admitted that we didn't want to wait in a line to be seated. And we wanted to be home early enough to slap on stretchy pants, flop on the couch, and enjoy the ice cream pint we'd been saving.

"You know who's kind of cute?" I asked once I'd swallowed my mouthful. "Wesley, the computer guy at school."

I'd been toying with adding him to my list of potential date options. Ford was number one, of course, and I wouldn't pull the trigger on dating Wesley if he continued to show signs of warming up. But, on the off chance that Ford retreated back into his protective shell, Wesley could be fun to get to know better.

Meredith shook her head and took a chip from the basket. "Nah. Too fair, too thin, too . . . vanilla for my taste."

Lizzie laughed. "You'd only like a guy if he was dark and hairy and came swinging a club at you."

We all chuckled as Meredith rolled her eyes. "I'd club him back."

"Exactly," Aryn responded. "That's your kind of love talk. Mutual clubbing."

"Good grief," Meredith sighed.

"If we're wrong, then tell us how things are going with Brooks VanOrman and the second annual show of horrors?" Ruby said as her head popped up over her menu. Her eyes nearly disappeared as she grinned at Meredith. "Halloween does seem to be your favorite time of year to haunt the man."

"Okay, first of all, last year was his first year as HOA president, and it was a happy accident when I realized he was upset about my outdoor Halloween decor," Meredith replied.

"Was he upset? Or were other neighbors upset, and he came to see you on their behalf?" Aryn asked.

"Brooks VanOrman speaks on behalf of the neighborhood, so it's one and the same." Meredith scooped up some salsa and crunched on it.

"Can you get kicked out of your condo over this stuff?" Lizzie asked with concern as she sipped her sarsaparilla.

"I doubt it." Meredith's face grew thoughtful before she shook her head firmly. "No. I haven't crossed any actual boundaries."

"Good. Then I'll still come over tomorrow with my Halloween stuff so we can get you set up right."

Lizzie's grin was kind of scary, and I shared an amused glance with Aryn before circling back. "Okay, but back to Wesley," I said. "He came to fix my computer during parent teacher conferences last week. He didn't say much, but he seems nice. My blind date with Shane didn't go well, but I'm wondering if Wesley might be a candidate. Anyone know if he's single?"

"Actually." Aryn did a little head bop, and her cheeks grew pink, which had us all zoning in, frozen mid-chew, to see what she'd say. "Wesley and I went to high school together. We, uh, sang in the concert choir and kind of knew each other."

"What does 'kind of' mean, exactly?" Meredith asked.

Aryn shrugged, trying to play it casual although she was failing. "He dated my best friend, so we spent some time around each other."

"Where is bestie now?" Ruby asked, laying her menu down flat on the table. "And was it a tragic breakup?"

Aryn laughed. "I haven't seen her in years. They dated our entire senior year of high school, but she went off to college in California, and I lost track of her. I don't know what happened between her and Wesley. I was pretty surprised when he showed up as our new computer support tech this school year."

"How surprised?" Lizzie asked. "Because your blush says you were shocked down to your knickers."

That blush had been fading, but it roared back to life, and I suddenly remembered a conversation we'd had recently about a boy in high school who had left sweet notes of encouragement in her locker even though he'd been dating someone else. I chose to keep the observation to myself, but a little excitement wove through me at knowing there might be a love situation brewing right under

127

our noses. I immediately let go of any thoughts about dating him. No way was I poaching that territory if it was a possibility for Aryn.

Aryn snorted. "We were only friendly in high school because we were thrown together a lot."

"I thought you said you spent 'some' time around each other. Now you're saying 'a lot.' Which is it?" Meredith asked, reaching again for the chips and salsa.

"Look, it's not a big deal. Hailey brought him up, so I'm just telling you that I knew him way back when and he's a nice guy." She paused. "Or was. Quiet, studious, but nice."

"Is he single?" I asked.

"Probably. He doesn't wear a ring," Aryn shrugged, trying to play like the answer carried no weight. "You could definitely ask him out." Her words and tone didn't match.

"Not all married men wear rings." Ruby's menu snapped back into place in front of her face.

"Have you asked him anything about the past fourteen years of life?" I pressed, playing like I wanted to know but really trying to decide how much Aryn and he had been talking already.

She shook her head. "I'm sorry, Hailey. Other than an awkward moment when we saw each other in the faculty lunchroom, we haven't really spoken."

Lizzie's mouth twisted, her disappointment matching mine. "So you're telling me that you run into this guy that you hung out with in high school and neither of you bother to chat it up? He's been working at Washington for weeks now. Nothing?" Aryn shook her head. "And you've never breathed a word of it to us? What's the story?"

"No story," Aryn insisted.

"I guess I can't date him then," I said, mostly to see how Aryn would react.

"Why?" Aryn asked, and her expression looked worried. Interesting.

The server came to take our orders, and when she was gone Meredith looked at me.

"Why would you want to date him?" she asked.

"Mer, just because you don't find him attractive . . . " I began.

"No, no." She waved her hands. "I mean, don't you have some little thing brewing with Ford?"

Oh, now all eyes were on me. I felt my own blush crawl across my skin. "I'm not sure?"

"Confusion is the gateway to attraction," Ruby said.

"I happen to know, for a fact, that Ford Whittaker stopped by your classroom during parent teacher conferences," Lizzie stated. "Was there more of him helping himself to your wrist?"

She made it sound dirty, and I rolled my eyes as I shook my head. "Hillary stopped by, and he was in tow. They were there for five minutes, maybe less." They all continued to gaze at me until I gave them a nugget to chew on. "He, um, asked me when the last time I'd been kissed was."

"Whaaaat?" they all said together, eyes and mouths gaping.

"I . . ." I shook my head, feeling a little embarrassed about even mentioning it. "He, well, it was kind of confusing."

"I guess so," Aryn stated, tilting her head. "When did that little switch happen?"

"Switch?" I asked.

"Oh, definitely when she was at his house and fell asleep on his couch. She's breached the castle; the conquest has begun," Ruby replied.

"Might have been earlier," Meredith joined in, rubbing at her chin. "When the whole ice skating thing happened."

"It was the opera." Aryn snapped her fingers. "That was a seriously romantic situation. I'll bet you looked smoking hot in your dress with your jewels, and his heart cracked open."

"What's her next move?" Lizzie asked the group.

I put my head in my hands. "You guys, I'm right here, and I'm not sure anything has changed or that I need to make a move."

"It's changed," Ruby stated. "And the ball is in your court. Time for a total score."

Everyone laughed while I blushed. I was grateful when the server returned with our drinks and fully planned to change the subject once we were all served. My friends, obviously, had other plans.

"All I'm going to say," Lizzie said as soon as the server walked away, "is that so far his actions don't match his words. He said he wasn't open to a relationship, but the man is acting all sorts of interested in you. Give yourself a high-five. He's a big score. Handsome, rich, darling kids, castle on the hill. I could only imagine not living paycheck to paycheck. He probably has an amazing kitchen, Hailey." Lizzie's face lit up. "Think of the dinners you could make there."

"You wouldn't even have to buy generic brands of everything. Real cheese, real eggs, real meat." Ruby silently clapped her hands.

"What kind of food are you eating?" Meredith's eyebrows dropped as she looked to Ruby, and we all busted up. "Don't you know better, being a nurse and all? The way you're talking I'm surprised your skin doesn't glow neon."

"The point is," Aryn called us back, "the money is nice, but the man seems perfect for you."

The others added their agreement, and I looked down at my soda. "Guys. I appreciate what you're doing here, but Ford is not a candidate."

"Why?" Meredith asked bluntly.

"Because I'm scared of Ford," I whispered.

Lizzie's hand landed on my forearm. "It's understandable. He's the type that could really do a number on your heart. I loved Jackson from afar for a long time. I know how that can make your chest feel hollow."

"Maybe you don't need to make a move," Aryn said gently. "Who are we to give you advice? A bunch of single thirty-somethings? Please."

"All you have to do is talk to him," Meredith stated.

My stomach swooped as the others looked to me. "Talk to him about what?"

"I don't know. Just don't shut him down all the time," she replied.

"Maybe the next time you're thrown together, you let down your guard a bit," Aryn said.

"I've been more open with that man than I have with anyone other than my parents and you four," I defended, agitated.

"Great," Meredith called. "Then when he asks you out, you'll say yes."

I blinked and shook my head. "He'll never ask me out. He's not interested in dating."

"Mm-hmm," Ruby said. "We've blown that theory out of the water. He brought you home when you were hurt and had your car towed and generally looks at you like you're dessert."

My cheeks flamed. "When have you ever even seen him in person? How do you know how he looks at me?"

Ruby laughed. "Your giant blush tells me all I need to know."

"Come on, Hailey," Aryn said. "I'll agree to talk to Wesley if you'll say yes when Ford asks you out."

I swallowed, wanting this conversation to end, now. "Fine. If he ever asks me out, I'll go. But it'll never happen because he's probably just a really friendly guy who likes to help out the honorary niece of his business partner."

"Yeah, because people are always helping out honorary nieces," Meredith smirked.

"Never say never," Ruby added.

"Things have really gotten interesting for our group lately," Lizzie sighed. "I'm engaged, Hailey is courting a millionaire, and Aryn might make love bloom in her classroom."

"Not bad for a bunch of thornback women," Ruby added.

"Lies," I mumbled under my breath.

"Total lies," Aryn seconded.

She and I clinked our glasses together and remained quiet while the conversation moved on to other things, both of us lost in our own thoughts.

CHAPTER SIXTEEN

I t turns out I had a chance to keep my promise much sooner than I'd have thought when Ford invited me out, but not in the way my friends had predicted. My grocery cart wheels squeaked as I pushed it along, glancing at my list and mentally mapping out the store. I typically made my list in the order of how the store was laid out. I found it efficient. However, today I'd made my list in the parking lot without much of a menu plan and just wanted to be done with this. I was pre-disappointed in myself, knowing I'd get home and find I'd missed some things, and then I'd have to be back here sooner than I wanted. On top of that, I'd end up adding a lot of junk that I really did not need. I'd already worked my way through the produce section and was walking through frozen foods when I heard a familiar squeal followed by my name being called.

I knew it was Hillary before I turned, just in time to see her smile flash a millisecond before she crashed into me. I staggered back a step, as I always did, using one hand to steady myself on the cart and placing the other on her shoulder.

"Hillary," I said in a chuckle. "Hello."

"Are you buying ice cream?" she asked.

"Thinking about it," I replied.

"Us, too. We have a pool party tonight, and Daddy said we could bring ice cream."

"That's the best part of any party."

I looked up to see Ford and Henry coming toward us. Ford, as always, looked delicious. Tonight he was more casual than I'd ever seen him, dressed in athletic pants and a sweatshirt. I noticed that tantalizing shadow of a beard on his usually clean-shaven face as he got closer and remembered him leaning close and asking me when I'd been kissed last. Fascinated by this new side of him, I wondered how scratchy his facial hair would feel against my fingertips and how it would feel to snuggle up to his soft clothes and smell his scent. At the thought I gave myself a mental shake.

"Hey," he said in greeting, his expression open and friendly.

I had a sudden flash of pleasure, remembering the last time I'd seen him and the promise of future sparring between us. I tugged down the hemline of my silk shirt as Hillary stepped away and looked behind her. Henry had his nose pressed to the glass of the ice cream case and was walking back and forth, calling out flavor options. It only took Hillary a second to join him, leaving Ford and me alone.

"Hillary tells me you're getting ice cream for a pool party. Neither of those seem like October activities," I said as I tucked my hair behind my ears with slightly trembling fingers.

"You're suggesting we give up two of our favorite things because of cold weather?" he teased. I dimpled and shook my head. He grinned as he continued. "We're headed up to Leonard's, actually. Connie invited the kids over to use their indoor pool. If you're into getting splashed repeatedly for two hours straight, lots of attempted drownings, screams echoing off the walls, and feeling chilled for hours afterward, you should join us."

The invitation made my heart skip a beat. Ford was inviting me to hang out with his family? That seemed really awkward and appealing, and maybe a little odd, but also tempting.

"Oh," I said without realizing it would be out loud.

"Oh?"

"I'm . . . why would you invite me?" I was so flustered that I couldn't seem to keep words from spilling out. "You're hoping I'm a temporary person in Hillary's life."

Hillary's yell from the end of the aisle interrupted us, although we continued to look at each other as her voice carried to us. "I want ice cream bars instead of regular ice cream," she said. "Henry wants popsicles."

Ford finally turned to look at his children, and I used his distraction to think quickly. What was his motivation? Did I want to go swimming at the Cox's house with the Whittaker family? I'd been in their pool a million times and knew they'd have no problem with me showing up, but . . .

Ford had finished settling the battle with his children, and his gray eyes were looking back at me. "You're overthinking it. I thought you might have fun."

I chewed on my lip and nodded. "But it's so unlike me to overthink something."

He chuckled. "Obviously it was a spontaneous invite, but it was sincere. If you're looking for a wild Friday night, you can join us." He tipped his chin down and gave me a look through lowered brows. "Unless you have another hot blind date that I wouldn't want to interrupt. Maybe this time you'll come away with a broken leg."

I huffed out a laugh and rolled my eyes. "So funny."

We watched each other for a moment, him patiently waiting to see how I'd respond. It was in those seconds that I remembered the promise I'd made my friends to say yes to an invitation from Ford. Okay, so they'd meant a date, but I could spin this and get everyone off my back if I played it right.

Plus . . . I wanted to be with him.

I wiggled my fingers. "I'm supposed to be easy on my wrist still."

"I'll do my best to keep the kids from manhandling you."

Hillary and Henry came running up, each with a box of ice cream treats, wearing excited expressions. Hillary bounced on the balls of her feet with a big grin. "We're ready, Daddy."

"What do you think of Hailey coming swimming with us?" Ford asked.

Henry and Hillary cheered. All three of them looked at me: Ford with laughter in his eyes, and Hillary trying to hold in a squeal. I glanced down at my grocery cart and thought about how I didn't have a suit or towel with me.

"We can follow you to your house so you can leave your groceries there and get your things," Henry surprised me by saying.

I was warming up to the idea of joining them. All I had waiting at home was an empty condo. Still, I wanted the security of having my own car there. It was something I tried to do as much as possible. I liked the comfort of knowing I could escape whenever I felt overwhelmed at gatherings. Besides, I had two legs that needed shaving, and I wasn't going to have them wait in my living room while I did that.

"I know where they live," I said, shaking my head as though I couldn't believe what I was agreeing to. "I'll meet you up there in half an hour."

The kids took off toward the checkout stand, and Ford followed them, walking backwards for a few steps. "I'm not bullying you into this."

I smiled. "I know."

In the end, it had taken very little convincing at all.

*****

Ford had been right—I was waterlogged. I'd not been swimming with children since graduating from childhood myself. I wasn't all that familiar with public pools, as most of the swimming I did was here at Cox's, which meant the group was typically small. Cox's two sons didn't live nearby, and they only had one grandchild so far. Even as a schoolteacher I was unprepared for the amount of screaming and

134

splashing that went on. And it was only two kids. The call of 'cannon ball' became the thing that made me shudder. After being thoroughly drenched several times, I figured out to turn my back toward the voice and hunch my shoulders. It was much better than a direct face hit.

Ford, for his part, was as active as the kids. He chased them around the shallow end, throwing them into the air and making them shriek as they flailed before hitting the deeper water. He did poses off the diving board and challenged the kids to a variety of races. I enjoyed the show, thinking how different he was from the man whose articles I'd read and polished pictures I'd seen. He wasn't the perfectly pressed businessman I'd initially met.

I enjoyed watching them have fun together but felt a little shy and unsure about how to interact with them myself, so I held back. When I was in a pool, I swam a few sedate laps and then lounged by the side chatting with the other women. Horseplay wasn't in my wheelhouse.

Tonight, however, I was the only woman around. Connie and my mom had gone out to dinner and a movie, so it was only Leonard in the house. And Leonard had never been one to sit by the pool, or really get into the pool as far as I could remember. After his boisterous greeting he'd instructed us to have fun and turned everything over to me since I knew it all anyhow.

On the bright side, it had given me plenty of time to observe the object of my infatuation, and there was no way I'd complain about that.

Hillary and Henry seemed to be winding down, and Ford climbed out of the pool, water sluicing off his shoulders and down his back as he walked to the side of the pool where large floaties were stored. He chose two and tossed them into the pool. I laughed along with him as we watched the kids climb on top, which involved flipping themselves over several times until Ford dove in and heaved them into place. Ford swam my way once they were lying on their backs, spinning in lazy circles and using their hands to flick water at each other.

I was sitting on the pool steps in the shallow end, the water up to my shoulders, and my eyes racked over him as he swam to me with broad strokes and gleaming skin. He took a seat on the same step and used one hand to push his hair into a slicked-back look that wasn't that different from his normal hair style. Water dripped off his lashes, making his gray eyes appear to glow as he smiled over at me.

"Hiding away from the action?" he teased.

I stretched my legs in front of me, letting my toes peek up out of the water. My eyes went to the red nail polish, and I was grateful to have something to focus on. "Did you know I'm an only child?" I asked.

He leaned back, propping himself up on his elbows and giving me a delicious view of his body. Not overly muscled, but lean, athletic, and healthy and . . . I was getting off track.

"I did," he replied, letting the unvoiced question linger in the air. 'What does that have to do with anything?'

"I don't know if that's the reason I'm more introverted or if it would have been that way even with ten siblings."

He nodded, his gaze watching his kids as they floated past. "I'm an oldest child and an extrovert to the core. Mom had a hard time keeping me at home to get chores and homework done. I wanted to be in the middle of the action."

My toes sank back down to the steps, and I pushed the ball of my feet against the rough floor of the pool. "I'm guessing you weren't spending your days at home reading books and cooking with your parents, then?" I swirled my hands in circles, creating little waves in the water.

"Nope." He chuckled. "I was too busy running for every student office I could and finding where the parties were on the weekends."

"We are so different," I said with a soft laugh.

I saw him nod. "True." But his tone didn't sound like that was a bad thing.

I looked directly at him, feeling confident in the moment. "Do you find shy people as confusing as I find outgoing people?" I teased.

"Not at all. The quiet thinkers are the ones running the show, and they get us big-mouths to go out and do the work. We need different kinds to get anything done." He looked back at me. "Do I make you uncomfortable?"

Normally a direct question like that, especially from someone like him, would have had me blushing, but tonight none of those emotions hit. Instead, I bit my lips while I thought about it. Yes, he made me uncomfortable, but it was more about how I wanted to crawl into his lap and wrap my arms around his neck than about his personality being unreserved. Some of my best friends were total extroverts--Ruby for example-- and I didn't feel uneasy around them.

He watched me for a second and then grinned. "I'm going to guess the answer is yes, and you're trying to find a way to politely tell me that it's not me, it's you."

I laughed, breaking into a wide grin, my dimples sinking into place. "Well, it's true. It's not me making trouble." I shook my head and put a hand lightly on his bare shoulder. His skin was warm, and the muscle underneath was firm. "I was actually thinking that some of my best friends are extroverted. It doesn't bother me." I dropped my hand back under the water and onto my lap.

His eyes found mine and then slid back to watching his kids. "Heather was as extroverted as I am." The shock of him mentioning his late wife made my smile disappear. "At first it was great to have a person who wanted to get out there and experience everything together with no hesitation. She didn't shy away from anything."

My heart sank, listening to him talk about her. The admiration in his voice was clear. "She must have been really fun," I said.

"Yeah, for a while. But then we became parents, and she really struggled with how that ties you down. She . . . "

When he hesitated, I wanted to nudge his foot with mine, something I would have done to one of my friends to keep them talking, but I didn't want to pry with our new and complicated friendship.

"You don't have to talk about her if you don't want to," I offered.

"Did you know she was a teacher? Like you?"

My eyebrows rose, caught off guard. "I had no idea."

He nodded thoughtfully. "Yeah, she taught high school math. She really liked it, but after Hillary was born it seemed like she couldn't settle back into her own skin and find her footing. Something about having a second child was overwhelming."

I wasn't a mother myself, but as a teacher I had a small idea of how much pressure, worry, work, and exhaustion could come with parenthood. "That must have been really difficult," I replied.

"We worked hard to help her find a balance. She loved her job, and I was supportive of that. We met with a therapist and decided to hire a live-in nanny. I did my best to help her schedule weekend trips with her friends a few times. It wasn't an easy time. My company was being built at the same time, and I wasn't always as available as I should have been."

I nodded, sympathetic to how hard that must have been for him to see his wife struggling, doing his best to be there for her while also building his career. Those years of life would have been very demanding.

"I'm sure you both did your best," I said.

I waited to see if he'd say more, but after a few seconds of him lost in his own head, I saw the shift from serious to playful, and he sat up with the bright smile that made my fingertips tingle.

"When is the last time you participated in a pool game?" he asked.

"Never," I said, watching as he stood from the steps and turned to face me.

"Look, I know you probably think that at forty I should grow up a little, but we all have to blow off steam now and then, right?"

I nodded, thinking about how my dad in his sixties still hadn't totally lost his boyishness. "Of course."

"Great." He reached for my hand, pulling me to stand. I floated toward him, the water providing no resistance until we were practically touching and I had to put my toes against the bottom of the pool to keep from pressing up against him. "Slide or diving board?" he asked, still holding my hand, our fingers flexing lightly together.

"I don't know. You pick, I guess?"

I couldn't have made a choice to save my life, not with the way his large fingertips were skirting up and down my palm.

He squeezed my fingers. "Okay, diving board."

He took my hand firmly and pulled me toward the ladder at the deep end of the pool, letting go of my hand when it was too deep to walk so that I could swim along behind him. I followed hesitantly, wondering what I was swimming into. Ford climbed out first, reaching a hand down to pull me up and out of the water. I stood, dripping, next to his side while he called his kids over.

"We're playing jump or dive," he said when we were all huddled together.

"I'm the caller." Henry raised his hand.

"Ah," Hillary griped. "Fine, but I'm caller next round."

"Caller?" I looked to Ford.

"Here are the rules. You get onto the diving board and jump off. Once you're in the air, Henry will call out what you're supposed to do. He'll call dive or jump—which is feet first—or cannon ball or jumping jacks. You get the idea. You have to do whatever he calls before you hit the water."

Okay, I understood the concept, but I wasn't sure how I was supposed to go from jumping in the air to executing a dive if that's what he called. It would require bending my body in half, midair.

A dormant sense of challenge filled my chest as Ford and the kids started trash talking each other. This was another thing I didn't have much experience with, so I kept my words inside my own head, but I felt their exhilaration as if it were my own.

"I'm first." Hillary hopped over to the diving board and climbed on. "No cheating, Henry."

"How would I cheat?" Henry cried, clearly offended by the very idea.

Hillary's little fists smashed against her hips. "By calling too late. You have to call as soon as my feet leave the board."

"Fine!" Henry marched to the side near the diving board and nodded to Hillary.

Hillary took off at a run down the length of the diving board and jumped into the air. "Jumping jack," Henry called.

Hillary's little limbs went spread eagle and then snapped shut before she landed in the water. She came back up with a big cheer, reaching a hand up to push the water out of her eyes. Ford nodded at me, and I gamely climbed up to the diving board. I didn't run down it like Hillary had, but I walked quickly and jumped off the end.

"Cannon ball," Henry yelled when I was at the high point of my jump.

I tucked my legs against my chest and wrapped my arms around them, slamming into the water with seconds to spare. A laugh built in my chest as I swam to the surface, and I came up with a smile that matched Hillary's. That had been fun. We played several rounds, with Henry adding in a special one called "bum bounce" that involved landing back on the end of the diving board with your rear end and bouncing off of it. We were all in stitches watching Ford try to figure it out the first time Henry called it, and after that it became a favorite. The backs of my legs were going to be fully scratched by the time this game was over.

When we were all breathless, hanging on to the side of the pool with big smiles, I called an end to the game. My wrist was getting sore from the pulling motions of the front crawl, and I needed dinner soon. They were good sports about it, the kids going back to their play and Ford swimming with me back to the steps. I climbed out, tired but feeling incredibly content, and wrapped myself up in a beach towel that was waiting for me.

When I turned back to face the pool, Ford was standing in waist-deep water, watching me. His eyes were focused, and my hands fisted in the towel at my waist.

"I'm glad you came," he said in a tone that was new to me.

This wasn't some passing comment from a friend or stranger but carried heavier notes of attraction that caused a shiver to follow a water droplet down my spine.

I knew I was attracted to him; it was something that I didn't fight but just accepted. Until that moment I'd never known how he felt about me either way, but here and now, it was apparent that the appeal ran both ways.

"Thanks," I managed, shaken and hungry for more of whatever was passing between us.

It was gone in a heartbeat, as Henry yelled something involving the word 'attack,' and I watched an object collide with the back of Ford's head. He reached up to touch his head just as a few drops of red hit his broad shoulders. He blinked a few times, pulling his hand away and looking at his fingers. He was bleeding. Dizziness and nausea hit me as I watched him put his hand against the back of his head once more. He turned his back to me to face his son, and I was relieved to see that it wasn't spurting or something. That would have been a real problem, and I didn't think it was the best time for him to find out just how unhelpful I'd be in a blood-filled emergency.

"What was that, Henry?" he asked, irritated and probably in pain.

"I'm sorry," Henry called, his face beet red.

"Ford, you'd better get out of the pool," I called, my voice strained. I was the only other adult here. It had to be me who helped, but I was fighting against getting super woozy. "Hillary and Henry, get out, please."

The two kids scrambled out of the pool and hurried around to where Ford was climbing up the steps, still holding his head. Stupid head wounds, I thought, why do they have to bleed so much? Ford came to stand in front of me, and I motioned for him to turn around, even though I absolutely did not want to see what was happening on the back of his head.

I released my white-knuckle grip on my towel, and it fell at my feet as I lightly tugged his fingers away to get a better look. I sifted through his thick hair until I found the source. I wasn't a pro, but I didn't think it would need stitches, and it seemed like it was already slowing down. My stomach heaved, and I unconsciously put a hand on his shoulder to brace myself as I looked away and took a few deeps breaths.

"How does it look?" he asked over his shoulder.

"No stitches. Just a good cut," I said breathlessly. "You'll be okay." I slitted a glance at the kids. "There's a closet in the pool house that has extra towels. Will you two please get some for your dad?"

The least we could do is get the blood wiped off his neck and shoulders.

The kids hustled off, and Ford turned to face me, causing my hand to fall off his shoulder. "Are you going to be okay?" he asked.

I looked up at him, knowing my face was pale. "I'm not a blood person."

"Any idea what hit me?" he asked, reaching out his clean hand and running it up and down my arm in what was meant as a comforting gesture.

The feeling of his skin against mine brought heat back into my cheeks and took away the dizzy feeling. "No," I whispered.

"You're getting some color back in your face," he whispered as his hand stopped its caressing and wrapped softly around my upper arm.

He swallowed and pulled me closer. It was like we were pretending that he wasn't bleeding from his head even though the blood was still dripping from the ends of his water-darkened hair onto his shoulders. I didn't dare meet his eyes, so I focused on the base of his neck as my forehead came near his lips.

"Take a few deep breaths." His voice was low, intimate, as though we were sharing a secret.

Another wave of light-headedness hit, and my clammy hands were heavy as they lifted until they pressed against the outside of his waist. I wasn't sure if I was bracing myself or embracing him.

"I'll be okay," he said.

His tone begged me to look at him. I felt his breath against my cheeks as I tilted my head back. His eyes were clear again, his expression grave. I nodded, and then his lips were feather soft against mine. I was aware of his hesitation, understood that he wasn't sure this was a good move, but for me it was pure heaven.

His mouth was soft and warm with a hint of rough bristle against my chin. I leaned into it; my mouth relaxing and welcoming before meeting his kiss with one of my own. His hand clenched tighter around my arm, and his thumb gave my bicep a slow stroke. There was no feeling in the entire world better than this.

He increased the pressure slightly, his mouth forming more firmly to mine, and I welcomed it, repositioning my head to get closer. It felt like my world was crumbling and being reordered, but in reality the kiss only lasted a moment, a heartbeat of time that could change everything for better or worse, depending on how we reacted. The kids' voices called us back, and he pulled away far enough to let a breath of air through. Just enough for me to whisper shakily.

"Wow."

He released me with an amused huff of breath, turning to face his children as I stepped back and bent to retrieve my towel. When I stood I was satisfied to see that I wasn't the only one practicing some deep breathing techniques.

That night, right before bed, Ford sent me a text.

Ford: Thanks for coming tonight

My stomach tingled and my face broke into a wide smile.

Me: I had a great time

Ford: I'm going to be busy hosting international visitors for the next week or so

It seemed a little random, so I replied with

Me: Okay?

Ford: I won't have much free time, but could I call or text you when I have a minute?

Oh, yes, yes he could. Delicious warmth spread through my limbs. He wanted to be in touch. He was telling me that he didn't want me to think he'd disappeared after our kiss. There was a crack in his wall, and I was more than happy to fill it.

Me: I'd like that

Ford: Goodnight
Me: Night

I didn't fall asleep quickly even though I'd completely worn myself out. I laid in bed for a long time, hugging my phone to my chest and running my fingers along my lips, reliving a kiss I'd never, even in my wildest dreams, thought would actually happen.

CHAPTER SEVENTEEN

A week later I stood with my hand wrapped around an ax handle, facing a target, while being both heckled and cheered on by my group of friends. Ax throwing was all the rage, and Meredith felt passionately about trying it out. If it had been allowed, she'd have put a picture of Brooks VanOrman's face on the bullseye. As it was, I didn't believe for one second she wasn't imagining it there.

"You don't have the muscles for this, Hailey," Ruby taunted from her spot behind the safety line.

I glanced over my shoulder and raised one eyebrow while pursing my lips. "It's not about muscles; it's about heart."

"That's right," Aryn cried. "You tell 'em."

"Bullseye, bullseye, bullseye," Lizzie and Meredith were chanting.

"Scoot your hand higher on the handle," Ruby said. I adjusted my hold because if anyone knew something about chucking axes, it was going to be her. "Perfect. Now pretend a bear is coming to attack your mom."

"Kill the bear, Hailey," Lizzie called.

"Kill the bear . . . kill the bear . . ." Aryn called.

I faced forward again and took a deep breath. I'd not spent much time with an ax in my hand, not being an outdoorsperson or dependent on wood to heat my home, but I did know enough to be slightly wary about flinging a sharpened blade through the air. I didn't think I had any aggression that needed purging, like Meredith, or anything to prove, like Ruby. But I also had no plans to be the loser this evening. The Whittaker family had introduced me to my competitive side, so I tightened my grip, counted to three, and stepped forward with my arm raised to hurl the ax toward that big red dot. I launched it with all my might and watched in fascination as it went end over end and then dropped to the floor a few inches from the target.

Huh. Maybe Ruby had a point about my muscles. I wasn't a very big person and none of my exercise routine was about building bulk. My face was a little red as I turned back to my friends who had stopped cheering and were moving their mouths trying to find the right words to say. Lizzie came through with "Hey, no big deal," before they all joined in, Meredith sucking her lips in to keep from cracking up.

"So, going to be adding weights to my routine," I said. "Because the bear is now mauling my mother."

That loosened them up, and we all laughed as I retrieved the ax from its sad place on the floor. I hung it on the wall, per our safety instructions, before joining my friends. Handing off the ax was a no-no. And yet, we didn't wear safety helmets, gloves, or goggles. Whatever.

Lizzie was up next, and she hustled to grab the ax from its hook. She took her place on the line, scrunched up her shoulders, lifted her arm, and then let out a bloodcurdling yell as she chucked that sucker with all her might. Her scream shocked us all into silence as we watched her nail a bullseye. She spun back toward us, curls bouncing and eyes dancing, and did a funny little bow before going to retrieve her ax.

Only, she couldn't get it out. She tugged and yanked, braced a foot against the wall, and finally gave up. She was giggling when she turned back to us. "Ruby?"

Ruby happily trotted into the area and pulled the ax out with a grunt. "Nice throw, Liz," she complimented. "I guess since I'm in possession, I'll take my turn now."

None of us argued, and Ruby took her place at the starting line while Lizzie came back to join us.

"It's bear attack time," Aryn teased.

"Take this bear!" Ruby called.

She wiggled her shoulders and did some strange thing where she licked two fingers and held them up to test the air or something. After letting her fingers sense whatever it was they were after, she smoothed back her long pony tail, stretched her calf muscles, and gripped the ax with two hands.

"If there really was a bear charging," Meredith called, "you'd already be a goner."

"Right now I'm staring down the bear and warning him that he's about to meet his maker," Ruby shot back.

We all snickered before Aryn replied, "He thinks you look tasty."

At this Ruby looked over her shoulder with a smirk. "That's what all the guys say."

Then, almost without warning after her huge build up, she spun forward and flung the ax. It rotated beautifully before somehow clipping the top of the target and boomeranging back toward Ruby. Five screeches filled the air followed by calls

144

of "duck," "dive," "watch out," and "holy cow." Ruby managed to jump out of the way as the ax passed her and landed two feet away from where the other four of us had huddled up and closed our eyes. Against an ax. At least no one had shoved someone else to the front.

"You can open your eyes now," Ruby said in an amused tone. "The danger has passed." We opened our eyes to find Ruby holding the ax and standing in front of us. "I expected better from you guys. Now I'm not sure you'd actually have my back in an attack situation."

We blinked at each other, and then I cracked a smile. "It's better to know now than to be disappointed in a real-life scenario."

"Speak for yourselves," Meredith said. "My eyes never closed."

"Yeah, but you did turn your back," Ruby replied.

"Well, this is interesting," Lizzie said. Her sly and scheming tone had us all looking her way. "Look who walked into lane four."

Our eyes all shot to two lanes down to find Ford testing out an ax. There were two other men with him, all of them dressed in suits and ties. They must have been some of the international businessmen he'd told me about during our phone calls this week. Phone calls that had made my heart fill with hope and excitement.

While their outfits stood out here, Ford looked oddly at home with an ax in his hand. It was like lumberjack met billionaire, and my breath caught momentarily. Memories of his warm lips pressed against mine, my palms against his skin, flashed through my mind, and I licked my dry lips.

"Is it just me or does it look like he carries an ax to his board meetings?" Meredith asked.

"Interesting," Aryn said. "I wouldn't have pegged him as an ax thrower. I'd have described him as suave. The kind of guy who gets manicures and keeps his neck shaved."

"His image is deceiving," I mumbled in a tone that made their eyes swoop my way. At their looks I held up my hands, palms out. "I don't mean anything by that. Only, I . . . there's more to him than meets the eye."

Ruby squeaked when it became clear I wasn't going to finish that thought. "This is getting juicy. Please, tell us about Ford Whittaker's secret side."

My entire face blazed, and I folded my arms. "I promise to spill my guts at dinner later, but not here and not with him standing barely a few lanes away."

Well. That response had them all giving each other dumbfounded looks and glancing between me and Ford. I was the quietest member of this troupe, so having me tell them I had juice to spill was intriguing enough to keep them from knowing how to react. Ruby had meant it as a tease. Of course it had been a terrible tactical error on my part, because now Meredith smelled blood. And there was nothing Meredith liked more than making people uncomfortable. Add in the fact that Ruby was guessing at a hidden romance brewing, and I was never going to make it through this without being humiliated.

"No, no, we'll back off," Meredith said in an epic lie. "But, I do think I'll at least wave to him. Just to, you know, be friendly."

Ruby, still holding the ax, said, "Me too. It's the neighborly thing to do."

Then my two dark-haired friends--one all bony limbs and determination, the other all voluptuous curves and silliness--called his name until they had his attention and then waved like he was a celebrity or their long-lost best friend. Aryn looked at me with empathy, and Lizzie sidled up close, supporting me with her presence.

"And to think I told Ford that extroverts don't bother me," I said, attempting to joke over the worried knot in my throat.

I didn't know if Ford wanted my friends to know about him or not. We hadn't gotten to any sort of real talk about our 'relationship'. We'd been chatting, creating a sort of tentative friendship. Of course, through those conversations he knew how close I was to these women but still . . .

"I'm acknowledging you said that and telling you that I'll wait to ask you about it, but know that in my head I'm thinking 'whaaat? When did she tell him that?'" Lizzie said.

"This has gotten much more interesting," Aryn said as Ford waved back and then turned to say something to the two other men.

"It's fine," I said, trying to convince myself as he started walking toward where my little group was standing.

"Maybe mentioning his hidden depths wasn't a good move," Lizzie said.

Aryn's eyes were bright but sympathetic. "Massive miscalculation."

"They're mostly harmless and only doing it to get under my skin. What's the worst than can happen?" My voice came out much shakier than I'd intended.

"My brain can't think that big," Lizzie sighed playfully. "Meredith and Ruby aren't a predictable duo."

Ford removed his suit jacket as he made his way to where we were, hooking it over one arm and then unbuttoning his sleeves and rolling them up. I was drooling so hard I needed a bib . . . and all my friends were watching me do it.

Meredith met him with a big grin, and Ruby sort of nudged her way in, talking at her top speed, which had Ford tilting his head like he was attempting to work out a problem. The two ladies talked, and Ford simply watched for a few seconds, never changing his expression from one of polite interest, before looking over their heads at me.

A tingle started in the base of my spine, remembering the way his eyes had looked before he'd pressed his lips to mine and lit me up inside. I clasped my hands together in front of me, wishing I knew what he was thinking right now. My cheeks heated. One side of his mouth tugged up, and I understood that he found the situation amusing.

Only in that moment did I realize I'd not been listening to what they were saying to him. My stomach swooped, and I leaned closer to Aryn.

"What are they saying to him?" I asked.

"A whole lot of nothing, really. Ruby's telling him her favorite ax weights--who knew that was a thing--and Meredith asked about his business. There's no rhyme or reason to it, and it's constantly shifting."

That explained why he hadn't yet spoken.

Until he did.

"Hi, Hailey," he said, his voice amused and warm as he basically interrupted their monologuing.

A smile bloomed on my face, and all my friends looked at me. They knew me well enough to see from my expression that stuff had happened.

"Hi, Ford," I replied.

Silence claimed us while my friends looked back and forth between us, and I took in everything about him that I could, from his mussed hair to the tired expression hidden behind his eyes. I could tell it had been a long week for him, and I wanted to ease his burden. I wanted to close the distance between us and wrap him up in my arms.

"Did you know there's a company that turns cremated remains into an ocean reef?" Lizzie blurted.

It was then that I realized how heavy and curious the silence had grown. I blinked and looked away from Ford, avoiding everyone else's eyes.

Meredith jumped on her odd statement. "You don't say?"

Aryn was also looking at her, so Lizzie grinned and swallowed. "Yeah. Let's say your dad was a big fan of the ocean and wants to be buried at sea, you can have him cremated and call this company that will mix his ashes with concrete to form this ball thing. Then they encase that in a reef ball or something and drop it into the ocean. It becomes a fish habitat and the start of a new section of reef. The circle of life."

"Why do you know this?" Aryn asked.

Lizzie shrugged. "You know it too, now."

I glanced back to Ford, who suddenly started laughing. We did, indeed, have that knowledge now thanks to Lizzie. It wasn't one I'd most likely be sharing, but it could come in handy if a social gathering got too boring someday.

"I'm always looking for things to discuss at business dinners," he chuckled, "so thanks for that." All of their faces melted under his power. "It was nice to meet you ladies," he said. "I'd better get back to my guests. Have a good night."

He gave me a nod, and we all said goodbye before watching as he made his way back to where the other two men had started throwing axes without him.

"Well, I was right in my first assessment," Meredith said. "The man is as smooth and delectable as strawberry ice cream."

"Strawberry ice cream is your smoothness measurement?" Ruby gaped at her.

"Yeah. What's wrong with that?"

"Strawberry ice cream has chunks of strawberry in it. Chunks are the opposite of smooth," Ruby joked.

Meredith rolled her eyes. "Whatever, the point is that he's everything I suspected. And he definitely has eyes for our Hailey."

I dug deep to come off cool and calm. "We've gotten friendlier lately."

"If by friendly you mean hot enough to make the devil sweat, then yes, you've gotten friendlier lately," Aryn piped in.

"Something I think we're all anxious to hear more about," Meredith stated.

She took the ax from Lizzie, marched to the throw line, and without pausing tossed the ax forward. It hit a dead bullseye. She turned, nodded once, and gestured for the door. I guess ax throwing was over then. We followed Meredith outside, and as I was passing the lane where Ford was throwing his ax, I glanced his way. He was holding the ax, but he passed it off to one of the other men and walked toward me. It was an unexpected move, and I tugged at the hem of my shirt. My friends all paused, but I was able to deliver a look that told them to keep moving, and I watched with relief as they exited the building.

Ford stopped a foot from me and, flustered, I blurted out, "I'm so sorry about my friends."

He shook his head, his mouth loosening into a smile. "Don't worry about it. I know they're important to you. It was nice to put faces to names. I'm assuming Ruby had the ponytail, Meredith was the other one with black hair, Aryn was the tall redhead, and Lizzie was the short blonde?"

I was delighted that he'd guessed correctly. "You're good."

"Just good at listening."

Out of the corner of my eye, I saw Meredith's car pull up in front of the big front doors of the building. "I should go. My friends are waiting."

"Of course. Until next time?"

I dimpled and nodded, offering a half wave as I turned and left the building. Meredith pulled quickly away from the curb, and we headed to Lizzie's house for dinner. She'd offered to cook her famous enchiladas, and we'd all happily agreed.

Entering Lizzie's house in October was like entering a Halloween shop that had exploded inside. Everywhere I looked were witches, goblins, spiderwebs, and an assortment of skeletons. Cauldrons topped every table with a variety of things crawling out of them. It was creepy, but in such a Lizzie-way that I was able to not get too hung up on all the morbid expressions of her favorite holiday.

We gathered in her kitchen and went about our assignments. Lizzie popped her already made enchiladas in the oven to warm them. Meredith directed table set up and arranged each dish as it made its way to the dining area. Aryn stood at the stove getting rice cooked. Ruby was chopping lettuce and veggies for the salad, and I was stirring together a fancy drink. It was easy, being together like this, and I never took it for granted. The warm kitchen, the happy banter as we easily chatted about our lives and experiences. Sometimes I thought it was sad that I'd been twenty-six years old when I had come to work at Washington Elementary and met this group of women. Twenty-six years before I'd made my first real friends and become part of my first sisterhood. I'd been the last one to join up. The others had been friends for years. But they'd welcomed me and overlooked my initial hesitance and tendency to be guarded, and they'd made me feel like we'd always known each other. Thanks to them I'd gained courage and confidence to more fully be myself.

I sometimes wondered how different my life would have been if I'd experienced this in high school or college. I'd always had associates and friendly acquaintances who I could spend time with here and there but never a bond like I had now . . .never a place where I would be missed or where I was truly needed to complete the whole. They were family to me, every bit as much as my parents were.

"Welp." Meredith clapped her hands together, making a few of us jump. "I believe we've been patient enough. Time for the tea."

I smiled as the others nodded and agreed. I looked down at the drink ingredients I was working with and wondered where to start. They were about to get a pretty big surprise.

"You guys know that Ford helped me after my ice skating accident," I said. They all nodded. "Um, and you know I fell asleep on his couch the next day."

"Yeah. We talked about it, in depth," Lizzie stated, a signal to get to the good stuff.

"Okay, well I ran into him after the parent teacher conference thing, and I ended up going to Leonard and Connie's to swim with Ford and his kids." I paused and ducked my head, tucking a piece of my hair behind my ear. "He kissed me."

I may as well have struck a match and dropped it into a barrel of gasoline. All thoughts of food and dinner prep were forgotten as they launched into volleys of shock and cheering and so much laughter and high fiving that I started to feel like I'd taken the state championship trophy in 'nailing it.'

"This is amazing!" Lizzie clapped. "How was it?"

"There's no way he's a bad kisser," Ruby said dreamily. "I hope you grabbed on and pulled him close and made sure those arms were wrapped around you nice and tight."

I giggled. "It wasn't like that. We were barely touching."

"Oh my gosh," Aryn said. "Those kinds of kisses make my knees weak." She playfully shivered and closed her eyes.

"I have to say, it feels good to be proven right," Meredith smirked. "I knew something was brewing there."

I bit my lips. "Then he texted me that night and told me he'd be busy this week with those out-of-town visitors we saw tonight, so he couldn't get together, but that he'd like to be in touch."

"And?" Lizzie asked.

"We've talked or texted every day."

"Swoon," Ruby called, slapping her hand to her heart. "This is better than baby kittens crawling all over your face."

I looked to Ruby, distracted by her statement, and played a mental video of kittens crawling on my face. I'm not sure I'd call that the best thing ever. The others seemed to be, momentarily, doing the same thing before Meredith called us all back.

"What now?" she asked.

I shrugged. "I don't know. I'm still trying to wrap my head around the fact that I seem to have fallen into a possible budding relationship with the man of my dreams."

"No one deserves it more than you," Aryn came over and gave me a one-armed squeeze. "I'm happy for you."

They all agreed, reaching out to pat my hand or shoulder, and we got back to our respective duties as conversation flowed to other topics. As the others chatted lightly, laughing and occasionally giving me a delighted look, I stayed quiet as the image of Ford, his hair dripping wet, his face close to mine, kept playing in my mind. Let me just tell you that no drink has ever been more stirred than the one I was making that night.

CHAPTER EIGHTEEN

A message on the interschool messaging system popped up on my computer screen after school a few days later, asking me to call Ford Whittaker and leaving his number. My hand froze over the mouse, and I reread the little box, unsure that I'd seen the message correctly. He'd never contacted me at work before, and even though I felt a little spark over seeing his name on the screen, I was curious what it could be about.

I wasn't going to be able to finish my lesson plan until I'd found out, so I stood and closed my classroom door before picking up my desk phone and calling him.

"Ford Whittaker," he answered authoritatively, and for some reason the business-y sound of it made me smile.

"Yes, hello Ford Whittaker, this is Miss Hailey Thomas returning your call from Washington Elementary School here in . . ."

"I know where you're located, Miss Thomas," he replied, cutting me off with a laugh. "I'm sorry I had to contact you through the school. Time is of the essence, and I was going to leave you a message, but your mailbox on your cell is full."

"Oh, yeah. I don't use voicemail. It's for old people," I teased.

He was silent, and I wished I could see his expression now. "I'll ignore the old people comment," he said in a totally dry tone. "Listen, the reason I'm calling is to ask you a favor."

"Oh?" Well blow me down with a feather, I did not see this coming.

"I sent off those international people this afternoon, but another group is coming to town tomorrow, and I'm hosting a dinner for them and their significant others or whomever they decide to bring as a guest. Anyhow, I thought it would make them all more comfortable if I had a guest, too, and I was hoping you'd be willing to come with me."

He was sort of asking me out, which caused unparalleled delight. "So what you're saying is that you're looking for a warm body to fill a chair?" I teased. "I'd be flattered, except you could have asked a chimpanzee to fulfill the same function."

"A chimpanzee spills their drinks more. Oh, wait . . . maybe I should ask someone else," he teased back, referring to that first meal at my parents' house and my drink tsunami.

I wanted to laugh, but I bit my lips and said, "I've never been asked to be an official companion and possible bodyguard."

"I don't need a bodyguard."

"Hey, I'm not making any assumptions about what this night will hold. Maybe one of the other women will set her sights on you."

There was a noise like the shifting of a leather chair, and I could imagine him leaning forward, elbows on his desk as we talked. "Doubtful," he replied.

Doubtful my foot. How any woman resisted him was beyond me. I'd sure done a terrible job of it.

"You can't convince me there's no chance of that happening," I said.

"If I tell you that I'd appreciate your bodyguard services, would that make you say yes?" he asked.

The bigger question was when had I become so comfortable with him? I was flirting and enjoying it so much. This banter had to be a result of the conversations we'd been having. I could picture his gray eyes filled with enjoyment, and I kind of wished this were happening in person.

"You'd really be checking an item off my bucket list. Where is this dinner?" I asked.

"I've reserved the private room at The Amaryllis."

"That must have taken a little bit of string pulling," I said with admiration. I knew for a fact that that particular restaurant was booked out for weeks, and forget about the private dining room being available in my lifetime. "That should impress your people. Speaking of impressing people, what's my role here? Am I silent and coldly beautiful, or chatty and warmly distracting?"

He chuckled. "It would be helpful if you didn't come across as a prisoner."

"How much do I like you?"

"What do you mean?"

"Hand holding, putting my head on your shoulder, giggling mindlessly at all the clever things you say, feeding you off my fork?" My toes curled in my shoes as the words flowed in a way I didn't know I was capable of.

"If you could avoid sarcastic replies to everything I say, that would probably be enough."

I grinned, even though he couldn't see me. "Okay. I'll do it."

"Thank you. I'll pick you up tomorrow at 6:40."

"I'll be ready."

"Uh, thanks, Hailey. For agreeing to come. It'll be nice to see you in person."

The sudden seriousness of his tone knocked me off balance, but I responded in turn. "You're welcome. See you soon."

I hung up and stood, tugging at the hem of my shirt as I beelined it straight to Aryn's classroom. It was time for a pow-wow.

*****

A knock sounded on my front door at promptly 6:40 p.m. the next night. I was standing in my room in front of my full-length mirror, tugging a little here and there on a strand of hair or the sleeve of my dress. I wanted to look good. I wanted to fit in with whomever we'd be dining with. Plus, I was a little nervous to be one-on-one with Ford for the first time. Every other time we'd seen each other it had been in a group of family or friends, and I'd always had that buffer. Although, I supposed tonight we'd have a buffer of other people, too. Maybe I should be less nervous.

To be fair, there was no way to mentally prepare myself to go from cyberstalking to daydreaming about to avoiding and then to going places with this man. This was new territory, and my heart was zigzagging through my chest as though it wasn't sure where to land.

My pale blue dress with lace overlay was tailored to my size but still loose enough to sit comfortably and eat food without being miserable. I was wearing the same strappy silver heels I'd worn to the opera, confident that I could add a few inches to my height without being taller than Ford. I'd put some curls in my short hair and done a few twists into a sort of updo that was fancier than my usual sleek bob, and I'd never admit how much time I spent on makeup. I was pleased with how the dress color brought out my periwinkle eyes and gave myself a cheesy thumbs up in the mirror before going to answer the door.

I opened it with a smile of greeting on my face, genuinely excited, and my face froze as I took him in. He looked immaculate in a light gray suit and vest with a blue tie, and I immediately dimpled without even thinking about it.

"You look great. You really will need a bodyguard tonight," I smiled.

"Only if the other men get any ideas about you," he said under his breath, but I heard it, and my feet wiggled in my shoes.

"We match." I gestured from my dress to his tie. "I hope you brought me a corsage before we hit the prom."

His lips tugged, and he surprised me by leaning in to wrap his hand around my elbow and brush his mouth against my cheek in greeting. "Do you have a jacket? It's going to be chilly by the time we finish."

My brain was busy for a split second, cataloging his smell and the feel of his hand on my skin. Only when he released his hold on me did I realize what he'd said, and I turned to grab the gray wrap coat that was sitting over the entry table. I beamed when I held it up.

"It's almost creepy that this is the same color as your suit. Maybe I should grab something else?"

He shook his head. "No. I don't want to mess up the whole ensemble you've got going."

"Oh, ensemble is a nice word. You're obviously a man of experience."

I draped the coat over my arm, and he stepped to the side, allowing me to come onto the small porch and turn to close and lock my door before we took the three steps down to the sidewalk. He nodded to the left, and we fell into step together as we made our way to guest parking.

"I was married for eight years. I'm familiar with the outfit selection process," he said over the light sound of my heels clicking along.

"Eight years, huh? Was your wife like me and took her time planning out all the details that no one else would even notice?" I said in a self-deprecating tone.

He shook his head. "Before the money, no. It was straight t-shirts and jeans. Later . . . yes. She got really into high-end fashion."

The odd tone he'd taken had me closing my mouth and avoiding any other mention of her. I didn't know a lot of about the mysterious Heather Whittaker, but what I did know was she wasn't a subject that Ford especially liked talking about, and this wasn't the right time.

We reached a sleek silver sedan, and I stopped and made my eyes wide. "Gray again? Ford, how did you know? Matching the car to the outfit is really high-level stuff."

The crack pulled him out of whatever trough he'd fallen into when thinking about his late wife, and he smirked. "I don't have a car for every suit."

"Right. You forget, I've been in your garage."

He reached the passenger door and opened it as I made my way toward him. "You have?"

"Yes. I ate your strawberries and cream birthday cake while sitting on the ground next to your Corvette."

"You ate on my garage floor?"

I nodded as I took my seat, and he closed the door. When he'd seated himself behind the wheel and backed out, I asked him about the people who would be at dinner and was happy to sit back and listen as he gave me a quick overview. It was best to be prepared, and for all my teasing, I understood that this was an important evening for him.

When we arrived at The Amaryllis, we pulled up to valet parking, and my door was opened by a young man in a crisp white uniform. I thanked him for his kindness and waited as Ford came around the front of his car.

"Have you been here before?" he asked.

"Yes. It's my mother's birthday tradition."

"Really?"

"Yes. Every year since they opened."

"Then I suppose you know your way around already."

The double doors were opened by another young man in uniform, and I startled slightly when Ford's fingertips brushed against my lower back, an indication that I should go ahead of him. It took a lot of willpower to play it off like gentlemen were always escorting me places rather than glancing his way with big eyes, but I pulled it off by focusing my attention on the employee and giving him a smile as I entered the beautiful lobby.

Once we were inside I felt a bubble of excitement over getting to come here two times in the same year, having celebrated Mom's birthday here in June. The Amaryllis was expensive, elite, and sought after. It was one of those bucket list type places where you almost pass out at the prices while screaming in excitement over actually being there.

In a flash I realized Ford could eat here weekly if he wanted while I was a pro-level budgeting master and penny pincher. We certainly lived different lifestyles.

Ford surprised me once again by lightly touching my shoulder and asking if he could take my coat. I'd been so caught up in the atmosphere of the place that I'd missed yet another employee coming from my side to take my coat and check it. I glanced over my shoulder at Ford and handed him the coat that had been hanging over my arm.

"Of course. Sorry."

Ford simply handed my coat to the employee without any comment, and I took the opportunity to square my shoulders, straighten my spine, and get my head in the game. Ford hadn't brought me here to gape like a hooked fish at everything or daydream about not living paycheck to paycheck. I wasn't new to this setting. Time to play it cool.

"If you'll follow me?" The maître d' bowed slightly toward us, and once again Ford's fingertips burned a hole in my back as he played the part of thoughtful escort.

I remembered the feel of those same fingertips, still damp from the pool as they wrapped around my arm and he leaned toward me . . .

I forced the thought down and followed the maître d' in his black-on-black uniform, avoiding the mistake of sight-seeing, and pasted on a serene expression when we stepped into the private room. This was one place I'd never been, and it was incredible. Made to look like an English garden, we'd somehow been transported outside of our small city. All the walls were glass, with hedges and pathways, flowers blooming, and even a fountain. On one end of the room was a wooden floor where a string quartet was playing something wonderful. I wanted to pause and listen, but I kept walking, reminding myself that I'd be able to hear them from the table. On the other end of the room was a large circular table, designed with intricate whirls and painted white and gold. Around it there were ten chairs, and all but two were already filled.

Worried that we were the last to arrive and had kept them waiting, I painted on my most apologetic smile as Ford gracefully skirted around me and offered his hand to the closest person.

"Welcome. I'm so glad you're all here and seated," he said graciously.

Conversation that had paused when we entered now kicked up again as the people around the table made introductions. I could feel their curious looks in my direction while Ford walked around shaking hands and the maître d' pulled out my chair to seat me in style. I thanked him before he bowed at the neck and exited the room. I watched Ford as he worked the table, putting on a charming show that I found incredible. I could speak to people and be polite, but I was never able to be the center of attention in that way. Well, at least outside of a classroom.

"And who is this lovely young lady you brought with you tonight?" one of the other women asked.

Ford turned to me. "This is Hailey Thomas," he said, extending a hand in my direction. "We met through my little girl."

The oohs and aahs that went around the table after that pronouncement had me convinced that he'd planned it out beforehand, knowing exactly how others would react to it. It sounded like he was a loving father and, aw shucks, he'd been lucky enough to meet a pretty lady. I kept my smile in place, but it was hard to keep my eyes from good-naturedly rolling as I thought, 'Yeah, and he wanted nothing to do with me at first.'

Instead, I turned to my left, where a middle-aged woman was seated and struck up a conversation with her. Her name was Gianna, and we hit it off immediately, a boon I hadn't been expecting. Gianna was a mother of three teenagers, she loved to cook, and she'd traveled as much as I had with my parents. By the time Ford sat next to me and the menus were passed around, I'd been filled in on the fact that everyone at the table was a player in the natural supplements world and they were hoping to score a deal with Ford as he prepared to go international. That's not what I had thought was going on here. I'd thought Ford was wooing clients, not that he'd be the one getting wooed. I said so to Gianna, and she laughed behind her hand.

"Oh, he did come up with the date, time, and location, but that's only after my husband's company had been after him for a long time. My Randy is so excited about this dinner; he'll probably not stop talking about it for months."

"Assuming it goes his way," I joked kindly.

She tapped her nose. "Exactly."

"Hailey?" Ford got my attention from my other side and handed me a one sheet menu.

"I've heard that they change their menu each month, so it'll be fun to try something new," I said cheerfully as I took it from him and began greedily scanning it.

The others were bent over their menus, too, each couple with their heads together discussing what they wanted to eat. I half expected Ford to pipe up and offer to order for the table, and when he didn't, I looked at him.

"You're not going to tell everyone what's good here?" I asked.

"No. I'm not."

"Huh."

"What does 'huh' mean?"

"It means that I saw you as the guy who orders for the table."

He turned slightly so he was facing me more directly and kept his voice low enough that no one else could hear. He put one arm along the back of my chair, his fingertips landing on my shoulder so feather soft I wondered if he realized he was touching me.

"You have some strange ideas about me, sometimes. I don't bully people, and I'm not pompous."

Nerves tumbled through my insides as the jokes were put away for a moment. "I guess maybe I'm still a little wary after the first time we met."

"Why?" he seemed genuinely confused.

"Because you accused me of scheming to get close to you, and then I watched you at your birthday party working the room like a politician. I figured you had a really high opinion of yourself and liked to be in charge of everything."

He didn't immediately respond but looked back at the menu with a thoughtful expression. His fingertips slowly grazed my shoulder, nearing my neck and then working their way back down again. I couldn't stop a shiver that caused one side of his mouth to inch up.

"Anything else I should know?" he said at last.

"No, nothing comes to mind." My voice was a timid squeak.

"Good." His eyes met mine, and he blinked slowly before apparently deciding to change the subject. "What do you think of this room?"

I let out a breath and cleared my throat. "Amazing."

"After we eat, the string quartet will play for dancing."

"Dancing? Really?" I took the chance to slip back into teasing mode--a place I'd feel most comfortable with him--and flashed my dimples. "Maybe you can use that opportunity to dance with some of the women and get the dirt on what this group wants from you."

"That's . . . okay . . . not really what I was expecting you to say." He reached for his water and took a deep swallow.

"What did you think I'd say?" I asked. "Oh, were you hoping I'd dance with the men and flirt their secrets out?" I glanced around at each one, pretending to think about it, and then back at Ford. "I'm game."

"For the love, do not play flirty spy with these men." He bit his lips together, and I knew it was to keep from smiling.

"I happen to be very, very," I leaned in closer to him, "very good at flirty spy." Such a lie. I'd never flirted in the past and was probably bumbling it up now.

He looked over to say something, and the words seemed to freeze in place as he took in my face mere inches from his. That same intense look he so often got came back into his eyes, and I felt like a book whose pages had suddenly fallen open. His arm, still on the back of my chair, shifted so that his palm skated across my shoulders as he moved back into his own space. I pulled back and cleared my throat, snapping my attention back to my menu.

"Anyone interested in appetizers?" Gianna's husband, Randy, called out to the table.

Heads popped up, and the look was so much like a documentary on meerkats that I'd recently shown my class that I had to clear my throat to cover my sudden laugh. Ford glanced at me, but when my eyes stayed trained on the menu, he returned to the group at large as he suggested a few starters that he knew were good.

"I was right . . . you did order for the table," I giggled under my breath.

"It's not my fault I know what's worth our while here," he replied, amused.

Randy waved over a server that I hadn't even seen lurking near a hedge and began repeating the list Ford had just given him.

"Poor guy gets to stand in a hedge waiting for us to need something?" I whispered to Ford as the waiter listened closely.

"I think he's paid well enough that he'd stand in the fountain if we asked him to," Ford replied quietly.

"Hmm." I watched the server for moment before leaning toward Ford again. "Do you think he makes more than I do as a schoolteacher?" I asked jokingly.

"Definitely."

"You could have lied."

"What would the point of that be?" he asked.

"Do you honestly think he makes more than me?"

"Possibly."

"Then the point of lying would have been to spare my feelings," I retorted. "I do have them, you know."

"Would anyone like drinks?" the server asked.

I was happy to turn slightly away from Ford and give him my order. Assuming Ford was paying, I made it expensive.

After the server left, I was more than happy to let Ford go back to his wheeling and dealing with the businesspeople while Gianna and I got back to a rousing discussion on a cooking show we both watched.

"I'm hoping to travel to see a taping soon," Gianna gushed. "Probably in the new year, seeing as this season gets so busy."

"I teach second grade, and from Halloween through Christmas, it's basically anyone's guess how things are going to go. The kids get all wired, the teachers get burnt out, and nobody has any time to spare."

Gianna giggled and placed her hand on my arm, a universal sign that things were about to get gossipy. "Ford said you met through his daughter. Are you her teacher?"

I shook my head with a smile. "I was for a short time last year, but we hit it off. So this year she invited me to her dad's birthday party because she said it was only for adults, and I was the only adult friend she had."

Gianna put her hands over her heart. "So of course you went."

"Of course I did. What kind of monster would say no to that?" I replied, crossing my fingers against my lap. Gianna did not need to know all the hullabaloo that had surrounded that event.

"And now you and Ford are dating?" she asked.

To stall, I picked up my water glass and took a sip. When I set it down, my pleasant face was back. "It's . . . undefined." I couldn't answer a direct question with a lie.

Gianna's dark eyes shot over my shoulder to Ford and then back to me. "So he's available?"

Oh, crap on a cracker. "Not really that either," I replied, unsure of what Ford would want me to share with business associates.

"Because my daughter seems like the kind of girl who would be really interested in a man of Ford's . . ."

"Kindness and great personality?" I hurried in before Gianna could say anything about his drop-dead gorgeous looks or his robust finances.

She recognized what I was doing and, in turn, what she'd been about to do. She had the grace to blush slightly, and we turned to other topics of conversation. I listened as Gianna included another woman at the table while reflecting on the fact that I couldn't wait to tell Ford that my assumptions, for once, hadn't been so far off the mark. There had definitely been an attempt on his person.

CHAPTER NINETEEN

I t was time for dancing, and while I couldn't wait to get out there, I'd eaten enough to wonder if I'd be able to roll myself on over. The others didn't seem to be suffering the same way and were delighted by the idea.

"I ate more salmon than a bear prepping for hibernation," I whispered to Ford.

He cracked a smile as Gianna clapped her hands, keeping him from responding.

"I didn't know we'd get to dance." She stood and extended her hand to Randy, eyes twinkling at the role reversal. "May I have the honor?" she said to him.

Randy's guffaw filled the room as he stood with a flourish and bowed to his wife. "I thought you'd never ask."

The couple strolled arm in arm down a magical pathway strung with lights until they'd passed the fountain and were mostly out of sight, hidden by hedges and flowering plants. Other couples followed suit, all happily commenting on how wonderful this place was. Ford and I were the last to stand, and I attributed it to him being the host of the evening. Either that or understanding I was in a bit of a fishy coma.

"Listen," I turned to him, putting my hand on his forearm, when the last couple cleared the hedge. "Maybe don't dance with Gianna. She's looking to set you up with her daughter."

His brow scrunched down. "How do you know?"

"She point-blank asked if we were dating, and I told her we hadn't defined it."

"First off, how old is her daughter? Eighteen? Secondly, that was gutsy to ask my date about my availability," he said, looking over the bush in her direction. I warmed at him referring to me as his date. "What does that mean, we haven't defined it?"

I sighed. "Don't pretend that you haven't spent enough time with women to know what that means. Guys love that phrase. It means what it sounds like it means. But she jumped on it when I said 'undefined' and mentioned her daughter, so I kind of put her off by saying you weren't really available, and it was a whole, you know, situation for a minute. She ended up dropping it, but I'm not sure if that's a permanent drop or a when-I-get-Ford-alone type drop, you know?"

He took a breath. "At the risk of hurting your feelings, you were supposed to outperform a chimpanzee."

I laughed and dropped my hand from his arm, the sound loud in the intimate space between us. "Yes, I know. Which is why I backpedaled so hard I'm surprised to find myself still here and not in another country."

He extended his arm, and I hooked my hand through his elbow as we started walking to the dance floor. "So does she think we're a couple or not?"

"At the end of it, I'm not sure what she thinks. She might think I'm too shy to admit that you're dating your daughter's teacher or that our relationship is so new that I'm afraid to give it a label."

"I can work with that," he stated. "Also, I was not a player as a young man, and I'm still not. I may be extroverted, but I'm not interested in drama or anything that uses the word 'undefined'. Do you dance?"

I stuttered a bit, trying to get my bearings and process all the little nuggets he'd just dropped. If he didn't like the word undefined, what did he think we were doing? "Yes, I dance," I finally stated. "For you I'll even dance gracefully, although graceful dancing wasn't part of the original favor."

"You have the most charitable heart of any woman I've ever met."

"That's probably the nicest thing you've ever said to me."

When there was space, we stepped onto the floor and Ford slid his arm around me, placing his palm firmly and flat against my upper back as he took my hand in his. I arched one eyebrow in acknowledgment of his apparent understanding of dance positions.

"You've got the stance down," I said, "but can your feet cooperate too?"

A smug little grin made its way onto his face as he led me into the beginnings of a waltz. I followed along easily, having taken dance lessons up until graduating from high school. Both of us were pleasantly surprised by the other's skill, and before long we were moving as one around the floor. I had no idea how Ford felt, but for me it was exhilarating. I couldn't hold back my delighted expression as the song ended. He smiled down at me with a satisfied look in his eyes.

The man could dance, he attended the opera, he had a good job, and was a kind father. It would have been enough to attract even the most discerning woman without the added benefit of him having a personality that I was really coming to appreciate. Him being delicious to look at only added to the allure. It was shallow of me, maybe, but I very much appreciated the view.

"Your dancing isn't undefined at all," I said. He responded to my quip by tugging me closer and squeezing me until I laughed. "You're good at it, you're good."

"You, too," he returned.

His arm continued to hold me close, which had me brushing up against him as we stood entranced together, both of us breathing more heavily than normal from the exercise, wearing big grins. The thumb of the hand that held mine lightly caressed the back of my hand, and my pulse leaped. His eyes shifted color, somehow darkening as his lips parted. His arm slid further around me until his fingertips were pressing against my ribs, and I was helpless in the moment, my head tilted back, reveling in the feeling of something so right building between us.

His voice was low, for my ears only. "Hailey, I know I . . ."

"Ford," Gianna called as she and Randy came up, clapping us on the backs. "That was wonderful. You simply must dance with me next and teach me some of your moves."

"Yes," Randy joined in jovially, "and Hailey can do the same with me."

Ford's fingers tightened around mine and I noticed his nostrils flare before he shifted back to a polite expression, released me, and stepped back. He looked to them both with charming ease and moved to lead Gianna to an open space. I mourned the loss of his closeness.

"Shall we?" Randy's arms were open waiting for me as the next song started.

I grabbed my skirt and curtsied with my dimples flashing. I'd be as charming as Ford had been. "Indeed, we shall."

I danced with Randy and then each of the other three men in succession before starting the entire rotation again. Eventually, I found myself back near Ford in what had become a game of musical dance partners. I was exhausted from keeping up the chit-chat, but also feeling relaxed and sunny from the dancing, by the time Ford and I were once again facing each other. My strappy heels, however, weren't made for this, even if I was thoroughly enjoying it, and my feet were squawking loudly.

Ford hurriedly stepped toward me, his arms open as he playfully darted looks around at the others, as though daring anyone else to try to dance with either of us. There was no hesitation from me as I stepped into his space and took his hand.

He was warm from the exertion, and I could smell that same scent I'd noticed so many other times as he gathered me close. The formal dance position from before was relaxed, with his hand resting at my waist rather than firmly against my upper back. My right hand was held lightly in his, his arm bent close to our bodies. The waltzing tunes had slowed into something more soothing, and conversations had fallen to intimate tones between all the couples who were back together. It was probably the restaurant's way of slowly bringing the evening to a close, and I appreciated the skill with which they'd planned out everything.

"Have these people convinced you to do business with them yet?" I asked, as we moved slowly, giving up on any official dance moves.

"Maybe. They're a group of strong negotiators."

I grinned, and it morphed somehow into a yawn. I was embarrassed and turned my head to cover it. I wasn't that tired, but most of my nights were spent at home quietly recovering from my busy days and even busier evenings as I caught up on household tasks and errands.

"Did they wear you out?" Ford's voice was mellow, and I found myself wanting to rest against him.

I fought against it and shook my head. "Them and the twenty-five children I spent the day with."

He made a noise. "My two wear me out sometimes. I don't know how you manage a herd."

I tilted my head toward the others. "The same way you manage one."

He chuckled quietly, and I felt it down to my toes. We'd closed the space between us without noticing, and I vacillated between pulling away or leaning in. He answered the debate for me, moving his hand from my waist to rest on my back. I let my head fall against him, and it was like something clicked into place as my ear touched his collarbone. Heat and light filled me, and in that moment I knew, I just knew, that somehow this man had the power to either be my everything or to leave me deeply wounded. It filled me with both joy and terror, and I faltered in our movements.

He read the stumble as me being tired, and he tilted his head down as he said, "How about we call it a night?"

I felt his words against my forehead. I nodded, unable to say anything, and reluctantly let go of him as he made his rounds, shaking hands and saying goodbye.

While he did so, Gianna came and placed her hand on my forearm. "Hailey, from where I'm sitting, that man is definitely off the market."

A blush crawled into my face, making my light skin a bright pink shade. "Gianna . . ." I argued, but she wouldn't hear it.

She gave me a quick hug and made her way back to her husband's side.

When Ford had finished his goodbyes and I'd done the same, he surprised me by taking my hand in his and guiding me through the restaurant. It felt natural to have my fingers wrapped around his larger hand. We didn't speak as the spell continued to weave its way around me. We stopped at the coat check and Ford helped me into the gray wrap coat that matched his suit so perfectly. Then his hand was on my back as we moved out the front doors and stood under the covered entrance while we waited for his car to be brought around.

"You were right," I said in an effort to be light and normal. "It's definitely chilly tonight."

He glanced at me. "Are you warm enough?"

"Yes. I'm fine. I grew up here, remember? I can handle the cold weather."

"That's right. You're a mountain girl at heart." He said it approvingly. "I grew up in Colorado, so I'm not too worried about snow either."

"What part?"

"In a suburb of Denver."

"Is that where you went to college?" I asked.

"No. I went to UCLA."

His car arrived, and he stepped forward to open the passenger door for me while the valet put the car in park. I thanked him and got in, happy to feel the heater already blowing. Late October was definitely cool enough that I'd been feeling it on my bare legs.

"So can I ask you a personal question?" I asked him once we were moving through the quiet streets.

"I'm not sure. They're not my favorite kind."

I folded my hands together in my lap and pushed on anyway, figuring I had nothing to lose. While I was seriously developing genuine affection for Real Ford, I still wasn't sure where I expected our association to go from here. Regardless, there didn't seem to be a reason not to ask, other than him possibly being annoyed with me, and I'd survived that already.

"How did your wife pass away?"

He was quiet, but I didn't get any angry vibes coming off of him, so I waited patiently to see how he'd respond. He cleared his throat and sighed. "She was killed in a car accident in London."

"It's lucky that none of the rest of you were hurt too badly."

"Luck had nothing to do with it. We were all back here at home. She was traveling alone."

"Oh," I replied.

He pushed out another breath, and I felt bad that I'd asked even as he seemed determined to answer. "After our kids were born and she struggled so much with postpartum depression, she became a different person. She . . . her words were that she couldn't find satisfaction in her current life. I was surprised by that because she'd wanted kids and a home and she had loved her job as a high school math teacher. She . . ." he cleared his throat, and I could feel the pain and confusion he'd felt. I almost told him to stop, but he opened his mouth and continued. "She was talented, kind, funny, athletic, and loved to serve people. She hosted the best parties, and everyone really gravitated to her. But she couldn't see herself like we did."

He took a deep breath and then his shoulders relaxed as the rest of the story flowed out of him in a way that made me think he was releasing a long-held burden.

"Anyhow, all of this happened around the same time that my company became really successful. She'd always been low-key, but she started to spend money as a way to feel better. She was shopping all the time. It wasn't only for herself, though. She bought things for me and the kids, for family and friends. Then she got into fashion, and she dove into it as a new passion. I wanted her to be happy, so I did my best to . . . well, we went to counseling and tried to find middle ground. She wasn't a bad mom, but she was having a hard time feeling comfortable in her own skin and that spilled over into our family life. We came up with a compromise that she'd take one big trip every six months by herself or with friends to some fashion capitals. It ended with her being killed while heading to a fashion show in bad traffic during a storm." He sighed and ran a hand along his chin. "In the end, it felt like we'd become strangers to each other. I was left with these two grieving children, but in a way, I'd been grieving for a long time as I watched her slip away from me."

Wow. I could see now why he'd reacted so poorly to feeling like I'd plotted to get close to him. It probably felt like the only draw would have been his money, which was a painful repeat of something he'd already lived. Obviously he wasn't having it. That had already destroyed a part of his life.

"That sounds very painful to watch someone you love struggle and then morph into a stranger."

"It was. I've worked hard to protect Henry and Hillary from all of it. She loved them, and they loved her. I hope they were too young to feel her pulling away little by little. Sometimes I feel guilty for thinking they might be better off with a dead mother than with one who was slowly abandoning them."

My throat felt thick at the thought of little ones waiting for their mom to come home and wondering where she was.

"No wonder you were so angry when you thought Hillary was trying to set us up," I mumbled more to myself than him. "You must have seen a teacher, who you know for a fact has a low salary, eyeing your wealth to take away her worries."

"I . . ." He paused. "I do owe you an apology for all of that. I handled it poorly."

167

I grinned at him. "The good news is that you've learned the truth about me. Your money is safe." I shot him a sassy look. "If I was after anything of yours, it would be that couch I slept on at your house. Expect it to be stolen at some point."

"You definitely rate higher than members of the ape family."

I laughed and let the subject drop, unwilling to pry any more tonight. It was enough that he'd been so open and that I now understood better why he'd been so resistant to me being around. I truly mourned for what him and his kids had been through. And Heather, too. She had my sympathy.

I could only hope that time would show Ford that I wasn't a risk. I'd been raised in the world of mental health and understood how it affected lives. I'd also been raised with money-- although not the amount he was functioning with--and was well aware of what it could and could not provide. If he'd let me, I could be an empathetic and steady person in his life.

We arrived back at my condo complex, and he parked in guest parking. We walked together to my front door in comfortable silence, and he waited while I unlocked the door and opened it before turning to face him.

"Tonight was fun," I said. "And, just so you know, I behaved myself and didn't flirt with the other men in order to get their secrets."

"Are you trying to make me feel better because I told you about my wife, and now I'm a tragic character?"

I dimpled. "Not at all. I thought you were tragic long before I heard about Heather."

His entire face transformed as he let out a snort of amusement. "I'm glad to know I'm leaving such a good impression."

"Goodnight, Ford," I smiled warmly at him.

I went to shake his hand, but he surprised me by pulling me in for a hug. It only took a second for me to relax against him and embrace him back. It felt so good and natural as my heart picked up the rhythm of his. Real Ford felt so much better than I'd ever imagined he could. The hug lasted far longer than a regular goodbye should have, and I shivered at the warmth growing between us.

He let go, but his hands moved to cup my face on either side, and he leaned in to press his lips to the place on my cheek where my dimple appeared. Kissing lightly, he moved to the same spot on the other side, his hands gently holding my face.

"I've wanted to kiss those ever since you flashed them at me at the dance recital while lying through your teeth about being happy to sit next to me. Those dimples are trouble."

A flush of embarrassment warred with the warmth cascading down my limbs. This close I could see stripes of white and blue circling together in the gray of his eyes, making them look like a blue sky filled with clouds.

I stuttered in reply. "I was not lying."

"Hailey, your nose almost grew two inches standing there with your pink dahlias and innocent expression." His eyes were warm with merriment as he leaned closer. "I would have given everything to have you tell me what you were really thinking. It drove me mad."

"I was thinking how much I didn't want to be around you," I whispered against lips that were moving closer to mine.

"And now?"

He pressed a light kiss against my mouth, stealing my thoughts and making my chest feel tight. When I didn't answer he kissed me again, his hands falling from my face to hold my shoulders. His mouth was so warm and so gentle. He wasn't insisting on anything, rather asking permission while letting me know how very much he wanted this. The kiss at the pool had been a surprise, but this time there was no hesitance on his part. I leaned in to the feeling, the knowledge, that he meant it.

My own hands raised to press against his chest lightly, not to push away, but to feel his heartbeat. The kiss shifted, his head angling slightly, and I dove into it wholeheartedly, feeling as though I was no longer connected to the earth. Ford's hands slid from my shoulders, one settling on my hip and the other pressing against the small of my back. I sighed against his mouth as my arms moved to circle his neck, eliminating the space between us. I was fire and ice as we fully connected, and he initiated another set of exquisite kisses. It was more than I'd ever thought I'd feel for someone.

He gently pushed me backwards, and we shuffled together--still kissing--until we were standing inside my house. He kicked my front door shut with one of his heels as his lips moved from my mouth to rest against my ear, his breath rapid and warm. "I'm not sure the neighbors should have a front row seat to this," he said.

"I'm not even sure what this is," I replied, turning my head to place a kiss on his jawline.

His arms tightened again, and he turned to meet my mouth once more. I'd never been kissed like this by anyone. I'd dated, I'd even had a few short-term boyfriends, but no one had tugged at my soul, demanding to be let inside, the way Ford did. His arms banded around me, and I wondered how perfect it would feel if my stupid coat wasn't bunching between us. It would probably have been a couple of degrees cooler, at least. The thought of me steaming alive inside this coat made me smile, which broke the melding of our lips. I dropped my forehead against his collarbone and pulled my arms down to wrap around his waist. I felt cozy and safe, and supremely happy, nestled against him, listening to our breathing settle.

I felt him swallow. "That was not part of the plan for tonight," he said in a raspy voice.

"I know."

"And sometimes knowing when to leave is a good thing, too."

"Just . . . give me one second," I said, feeling brave and reckless for the first time in my life. I pulled out of his embrace, and he released me, watching as I unwrapped my coat and pulled my arms from the sleeves. I draped it over my couch and then stepped back to where he was standing. "That's better. Now, where were we?"

I grabbed the lapels of his suit jacket and tugged him toward me, leaning up on my toes until our mouths met once more. He laughed against my lips, but it was short-lived as I demanded he meet my kisses with some of his own. He complied quickly, his arms wrapping about me until I wasn't sure I'd ever be able to fully breathe again. This was better than a thousand daydreams and a million hopes. I felt alive and whole and so, so, so cherished by him.

"You're beautiful, Hailey," he murmured against my cheek. "You're smart, and funny, and so . . . unexpected."

I liked that I was getting under his skin, that I was keeping him on his toes. I adored that he found me beautiful. He released me, and I did the same, tucking a strand of hair that had fallen out of my updo behind my ear.

"I really better go," he said, and I nodded.

"Yeah."

He looked as jumbled up inside as I was. His eyes were glowing, his lips pink from my lipstick, his hair a little disheveled. I took a mental picture, wanting to remember him this way.

"Goodnight," he whispered.

"Goodnight."

He stepped out, and I stood watching my door close, soaking up the last few sparks of attraction before they flitted away.

CHAPTER TWENTY

The next day a chiming sound pulled me out of planning my math lessons for the coming week, and I shuffled the papers around on my table at home until my phone surfaced. My face lit up as I saw Ford's name. I'd thought of him obsessively over the past day. . . possibly even more than when I used to daydream and make up silly stories. I excitedly clicked on the message.

Ford: Are you going to the Halloween Fair on Main this weekend

Me: Thinking about it

Ford: I have a favor to ask

I grinned and replied:

Me: I know a great chimpanzee

Ford: I think I'd rather go with you, if that's okay

My face felt warm, and my smile grew. Ford was admitting he wanted to spend time with me. I could hardly believe it.

Me: Okay

Ford: We'll meet you at the big pumpkin on Saturday at 5

Not only was he asking me out, but he was asking me to spend time with his family in a very public setting. This was a big move. While a tiny part of me hoped for some alone time with him in the future, this was . . . easier, somehow. So I was happy.

So happy, in fact, that I forgot to play it cool and simply blurted it all out at the Recap and Recoup session the next day.

"I went with Ford to dinner at The Amaryllis. We danced and had the best food, and at the end of the night, he kissed me breathless. Now I'm going to the Halloween Fair with Ford and his kids this weekend." I said the words so quickly it seemed to take them a minute to catch my meaning.

"Come again?" Meredith asked as they all looked at me with varying degrees of surprise. "Because last time we talked about Ford, he'd kissed you very lightly at the pool. There have obviously been some developments since then."

I shook my head and waved my hands. "I've been a little distracted."

"This is kind of a big deal," Lizzie said while clapping her hands together. "The fair is a big event. Everyone goes."

"I know," I grinned.

"Seems like you're excited about it," Aryn said.

I bit my lips and nodded. "Yeah."

"Can we get back to the kissing-your-face-off part?" Ruby cried, looking at us like we were nuts for skipping over that.

Sound exploded from all my friends as they dropped the façade of calm support and went ballistic. I could hardly separate out their words, but the general consensus was that they assumed Ford knew his way around a pair of lips and that I had a serious issue with keeping things to myself. I was laughing breathlessly by the time I got them settled down enough to tell the whole story. By the time I finished, they were unusually quiet, processing.

"Okay, take us back a bit. How hot was he in that swimming pool?" Ruby asked into the stillness. I closed my eyes and blushed enough that they all whistled. "That's pretty hot," Ruby stated.

"Seriously, he comes off as this total businessman, stiff suit," Meredith said, but not rudely.

"When you first met me, I hardly strung two sentences together," I reminded her. "Now I'm a regular blabbermouth."

Aryn arched an eyebrow. "You're far from a blabbermouth, but I get what you're saying. First impressions aren't everything."

"And people warm up," Lizzie supplied.

"Do you really like him?" Aryn asked.

"I'm starting to," I replied. Which was a total lie because I'd been starting to like him for quite a while now, but I hadn't allowed myself to admit it.

"Tell us about the kissing again," Ruby wiggled her eyebrows.

"I had to take my coat off," I dimpled, and they brought the walls down with their cheers.

*****

I was lounging on my bed, flipping through my e-reader trying to settle on a book the next night when my phone rang. I glanced at the clock, wondering who would be calling at nine p.m. When I picked up my phone and saw Ford's name, I smiled.

How was this happening? I wasn't the girl who got wishes granted this way.

I'd assumed there would be no contact until the fair on Saturday, even though I had been feeling bummed about it. I wanted him to set the pace since he had so much more skin in this game, but being patient wasn't as easy in this situation as it had always been in the past. I set down my e-reader, tugged my covers up, and slipped down into my bed, looking at the ceiling.

"Hello?"

"I've been thinking, and I feel like maybe Shane was onto something," he said by way of greeting.

"Shane? My blind date?" I asked.

"Yeah. So I've come up with a list of questions I'd like you to answer." His voice was playful and open and . . . super flirty if I was reading this correctly.

I shook my head and giggled. "Should I be nervous?"

"Only if you're a serial killer, but the background check I ran on you came up clean."

At this I laughed. "Alright. But this has to be a two-way street. You have to answer some questions about yourself, too."

He scoffed. "Sweetheart, I've been an open book since day one."

I knew he'd said sweetheart the way you'd say it playfully to anyone, but it still made my toes curl under my sheets. "Agree to disagree. What's your first question?" I actually heard a paper rustling, and I couldn't help but tease him. "Do you have an actual list? I thought you were joking."

"Of course I have a list," he scoffed. "I looked it up online. This is serious business."

"Exactly what position am I interviewing for here?" I asked in mock-seriousness.

"That's yet to be determined. You're either going to be my date or the lady who cleans the tires on my cars. It all depends on how you answer these very important and scientific questions."

"I'll bet you ask these questions to all the ladies."

"Why do you think my car tires are so shiny?"

At that I laughed out loud, and he chuckled along at my reaction. Delighted, I squeezed my free hand into a fist and kicked my feet.

"Okay, well, I can't wait to get started. I think."

"Alright." He cleared his throat theatrically. "First, what's your weirdest habit or quirk?"

"Oh." I blinked a few times and chewed on my lip, trying to think what other people would find quirky about me.

"I'm worried that it's taking this long to answer."

"I . . . I don't think I have any quirks. I'm really . . . normal?"

"Is that a question?" he joked. "Come on, everyone has their little quirks or habits that they think everyone else does but really no one else does it."

"Okay. I, um, I tug at my shirt or smooth down my hair when I'm nervous."

"I've noticed that."

"Great," I muttered, feeling awkward.

"It's nothing to be ashamed of. Want to know mine?"

"Yes."

"I have a watch, but I always carry it in my pocket instead of wearing it on my wrist. And before you ask, no, I don't want a pocket watch, and yes, I understand that my phone has a clock on it. It's a quirk, and I stand by it."

"Does it have a watch band actually attached?"

"Yes. It's blue."

I giggled. "That's weird, Ford."

"Exactly. Next question. Who is your celebrity crush?"

I puffed out some air. "I don't really crush on celebrities."

"No lies. I know there's a guy out there, on the big screen, making your eyes get all big and dreamy. Spill it."

And I knew, I fully understood in that moment exactly why people followed Ford around like a fly to honey. He was funny, leading you through conversation effortlessly. What I'd seen as arrogance was confidence and calm. This man would make such an interesting life partner.

"Okay. There is one guy," I hedged.

"I knew it."

"It's Idris Elba. The man is the whole package. Handsome, suave, classy . . ."

"Well, okay. Looking up Idris Elba as we speak." He put me on speaker, and I laughed as I heard him mumbling to himself. "Yep, solid choice," he said a few minutes later. "Totally drool-worthy."

"Oh my gosh," I cried, wanting to hide even though he wasn't in the room with me. "Now you have to tell me yours."

"Easy. Michelle Pfeiffer in the movie Stardust, 2007ish."

"That's awfully specific."

"I take my crushes seriously," he said, deadpan. "Moving on."

My smile was making my cheeks ache as he guided me through more questions, but eventually the tone changed, and we entered territory that I wasn't sure we had touched on before. We talked about our childhoods, our wins and losses, our college years, and our careers. It was more than I'd shared with anyone other than my women friends. As the conversation flowed I felt myself relaxing and trusting it to him. However, my heart felt like it stopped beating and my breath caught in my chest when he said:

"I think what I've realized is that I have to be more than only attracted to anyone I bring into my life or my kids' lives going forward. I have to be with someone who is a friend, too. Heather and I, we were young. It was hot and heavy, and it went quickly. I wasn't thinking about the long term; I was thinking about the now and, honestly, my hormones were involved, big time." He paused, and I wasn't sure what to say, so I did the thing I was best at and stayed quiet, listening. "That makes it sound like we weren't friends. We were, but not . . ." He made a sound, and I could picture him trying to figure out what to say. "It's important to me to get to know someone better before jumping into anything."

"I totally understand, and I think you're smart. You have different parameters as a forty-year-old parent than you did in your twenties. You can't risk Hillary and Henry being hurt," I replied softly.

"I can't risk me being hurt again, either."

Oh, wow. I ached for him, for the loneliness I could only imagine. I'd never been married or a parent, so I could only empathize with how hard it would be to be let down by, and eventually separated from, the one you were supposed to be going through it all with. The daily tug-of-war between business and fatherhood had to be exhausting. I wished I could see his face and promise him that the only thing I'd really ever need in life was just to be loved by someone. To have a place to belong. But it was too soon for those words, so I said what I could at the time.

"Friendship is important to me, too."

"I'd like to be your friend," he said, and while the words were vulnerable, the tone he used was strong and decided. "I'd like that a lot."

"Me, too," I smiled into the darkness. "A lot."

CHAPTER TWENTY-ONE

The fair was crowded, as it always was, and I had to battle my way through the hordes of people to get near the big pumpkin Ford had set as our meeting place. I was wrapped in a tan wool coat that fell to mid-calf completed with a scarf over a soft, gray sweater. My jeans were cold against my legs, and I tugged my coat tighter around me. I loved the fair, but the weather this time of year wasn't my favorite. Still, the scent of pumpkin and spice rising from the steaming cups all around me was enough to keep me from being too grumpy. That and the fact that I was sort of on a date with the guy I'd been playing pretend about for a long time.

While I'd sternly cleansed my mind of the daydreams, I hadn't had any luck convincing my heart to entirely let go of hope—especially after the conversation a few days ago where we'd talked for two hours about everything under the sun and ended by admitting we'd like to get to know each other better. It was a huge leap I'd taken from internet stalker to attending a fair together, and I felt a little jittery as I neared our meeting place.

Ford was standing with his back to me, watching his children climb on the playground nearby. I recognized him anyway: tall, dark blond, casual stance, dressed like he'd stepped out of a fashion magazine in dark jeans and a blazer. I paused a few steps away as a couple approached him and Ford turned slightly to shake their hands, a broad smile on his face. The three of them chatted easily, Ford laughing and charismatic as he conversed. Then three more people joined, and somehow Ford became the center of it, the sun they were all orbiting around.

Admittedly, I got it. I'd long known he had that certain quality that drew people in. And I'd also known that he liked being there in the middle, enjoying the spotlight and being around other people. But even though I accepted that about him, it caused a little pang in the center of my chest, hard enough that I reached up to rub the spot.

How did I think we'd blend our two very different personalities? One of the things that had drawn him to Heather was her exuberance. Would he find fault with my tendency toward quiet?

The motion of me lifting my hand caught Ford's eye, and he glanced my way, his expression lighting up as our eyes met. I did my best to offer him a happy face, although it felt flimsy and unsure. Should I join that group or wait for him to wrap it up? What role did he want me to play in this scenario? I wasn't a barge-into-conversation type. Was this relationship developing between us supposed to be public knowledge? He had, after all, asked me to the fair, which was an incredibly public event.

He was still talking to the others, but his eyes were so focused on me, taking me in as though I were the most interesting thing there, that the others with him started to notice his distraction and turned my way too. They scanned the crowd to see what had caught his attention, but they never settled on me. I shook my head and waved at him, hoping he understood that I was content to wait until he was finished with his conversation, but his eyes rolled humorously, and he patted the first man on the shoulder, excusing himself with a smile.

"What are you doing over here pretending you don't want to talk to all those strangers?" he said with a chuckle before lightly grasping my elbow and brushing his lips against my cheek in that dimple spot he seemed so fond of. "You're supposed to be my bodyguard."

His easy manner and warm acceptance of my personality helped me relax. The look on his face didn't hurt either. There was a new familiarity between us after the dinner date and the late-night conversation, and it was palpable in the way we gazed at each other as though we'd discovered something new and filled with possibilities.

I flashed him those dimples I knew he liked so much. "You might have been negotiating a business deal to take over running the playground or to protest pumpkin spice drinks, and I didn't want to get in the way."

My eyes caught the interested looks of those he'd been talking to, and they all found themselves suddenly busy. Odd. I'd never been the person people were watching, but it was probably big news that Ford was here with someone. Maybe. Or maybe they were nosy, plain and simple.

"Come on, the kids are probably getting bored of the slide. Let's get some pie." His hand was still on my elbow, and it slid down to squeeze my fingers lightly before he let go and stepped to the side to allow me to walk with him. "You look really nice."

I glanced down at my outfit and brushed my hand down my shirt, tugging at the hem. "Thanks. You, too."

"This old thing?" he said in a playful old woman Southern accent that made me laugh. "I'm assuming that growing up here you've been to the fair before?"

"Every year," I nodded, falling into step beside him.

"This is our first year."

My jaw dropped, and I opened my mouth wide. "Why?"

"I'm not much for fairs, actually. But the kids were begging, and I thought maybe it would be a good way to get this woman I know to spend some time with me." His eyes danced down at me, and I had the strangest urge to grin like a lunatic. "I was prepared to bribe her if I had to."

"Who is she? Can I meet her?" I asked. "She sounds like a gem."

We came to a stop at the border of the playground, and he opened his mouth to reply, but a woman planted herself in front of Ford and greeted him with a sunny look. It was quickly apparent that she was a neighbor and was really into gardening, so my attention drifted to where Hillary and Henry were playing tag with a group of kids. They were laughing, cheeks pink and eyes bright as they ran, calling out to each other. It made me smile.

I turned back to Ford to point out how hilarious Hillary was being only to find that, somehow, I'd become slightly separated from him, and now there were like five people chatting around him. Once again, he'd become the center of the group of smiling people. Did he even try, or did it just happen?

I watched in amusement. I was a people watcher, not a people entertainer. Ford seemed to notice the distance at the same time I did, and he shocked me by reaching out a hand to me. We weren't so far apart that I'd have to reach far to take it, but I paused wondering what he hoped to accomplish by bringing me into the group. I'd have nothing to say to these strangers. Ford thought I was chatty and could be witty, but what he didn't know was that I was only those things with him. Okay, and my four best friends and parents. But no one else. Even Shane had told him at the ice rink that I never had anything to say. I wasn't actually capable of that easy behavior without certain perfect parameters. I was the flower that had to have the ideal soil in order to bloom.

He wiggled his fingers, still talking and entertaining the others, but the message was clear. He wanted me near. So, I stepped closer and took his hand. He wrapped his fingers around mine and tugged me against his side, seamlessly introducing me.

"This is Hailey Thomas. She teaches at Washington Elementary," he said to the group.

"Nice to meet you all." I inwardly cursed my cheeks for pinking up.

There were a few welcoming words before they returned to the conversation they'd already been having. Ford kept my hand tightly in his, and I focused on how it felt, the difference in size, how his hand was so warm and strong. I was mushy inside over the message it was sending to the group. These thoughts were dangerous because they were making me feel tingly, and I wanted to lean into his side, press my cheek against his shoulder, and huddle up against him, which was probably something I had no business doing.

"Well, we'd better find my kids and get moving." Ford's voice broke into my thoughts, and I realized I had been leaning a little after all.

I straightened as he said his goodbyes and the group broke apart. Feeling suddenly self-conscious I released his hand and walked slightly ahead of him toward where I'd last seen the kids. Ford waved them over, and Hillary arrived with a big hug for me. Henry was a few steps behind, smiling too, but minus the hug.

"We have to get pie, Daddy," Hillary cheered. "You promised that when Miss Hailey got here we could get some."

He looked at me. "We take our promises seriously in this family."

I nodded. "Pie."

"I saw the pie stand over there." Henry pointed to his right.

Hillary bounded ahead, skipping and calling to Henry to keep up. I quickened my pace, expecting Ford wouldn't want to lose his kids in the crowd, but he was relaxed, following them with his eyes and an indulgent smile. Ford greeted more people as we walked, seeming to know at least half of the population. His hand occasionally found my back or my elbow, keeping me from being jostled or slowing me down while he greeted someone. I didn't know how to feel about the fact that he was so blatantly signaling that we were there together, but mostly I was on cloud nine.

When we arrived at the pie stand, Hillary and Henry were already in line arguing over which flavor of pie was the best. I got in line with them, telling them that the pies were sold by the slice and they could both have whatever they wanted. This seemed to be the right thing to say, because the argument died down as they began reading the menu board. I studied it myself, but it was only out of habit. I already knew I'd be getting a big fat slice of pumpkin pie with a dollop of whipped cream bigger than my face. It was tradition, after all. I turned to ask Ford what he wanted, but he was once again chatting it up with a group of people.

"How on earth does your dad know so many people?" I said to Hillary.

She shrugged. "All adults do. They don't care if you're friends or not; they just talk to each other."

I was suddenly reminded of myself around age ten, going to the home repair store with my dad and asking him how he knew everyone there. He said he didn't, that he just liked to talk to people. It had been confusing to someone like me who could talk when required but didn't necessarily want to converse with strangers.

"You're probably right," I replied.

"What kind of pie are you getting?" Henry asked me.

The three of us fell into a good-natured debate and ended up agreeing that we'd never agree. I was smiling at their antics and arguments when I felt Ford slide in next to me.

"I'm so sorry," he said leaning down, the warmth of his breath raising goosebumps on my neck.

"You're a popular guy," I replied with a shiver.

"It's my cologne. It has pheromones."

I blinked and then a laugh burst out. I covered my mouth with my hand to reign the sound back in before everyone looked at us. "That explains it."

"No one can resist bobcat scent." He straightened with a smile.

I nodded, biting my lips, my dimples pushing into my cheeks. "Irresistible for most."

"For most?"

I pointed to myself. "Not for me, of course. I'm impervious to wildcats." I scooted forward in line with the kids, and Ford followed. "In fact, I'm buying the pie today in order to prove how honorable my intentions are." He started to shake his head, and I shook mine back at him. "No arguing. Besides, I purposely ordered the most expensive thing I could at dinner last week, so it's fair."

His face split into a bright grin. "You purposely did that?"

"Yes."

"Joke's on you, then. I didn't pay for that meal."

"What?" I whispered, guilt flooding me. "Who did?"

"Randy. He invited me, remember?"'

The line moved forward again, and this time, Ford stayed close, so close I could feel his shoulder brushing mine. "I'm a terrible person," I whispered.

"Nah. Just really bad at knowing who is actually paying for things."

Before I realized what was happening, he handed the pie stand cashier a few bills while the kids ordered. He was slightly bending forward to reach the cashier, and it put our eyes level as I glanced at him. I could see the way he was enjoying this, and my heart completely halted in my chest, realizing I was enjoying it, too. So much. I swallowed hard, and he watched my throat work before he stood up straight and reached for our pie slices. Hillary and Henry already had theirs and were finding a place to sit. Ford balanced his and mine in his hands, and I fell into step behind him, following the kids, their giggles leading the way, until we found a free bench and sat down in a row.

"Why did you purposely order the most expensive thing the other night?" Ford asked as we all bit into our food.

I closed my eyes, letting the pie rest happily in my mouth for a moment before chewing slowly. I opened my eyes to find him watching me with a happy expression, and it did strange things to my stomach but not enough to keep me from fully enjoying the pie and cream before swallowing and clearing my throat.

"I can't remember. I think you said something irritating."

He gave a brief nod. "It's possible. Your revenge tactics could use some work."

I pretended to think about it and shrugged. "I'm an only child. My revenge skills are seriously underdeveloped."

The four of us chatted comfortably about everything and nothing much while we ate. The kids told me what booths they wanted to see, and Ford vetoed a few of them with teasing eye rolls that had the kids laughing. Through it all I felt surprisingly content. Comfortable. Like I was sharing a piece of pie with one of my friends, only there was a simmer below the surface of pure attraction. It was a new feeling, and it made me realize how much I really had been missing out on in past relationships.

"Miss Hailey, can you fix my hair? It got stuck on the swing, and now it's all out," Hillary asked as Ford and Henry carried our trash to the can.

I turned on the bench and began braiding new pigtails while she chatted happily. It felt so natural, sitting there in the autumn sunlight, braiding her blonde hair, that I wanted to pinch myself.

Some commotion caught my attention as I finished the second braid, and I looked up to see Aryn and Ruby headed my way with delighted looks on their faces. Ford was behind them, carrying napkins to help his kids clean up by wiping their faces. I made the mistake of glancing over their shoulders at him just as my two friends arrived. Their eyes shot toward him, then at each other, then at me as their smiles changed from happy to see me to slightly devious.

"Hey,"' they said to me in eerie unison.

"Hey," I said back, wary.

"How's the fair going?" Aryn asked.

"Anything tasty on the menu?" Ruby winked.

I shook my head and blushed, which was basically asking to be teased by these two. "What brings you here?" I asked them.

"We always come to the fair." Aryn shrugged innocently.

"We love seeing what kinds of things are up for grabs." Ruby winked her other eye, and I had to laugh.

"Stop that," I said. "You're scary."

She pouted her lips out. "I was going for provocative with a hint of innuendo."

"Yeah, that's obvious," Aryn teased. Then she looked to me and dropped her voice, watching Ford who had called his kids over to the garbage area to clean them up. "How's it going with Mr. Yummy?"

I shook my head. "Please do not call him that."

"Mr. Delicious?" she offered.

"Mr. Scrumptious," Ruby stated.

"Mr. Mouthwatering," Aryn raised her eyebrows.

"Mr. Get in my belly," Ruby tapped her stomach.

"Line crossed," I rolled my eyes with a giggle and covered my face with my hands.

Aryn patted my shoulder and wiped her face clean of her teasing expression. "He's coming," she hissed.

I dropped my hands from my face and went slightly rigid with discomfort. The last time some of my friends had interacted with him it had been at the ax throwing facility, and he'd been cool with it, but today they were clearly in top form and I wasn't sure what to expect. I was partially grateful that it wasn't Meredith but also worried about what would come out of Ruby's mouth.

"Ford, you remember Aryn Murphy." I pointed. "And Ruby Jenkins. You met them at ax throwing. They both work with me."

"And we're her very best friends," Ruby added.

"Nice to see you both again," he said, reaching out to shake their hands, flashing that handsome smile he wore so perfectly. "Hailey has told me a lot about you."

If I wasn't mistaken, both of them got slightly glazed-over eyes before they snapped out of it. Yeah, he was definitely yummy.

"We had pie," I said, awkwardly.

"Pie is good," Aryn mumbled, blinking.

"Pie seems pretty serious," Ruby's eyes slitted. "What are your intentions with our friend? Are you going to feed her and leave her?"

I was absolutely frozen in place by an acidic mix of shock and horror boiling in my stomach. I couldn't have spoken if I wanted to.

Ford, however, was cool and confident, as always. I was amazed as I watched him laugh, taking Ruby in and seeming to enjoy the challenge she offered.

"I can promise you I'm not eating pie with anyone else," he said.

Ruby nodded. "That's good. I guess I just have two questions for you, then."

"People seem to be really into questions lately," Ford said, giving me a look that had me smiling back at him.

Ruby's face, however, was intense when we looked back to her. Ford nodded and tucked his hands into his pockets, one leg bent, smiling down at her, giving her the green light. I, however, was going home with a massive crick in my neck from worrying over what was about to pop out of her brain.

"What's the weirdest way you've gotten hurt?" she asked.

I blinked at Aryn, and her expression told me I wasn't the only one wondering what that question had to do with anything.

"In the shower I sneezed really hard and slammed my head against the glass shower door. It shattered, and I had to get stitches on my face." He pointed to a spot on his left cheek.

"What was your childhood nickname?"

Again, Aryn and I looked at each other with matching confused expressions. This time Aryn smirked, and my mouth tugged upwards. Only Ruby would think these were pertinent questions.

"Pickle Pop because I liked to freeze pickles and eat them."

"Ewww," the three of us said in unison.

He shrugged with a chuckle. "I'm not apologizing. They were good."

Ruby nodded once, sharply. "Those were my only questions. I needed to know if he's good enough for Hailey."

"I'm not," Ford stated. In fact, he stated it so simply and genuinely that it felt like the actual air stopped moving around us. "I can be bossy, and demanding, and laser focused." He looked at all three of us one-by-one. "I'm lucky she's willing to eat a piece of pie at the fair in my company."

"Oh my gosh," Aryn whispered, giving me eyes loaded with stars.

"Good to know," Ruby stated, maintaining her serious interviewer persona.

"She's the best of us. She's nice, and calm, and classy." Ford nodded as I prepared to melt into the pavement. "But you should know, she hates bodily fluids and camping. So maybe stay away from those things."

"Although," Aryn added, "she's a boss at rowing river rafts."

Ford glanced at me, amused and questioning, but I still felt frozen by all that was happening. So I raised one side of my mouth in an embarrassed smile and shrugged.

"I'll remember that," he said, keeping his eyes on my face, taking me in and analyzing everything he saw.

"See that you do," Ruby replied.

With that, Ruby and Aryn said friendly goodbyes as though they hadn't kicked up waves and walked away. But Ford, his eyes never left my face, and warmth crept into my chest.

"You don't give yourself enough credit," I managed to say. "You shouldn't put me on a pedestal like that."

He bent low and pressed the lightest of kisses to my lips, right there in broad daylight. "You'll lose this argument every time," he said.

And I couldn't imagine wanting anyone more than I wanted him.

CHAPTER TWENTY-TWO

The tears were never going to end and I was never going to be okay and my life would always be horrible from here on out.

At least that's what I told myself Wednesday night as I laid in fetal position on my couch, covered in a throw blanket with a damp tissue balled in my fist. I still couldn't make sense of the fact that my principal had called me in that afternoon and told me I'd need to find a new school for next year. Washington Elementary didn't have enough enrollment for two second grade teachers, and since I was the most recent hire, I'd be the one to go. She did throw me a little bone, saying that if enrollment went up, they'd be happy to rehire me the following year.

It hadn't helped.

My stomach ached, my chest felt hollow, and my eyes were raw.

It had taken every ounce of willpower and self-discipline I had to get out of the building with a cheerful face. Only once I'd pulled out of the parking lot did the tears begin. And they hadn't stopped even once in the past hour. Every time I'd felt I was coming up for air, I'd think about leaving my friends, my chest would heave, and the tears would flow again. After thirty minutes of sobbing, I'd texted my mom, asking her to call me when she was done with patients for the day. I hadn't told my friends yet, and picturing their faces caused another round of moaning sobs to begin.

My phone rang on the coffee-table, and I reached for it jerkily, sniffling loudly, wanting more than anything to hear my mom's voice. Even at thirty years old, I still wanted her comfort and advice.

"The worst thing happened today," I wept.

"What happened?" The voice that responded did not belong to my mother.

I gasped and hiccupped and held the phone away from my face to see the display screen, knowing already it was Ford. We'd slipped into the habit of talking every night, but it was much earlier than I usually heard from him. Most nights we talked after his kids were in bed. I held the phone to my chest and took a deep breath. We were not in a place yet where I was coming to him with my problems. In fact, as a general rule, I pretty much kept problems to myself.

"Hailey?" I heard him call.

I hurried to sniffle and wipe my nose, sitting up and taking another deep breath. The tears were still falling, but maybe I could hold it together enough to have a brief conversation.

I put it back up to my ear. "Yeah, hi. I . . . thought you were my mom," I stammered. My voice wobbled, and I grimaced.

"What happened?"

I fought back against another wave of emotion. "I had kind of a rough afternoon. No biggie." I took another deep breath and cursed the way it was uneven and raspy. "What's up with you?"

His voice was amused. "Nice try. I was calling to invite you up for dinner if you're free, but I'm much more interested in hearing what has you so upset."

"Yeah, I'm not sure I'll be able to make it tonight. I have . . . other things going on. Rain check?" I tried to sound upbeat, but it honestly came out so much like a child trying to be brave that I closed my eyes, causing some tears to fall.

"Do these other plans involve tissues and being wrapped in a blanket?"

"I might get some ice cream, too."

"Sweetheart, what happened?" his tone was coaxing, asking me to give up my walls.

"It was only a thing at school. I'm really okay."

He paused, and I could picture his face as he changed tactics. "I don't know everything about you, yet, but I do know you're not the type to cry without reason."

"Maybe I bawl my eyes out every night," I said, surprised to notice it was getting easier to hold back the tears. In fact, I felt a smile tugging and reached up to feel it with my fingertips.

"I doubt that. But, if you don't want to talk about it with me, I guess I can respect that."

"Thanks."

"I'm not letting you go, though, until I'm convinced you're okay. Safe topics of conversation could include the weather, recent changes in traffic congestion, or how to pick a ripe watermelon."

"I was kind of cold today. And I miss the fall leaves. Now it's all brown," I sniffed again and leaned back into the couch.

"It took me ten minutes longer than usual to get home today thanks to congestion on Main Street. I'm thinking about taking alternate routes home."

"That's a smart plan."

"Tell me about your last boyfriend."

Well, that was out of the blue.

"Why?" I asked, totally baffled.

"I'm curious."

"That wasn't on the list of approved talking points," I hedged.

"Tell me anyway."

A sudden irrational bravery took over, and I tugged the blanket tighter around me. "Okay. His name was Garron."

"Garron sounds like a punk."

I laughed. And then, I was so surprised by the fact I could laugh right now that I did it again. "He was not a punk. He was nice. Academic. We went to a lot of nice, cultural, brainy type things together."

"How long did you date?"

"A couple of months."

"Why did you break up?"

"I . . ." I paused, thinking. "I guess because it wasn't really . . . I felt like it wasn't a big deal if we didn't see each other. I think I was lonelier in the relationship than I was without him."

My cheeks heated over the vulnerable admission, and I was so grateful to have the barrier of the phone between us.

"I know how that can be, to feel lonely in a relationship."

Oh. Okay. Talk about your stunning admissions. "I'm so sorry," I replied, in a soft voice.

"Emotionally, she left me before she died. I sometimes wonder what would have happened if she'd lived. Where we'd be now." I didn't know how to respond, so I made a sympathetic noise and hoped he'd keep talking. "I didn't even think about finding someone else. I didn't want to risk it again, you know?"

"Yeah. You told me that the first time we met."

He huffed out a breath. "I was a jerk."

I chuckled. "A little bit. But, knowing you better now, I can understand why you said it."

"The thing is, I'd never said that to anyone else. After I blurted it out to you, I was horrified about it."

"Really?"

"Yeah. Definitely. Then I find out you know Leonard, and I'm at dinner with your parents, and all I kept thinking was how rude I was to you the first time we met."

I smiled. "You really did jump to conclusions there. But Hillary wasn't helping, the way she kept throwing us together."

"Hillary really, really likes you."

"I like her, too."

"So, that blind date you went on . . ."

I laid my head back against the couch. "That mistake of an evening?"

"Does that mean you're looking to date again?"

"Yeah," I nearly whispered the word, my throat feeling thick, wondering what this meant.

"Most of the time I think I am, too, but then sometimes I'm not sure. There's been a lot going on in my head these past months."

The admission made my breath hitch. Oh. And yet, I could respect that, and was grateful for the honesty. I knew I needed to say something, but so many thoughts were running through my head. The way he'd kissed me, asked me to the fair, called me tonight to see about dinner. What was he doing if this wasn't dating? Was he as mixed up as I'd been? It sure sounded that way.

"Are you there?" he asked.

"Yes, sorry."

"Are you ready to tell me what happened today?"

I guess we were glossing over what he'd just told me, and oddly, I found that I was okay with that too. I didn't need to go through another difficult conversation today, and there was no way I'd be pushing him or admitting to him that I'd developed feelings for him. Just like I didn't want to be bullied, he deserved to move at a pace he was comfortable with. So . . . moving in a new conversational direction seemed best.

"I found out that I need to find a new job for the next school year," I said on a deep breath.

"But you love where you teach. All your friends are there," he sounded as shocked as I'd felt.

Tears welled again, and I pressed my hands to my eyes. "I know." I did my best to tell him what my principal had told me while holding back the waterworks, but my voice was getting watery again.

"Do you need company tonight? I can come over."

The offer was kind, but I knew if he came over to comfort me, I'd end up giving him my entire heart. Better to practice patience. I could give him the gift of time even though I would have given anything to have his arms around me and his strength giving me much-needed courage right now.

"No, thank you. My mom will be coming over."

"Right," he replied. I held my breath and waited to see what he'd say next. "I'm really sorry that happened."

"Thanks."

We said goodbye, and as soon as the phone was back in my lap, I crumpled into a sobbing heap again.

*****

Knocking on my door pulled me out of my TV stupor, and I glanced down at the phone sitting on the couch next to me. It said 9:30 p.m., and I blinked, surprised I'd been sitting in the same place for hours. Had I had dinner?

My eyes ached from crying, and I rubbed at my face as another round of three knocks sounded, reminding me of what had tugged me back into awareness in the first place.

I stood, stumbling a bit as I was currently wrapped in a blanket burrito and it was caught around my legs. I tugged at it and freed myself, dropping the blanket in a heap on my couch as the doorbell rang. My goodness, this visitor was impatient.

I'd had a good vent and mini therapy session with my mom and was feeling better emotionally but also so very drained, and I just wanted this person to stop making noise so that I could slink off to bed.

My stomach rumbled as I undid the deadbolt and pulled the door open.

The smell hit me first. Onion rings and a burger. The brown paper bag had greasy spots on its side, and saliva filled my mouth. I looked at the face above the bag and would have teared up again if I'd had anything left in me.

"There's no way I wasn't coming to see for myself that you're okay," Ford said.

His tone told me he expected an argument, but I simply swung the door wide and let him in. He brushed past me, and I followed that food bag with my eyes before closing the door behind him.

He walked straight into my kitchen, set the bag on the small table, and then marched right back to where I was standing, feeling like my tether to the earth had been cut. Without even a pause he slid his arms under mine, wrapped them around my waist, and hauled me up against him, pressing my body close to his and dipping his head to kiss my cheek.

"Hi," he said against my skin.

An entire battleship of butterfly fighter pilots was loosed in my chest as I lifted my arms to circle around his neck. "Hi."

We didn't speak for a few precious minutes, just enjoyed the closeness and the silent communication. He'd come for me, and I was allowing him in. That was enough for now.

His hands coasted up and down my back, comforting but also stirring up some very interesting feelings that might not be what he'd bargained for. I pressed my nose into his neck, and then my lips moved to take its place. His skin was so smooth, and he smelled so nice. He was wearing a sweatshirt that was cozy against my cheek and under my hands.

I reached up to the back of his head and turned him into the position I wanted him in. Specifically, kissing position. He was more than willing to give in, and he met my vulnerable kisses with patience and comfort, holding me close and molding his body to mine until I wasn't sure even the slightest breeze could get between us.

His hand moved to my hair and tugged my head back until he had access to press a lingering kiss under my jaw. His breathing was rapid against the sensitive skin. Chills skittered up my back and down my arms.

And then, my stomach rumbled again. It broke the spell, and he laughed as he slowly released me.

"Sounds like you're going to need some actual dinner and not just me," he joked as he slid away and moved toward the table again. "Go sit down, and I'll serve you."

"This is the best room service I've ever received," I replied, smoothing my hair back into place.

"Sorry it took so long to get here. I swear kids have a radar of some sort that tells them if their parent has somewhere else to be. They were on one tonight, stalling about bedtime like real pros. I finally just turned them over to Ellie. I was hoping you'd still be awake."

"I was awake-ish."

His smile was sympathetic. "Emotional stupor?" he guessed as he crossed to where I was sitting. I laughed. "I was also assuming you hadn't eaten. You're clearly starved by this point, considering the sounds your stomach just made."

"You've saved a life tonight."

He handed me a bacon cheeseburger and a stack of onion rings complete with dipping sauce. I dug in, well, at least as much as someone with a real thing about manners can dig in. While I happily chewed, nearly moaning with pleasure, he kept up a light stream of conversation about nothing at all. As food filled my stomach and his presence filled everything else, I began to feel drowsy in that warm, completely satisfied way that's so rare.

190

I wiped my face and hands on a napkin and then scooted next to him on the couch and put my head on his shoulder without any hesitation or doubt at all. His arm came around me, and he stroked along the outside of my arm.

"I hope you know how much this means to me," I said softly, a yawn working its way out. "I would never in a million years have taken you up on your offer to stop by, but I'm glad you did."

He kissed the top of my head. "Wild horses couldn't have kept me away . . . but wild children nearly did," he chuckled.

I closed my eyes, and my breathing became peaceful and even, and before I knew it, I'd drifted to sleep in the one place I truly wanted to be.

CHAPTER TWENTY-THREE

I'll sue the school, then the district, then the state!" Meredith cried, standing up from her seat on my couch the next night . . . the very couch where I'd fallen asleep on Ford before he'd tucked me in and let himself out. "They can't get away with this. You're too valuable to the school."

"She probably already has some protest posters drawn up," Aryn said to me out the side of her mouth.

Meredith did a lap around my living room, waving her arms in the air. "I'm not kidding. The other second grade teacher is like two hundred years old. She should retire."

"She's forty-five," Lizzie stated with an amused expression. "Hardly decrepit, unless you're planning to fall apart yourself in ten years."

"She's got lower test scores than Hailey does." Meredith put her hands on her hips.

"Is that true?" Aryn asked me.

I shook my head. "No."

"We like Hailey better," Ruby injected.

Meredith pointed at Ruby, an annoyed jab that I knew came from love and disappointment. "That. That's the real issue."

I smiled, warmed by the reaction of my friends to the news that I had to leave. "I'm so sad that I won't see you every day. Washington has become my second home."

"Hey, I'm moving in January, and I'll be five hours away. Where was all the protesting about that?" Lizzie teased.

"You're moving because you're getting married to the guy you've been in love with since you were fifteen. Hardly the same thing," Meredith replied. "We're celebrating with you. We're mourning with Hailey."

"So I get a going away party?" Lizzie's eyes gleamed.

"Yes. Of course." Meredith stopped pacing and pointedly nodded my way. "Can we focus on Hailey now?"

Lizzie regally nodded and gestured in my direction, which had the rest of us cracking up.

"How are you feeling about all of this?" Aryn asked.

After my cryfest the day before, I'd been fairly unemotional and factual when I told my friends to come to my place tonight and then told them the whole spiel. The tears were near the surface, especially looking at their faces and seeing their upset as I finished my story, but I'd kept them in, not wanting to embarrass myself by totally falling apart in front of them. I'd cried enough the day before to last me several months.

"I'm disappointed. A little scared, if I'm honest. I know there are other elementary schools in the city, but I found all of you at Washington, and I'm really upset about moving." I looked at them, and they all wore expressions that mirrored my own melancholy one. "How will I get by without Recap and Recoup?"

Suddenly they all moved toward me as one, and we were in a group hug, all leaning into a heap on my couch. There were a few sniffles, and Lizzie patted at her eyes.

"It's unfair," she whimpered.

"This means next year it will only be me, Meredith, and Aryn," Ruby stated.

Everyone pulled back and looked around at each other. It was a sobering thought, that after four glorious years the group was breaking up. How could this be?

"I think the real victim here is me," Aryn cracked. "Alone with Grumpy and Dopey."

She pointed at Meredith and Ruby, and we all burst out laughing as the two of them picked up throw pillows to slap Aryn with. Lizzie dried her eyes, and I swallowed against my own tight throat in spite of everything. It felt like a big shift was upon us.

"Let's make a pact," Ruby said, putting her pillow weapon back in its place. "We will commit to monthly dinners."

We all nodded as Lizzie moped. "I can't commit to that. I'll be living in Moab. Maybe you could video call me, too?"

A chorus of yeses answered her request.

"Once a month isn't enough considering we're used to being together every day," Meredith said, taking a seat for the first time in a while. "What if we do twice-a-month dinners?"

"Plus any extras we want to do. Movies, working out, phone calls . . ." Aryn added.

I nodded. "Yes. That would mean the world to me. Well," I looked around, "to all of us."

Lizzie folded her arms. "I'm trying to decide if I should be bummed that you're planning all of this knowing I'll be gone."

"You're running off with your prince charming, I doubt you'll miss us for long," Meredith replied, tongue-in-cheek.

Lizzie smiled and laughed. "You're right. He'll keep me happy."

"We'll miss you, Liz," I leaned over and patted her arm. "We're so happy for you."

"Less than two months to the wedding," she grinned. "I'll be Lizzie Walker. Elizabeth Duncan Walker."

"It's been a long time coming," Aryn said warmly.

"You've all been so nice to listen to me talk wedding plans during half of our Recap and Recoup sessions," Lizzie laughed.

"We've loved it," I assured her, meaning that genuinely. We were all so very happy for her.

"You might be moving," Meredith said, "but the sacrifice will be totally worth it."

Lizzie nodded. "Doesn't mean I won't miss you all so much."

"Hey now," Ruby called. "We're thornback women, bonded whether near or far. And don't you forget it."

*****

Sunday evening I made my way up to Leonard and Connie's house for dinner. I still didn't feel very much like a ferocious thornback woman, but I'd done enough licking my wounds. I wanted to see my parents and, yeah, food is always a draw. It was Cox's turn to host, and I'd brought a plate of homemade cookies to deliver to Ford and his kids after dinner. Two could play the drop-by game.

I was feeling more upbeat about my work situation, thanks to the promises of my friends and the awareness that our job wasn't the only reason we were a group. I'd also come to accept that life was full of changes, and maybe this new path would open some doors that I needed to walk through.

I hadn't seen Ford for a couple of days, though. He had called me after my friends went home the other night, and we'd had a nice conversation, but I could feel something almost hesitant, and I wondered if I'd scared him somehow. He'd also texted a few times after that, checking in, nothing major, and I realized how much I'd grown to love talking to him daily—how much I'd fallen in actual love with him. That was another reason I was hoping to pop by. I needed to see his face and read his body language. I ached with wanting him but loved him enough to give him space if that's what I discovered he needed.

I found my parents and the Cox's in their massive kitchen, already seated at the table, laughing and sipping on drinks. They all greeted me with a cheer, and Mom and Connie both gave me hugs, knowing I felt fragile at the moment. I took a seat near my mom as the doorbell rang. It was at that exact moment that I also noticed three more places set. It was unusual to have extra guests at Sunday dinner but not totally unheard of when we came to Cox's. Leonard was nothing if not social.

"Miss Hailey," a little voice squealed as a familiar blonde head lunged in my direction from the front hall.

I didn't have time to stand before Hillary had launched herself at me, wrapping her arms around my neck from the side and placing her little cheek on my shoulder. I tilted my head to lay against hers, soaking up her energy and warmth. Unexpected emotion flooded me at the feel of her little arms around me. I'd grown to really care for her and Henry, too. Henry was the quieter, more serious Whittaker, and I felt a tug in my chest as he came near and put a hand on my shoulder.

"Hi," he said with a small smile before taking his seat at the table.

"Hi buddy," I replied. "And hey Hillary," I said to her, reaching a hand around to squeeze her shoulder. "I didn't expect to see you here."

Hillary stood straight and started into an explanation, but even though I kept my eyes firmly on her expressive face, I was hyper aware of her dad entering the room and greeting the others. His voice was deep and sent tingles jangling up the backs of my legs. I wanted to follow his progress, drink him in, see if he was his same old self, but I was also a little frightened of what I'd see—or show.

Ford had always had a way of looking at me that made me feel like he could see into my true feelings, and I didn't want him to deep dive into my heart and find things that he wasn't ready for. So I kept my eyes trained anywhere but at him as everyone took their seats.

He sat across from me, between his two children, and I couldn't soak him in without being obvious. My parents and the Cox's had no idea that we'd ended up in some sort of half relationship. My parents knew we were friendly but not the whole truth.

Ford nodded when I finally looked his way and offered a smile. He looked . . . tired and maybe a little worried, his face lacking its usual carefree exuberance. I returned the greeting, feeling the strain in my own face, before becoming seriously interested in what Leonard was saying from the head of the table.

It was more obvious than ever that I needed to get him to myself at some point. I didn't want to assume that I was the cause of stress because that felt a little arrogant and dramatic. Maybe something had happened with his business or one of the kids was struggling. Regardless, I wouldn't sleep until I found out for sure what was happening.

And if I was the cause of his worry? Well . . . I'd deal as best I could.

As I watched Leonard talking, my thoughts ran free. Did Ford know I'd fallen for him? Did he know how happy I was that he was there because just having him in the same room made my heart feel a little stronger? I wished he was sitting next to me where I could feel his warmth and smell his scent and maybe sneak in a side conversation. I sighed, and Ford's head popped up, which drew my eyes to him. His were questioning, and I merely shook my head and bit my lips, not knowing how to answer him here.

"Leonard said we can swim after dinner," Henry told me from across the table as the food was being passed. "We could play jump or dive."

"That's a fun game." I smiled at him, both happy and sad that he'd finally warmed up enough to want me to join in.

"Did you bring your suit?" Hillary asked.

"I didn't. I'm sorry."

"Maybe Miss Connie has one you could borrow," Hillary suggested helpfully.

I glanced at Connie who looked at me with a questioning expression. I knew she had extra suits. She knew I knew she had extra suits. But she needed to know if I actually wanted a suit. I gave the most subtle head shake I possibly could, and Connie picked it right up, apologizing to Hillary for the fact that the suits were all in the laundry.

I didn't think I could play with them until I made sure their dad was okay.

When I looked back to Hillary, my gaze caught Ford's. He raised his eyebrows, having clearly noticed the exchange between Connie and I, but I only smiled pleasantly and went back to eating.

Halibut and asparagus were some of my favorite foods, but it was tasteless in my mouth. Each time Ford joined in the conversation, I pictured dancing with him at his business dinner, him pressing bold kisses to my dimples later, holding on to his shoulders as he kissed me merely yards from here in the Cox's pool house. I imagined him quietly slipping out of my house the other night and how at home I'd felt snuggled up against him. Had that been the moment I'd crossed a line?

Warmth crept into my face, and I took a shaky sip of my water.

Before too long conversation turned to me, and while Connie knew all about my change in situation, I filled Leonard in about having to find a new place to teach next year.

"Oh, honey, I just can't get over it. You love that place. Your friends are there. You've found your home," Connie said with genuine sympathy.

"You're leaving Washington?" Hillary asked, her eyes growing round.

"I'm afraid so," I replied. "I'll be there through the end of this school year though."

"Where will you go?" Leonard asked. "I know the superintendent. I could put in a good word."

I shook my head. "That's sweet, but I have some time to figure it out."

"I don't want you to figure it out," Hillary whined.

I looked kindly at her. "I couldn't stop this from happening even if I tried," I said to her. "Things change, and life has unexpected twists and turns. I wish it could have always stayed the same, but sometimes the new path can be even better."

"Are you scared?" Henry asked.

I nodded. "A little. I'm really comfortable where I am now."

Talk shifted to my parents, and my mom shared about some research she'd stumbled across that had her fascinated while Dad told us about a student's paper that had made him howl with laughter. Everyone joined in the amusement, except Ford. I could feel his eyes on me, and when I looked at him, a spark of some powerful emotion radiated off him, hitting me in the chest. He was sitting stick straight, his fork slightly raised with a chunk of salad dangling there. His eyes, usually so gray, seemed darker. I felt that look down to my bones, and without thinking I scooted back my chair.

"Excuse me, I'll be right back."

I stood and walked briskly out of the kitchen and straight out the front door. I stood on the porch with a hand to my chest and took a deep breath, my mouth forming a circle as I let it slowly flow out. That man muddled my head and made my emotions take a dive.

"Hailey."

And there he was, closing the door behind him and walking toward me where I was standing at the end of the front porch, leaning on the railing, my hand still resting on my chest.

"Hi." I managed when he continued to do nothing more than take me in.

He seemed to notice everything, from the way my hair was tickling my jaw to the way I'd started to shiver lightly in the chilly November air. He was holding his jacket, and I found it interesting that at some point he'd stopped to grab it. He leaned toward me to wrap it around my shoulders. It hung loosely, providing warmth and the scent of him in spades.

I was sunk. He was the only place I wanted to be.

He took another step closer until I had to look up to meet his eyes. I could see those tempting flashes of gray growth in his beard and remember how they felt under my fingertips. His eyes were bright, and I had this feeling that the walls were fully crumbling at last.

I put a hand lightly against his chest. "Ford . . ."

I didn't know what I wanted to say.

He startled slightly at my touch and reached up to lay one of his hands over mind. "I couldn't stop this from happening even if I tried," he said in little more than a whisper. It was the sound of a person discovering something profound. "I was really comfortable where I was, but things change, and life has unexpected twists and turns." I pulled in a breath as I realized he was repeating back to me the words I'd said to his children a minute ago. "I wish it could have always stayed the same, but sometimes the new path can be even better."

"I . . ."

He leaned down to press a kiss against my forehead. "Let me finish. I told you the other night that I'm not sure I'm ready to be in a relationship again." I nodded, feeling his lips feather light against my skin. He put his hands on my outer arms and stood there, gathering his thoughts. "I've been scared for a long time."

Of course he had. He may be a confident and gregarious man, but he also loved deeply, and I knew that. "I know you were hurt. I don't blame you for not wanting to possibly be hurt again."

"It's hard to trust or to take that leap of faith again. Especially with kids involved. I'm the only parent they have, their only stability."

His forehead remained resting against mine, and I lifted my hands to rest on his waist. I needed to touch him; I loved touching him.

"I'm not asking you for anything, only to know that you can trust me."

Some of the strange tension left his body, and his shoulders shifted down even as his head lifted to see me better.

"You may not be asking me for anything, but there are important things that you make me want to give you, and they're the biggest risk of all."

I understood exactly what he meant. The heart was a much harder thing to hand over.

"In the interest of full disclosure, I can think of a few reasons that you should be wary of me," I said.

His hands left my arms and landed on my hips, shifting underneath his jacket as it hung over my back. "Like what?"

"I'm pretty introverted, especially with strangers or in big groups. I might be too quiet for you," I said.

"I like that about you." His thumb coasted up to the bottom of my rib cage and back, raising goosebumps on my spine. "You're peaceful."

"I internet stalked you for months and made up stories about you in my head."

He pulled back, keeping hold of my waist, to look me full in the face. "You did?" A grin lifted his mouth. "Tell me more about that."

I shook my head and blushed. "Another time. For today all I'm going to say is that Fake Ford was pretty great, and you've managed to surpass him."

"Oh my gosh, you are a schemer after all," he laughed. "How flattering."

I opened my mouth to defend myself, but he leaned down and kissed me, deep and slow, until heat gathered under the coat I was wearing. He kissed me like he'd been thirsting after me, and I bunched his shirt in my hands, leaning up, wanting closer contact. After a few more kisses, he pulled away again, his eyes tracing my face.

"What else do I need to know about you, Miss Thomas?"

"I wore that sparkly wrap dress to your birthday party and talked to all your friends I knew just to prove to you that you'd been wrong about me."

His eyebrows rose. "Really?"

"I didn't want to sit by you at Hillary's dance recital. I was lying through my teeth."

At this he laughed, and I could feel the vibrations against my hands. He moved his hands from my waist and tucked them against my lower back, pulling me in tighter.

"I knew it. Whenever those dimples appear I think 'there's no way I'm not being played right now,'" he said warmly.

I turned my head and pressed my cheek against his collarbone. "It terrifies me to say all these things, you know. You're not the only one who's vulnerable here."

"Should I return the favor?" he asked. I nodded, urging him on without saying the words. "You scared me to death the first time I saw you. I already told you how badly I felt for accusing you of anything, but it was because I'd taken one look at you and something got knocked loose in my chest, something I didn't think could ever move again."

"Your heart?" I joked.

He lightly pinched my back, and my squeak turned into a giggle. "Yes, probably. Hillary was already head-over-heels for you, and it was an involuntary defense mechanism to push you away and make it count."

"It was kind of mean."

"It was a failure. After that, you were everywhere. And every time I saw you, I only wanted to see you more. I should know better than to fight with myself. I always lose."

I leaned up and pressed my lips against his throat, feeling his pulse there and the way his hands tightened on my back. "It was the same for me. Only I was busy beating myself up for ever having daydreamed about you. I was so humiliated by my behavior and how I was practically already half in love with you . . ." I hurried to cut off my words, but his sudden stillness told me he'd heard my confession.

He cleared his throat. "How do you feel about dating a man ten years older than you?"

I pursed my lips thoughtfully. "A man of experience, with roots, and an understanding of real-life responsibilities? I'm good with it."

"I'm already going gray, and you're still so young with so much available to you." His hands coasted up and down my back, making me want to arch against his fingertips. "I'm a father."

One side of my mouth tilted up. "So, you're saying that's a permanent thing? I wasn't sure if they were on loan or . . ."

He chuckled. "I want to make sure you really know what you're taking on. It's a lot. I'm busy with a business and my kids and community involvement."

I tucked in closer. "It sounds to me like we'll take it slow. Maybe your assistant could pencil me in for some sort of face-to-face every couple of weeks."

"My assistant is staying out of this."

I smiled. "I know you're busy. I'm not asking . . ."

"Hailey," he stopped me. "Start asking. You deserve things, and I'll do my best to give them to you."

Pesky tears filled my eyes, and I had to work my throat to not sound weepy when I replied, "I'm asking for you to take a chance on me. And I'll do the same with you."

"I'm afraid you're the one taking the biggest risk, here," he said against my hair. "Older man, single father, busy business owner, extrovert . . ."

"The only risk is not trying at all," I replied.

He tilted my head back and found whatever he'd been looking for in my eyes because his own grew warm and serious. "Just so there's no wondering here, I'm more than half in love with you, Hailey Thomas. I am one hundred percent all yours."

One of my dimples flashed, and his warm mouth came against mine, giving and taking until I was a breathless, mindless heap in his arms.

Everything I needed to know was in that kiss. Everything.

THE END

EPILOGUE

September . . . The following year

I put down my lesson plan and glanced at the clock. Five p.m., time to wrap up my day. Smoothing my hair behind my ears, I looked toward the classroom door when I saw movement. A blonde head, followed by another, followed by Ford filling the doorway. The butterflies I always felt at seeing him launched, rising up in celebration.

Hillary hurried toward me, waving an envelope. "You should come to my dad's birthday party next week," she said, giggling at the end.

I took the invite from her and read it over. "I don't know." I made a serious face. "Your dad doesn't really know me, and this seems like a special occasion."

Hillary laughed again and ran back to Henry, grabbing his hand and tugging him out into the hall as Ford came to stand next to my desk. He brought his familiar scent with him, and I breathed it in.

"I really hate to push myself onto the guest list," I said with a grin.

"No, no, by all means, come." He scratched at his chin. "It's just, I wonder if Hillary is plotting something." He reached for my hands and tugged me up to standing, pulling me flush against him.

I leaned forward and onto my toes, pressing a light kiss to his lips. "I have no idea why you feel the need to tell me that."

"You know, Hillary has been having daydreams about getting a new mom."

His hands skated down my back, causing the same familiar shivers they always did, and I snuggled in closer as I said, "To be clear, I really don't want anything from you."

He bent and kissed me again, this one a little deeper than the last. My hands slid up to his shoulders, and I deepened the kiss further, forgetting for a moment that we were in my classroom in a new school, a place where I was still trying to make a good impression.

"Do you think your new principal is okay with you doing this in your room?" he teased against my mouth, having somehow read my mind.

"I guess I'll just have to avoid you from now on."

I stepped out of his arms and turned off my computer, packing my things as a hum of awareness moved through me. It was always this way when Ford was nearby. The year we'd known each other hadn't dimmed it, and the more we worked on fitting our lives together, the more I realized that being with someone so opposite from me was the best thing that had ever happened to both of us.

We'd developed a comfortable push and pull, a balance of nights home at one of our houses and nights out attending events. Wherever we were, we were unified, and I'd grown better at expanding my social circle. Ford, for his part, had gotten better at being present in the moment. He was often in the kitchen or doing a puzzle with his children when I stopped by a few times a week. His gaze still took me in as it always did but gone were the shadows that he'd been running from.

I picked up the envelope with the invitation and waved it at him. "You're getting pretty old, you know. Forty-one. Everyone will think you've robbed the cradle, dating someone as young as me."

I started to move around him, but he snagged my arm and smiled down at me. "I think to be safe, you'd probably better marry me."

I assumed he was teasing, even though it thrilled me to hear those words, and I laughed as I leaned closer. "Okay."

But, before my mind could grasp what was happening, he was bending down to one knee, his hand diving into his suit pocket. I heard giggles behind me as Henry and Hillary appeared with balloons and a bouquet of those bright pink dahlias I'd once taken to Hillary's dance recital.

I looked back at Ford. His face was as serious as I'd ever seen it, and his look of pure love and devotion caused tears to well in my eyes.

"Hailey, a year ago we met, and the second I laid eyes on you I knew you'd be someone important in my life."

"Ford," I whispered his name, reaching a hand toward him.

He took it and continued, "I love you, Hailey. You've healed me, you've healed my children, and you've brought so much happiness into our life. You make our family complete. Will you marry us?"

Ford opened the ring box, and Hillary and Henry stepped forward next to him, each holding out another item of jewelry. Hillary had a gold bracelet and Henry a gold necklace, both with a heart charm on them. I burst into tears and reached for all three of them, creating an awkward hug situation where Ford's face was basically pressed into our stomachs as he was still on his knees.

"I love you all so much," I cried.

Henry and Hillary solemnly gave me their jewelry items, each helping me put them on, and then it was just Ford, still kneeling there, so patiently waiting.

"Of course, I'll marry you," I said to him. "I love you more than anything in the world."

He slid the ring onto my finger and stood, gathering me in his arms and holding me close. Only then could I feel the nerves running through him, and I pulled him closer.

"This is the kissing part," Henry muttered. "Let's go."

Hillary followed as they left the room, but I only had eyes for Ford.

Henry had been right, after all. This was the kissing part.

Dear Reader,

Thank you so much for reading Hailey's story. If you've been with me for a while, thanks so much for coming back. If you're a first-time reader, welcome aboard!

If you want sneak peeks, updates on my writing, and information on book releases --without depending on my mood-based social media posting -- you should sign up for my author newsletter. I send twice a month, and I try really hard not to be annoying. I'd love to have you!

You can find my newsletter sign-up through my website at www.aspenmariehadley.com

COMING SOON

Up next for the Thornback Society friends is Meredith's story, *A Class of Her Own*, coming December 1, 2022. Keep reading for the description and a first chapter sneak peek.

Description:
Meredith Atwood has been described as a lot of things. Her friends call her determined, strong, and dedicated. Her enemies, well, their words are a little less flattering. But, Meredith doesn't have time to worry about appearances, especially not when she finds herself locked in a life or death battle with her new HOA president – a man, incidentally, who didn't even want the job that should have been hers.

Brooks VanOrman doesn't have a lot of time or interest in fighting battles. However, when he finds himself unwittingly in the position of HOA president, he realizes he's going to have to start caring, and soon. To complicate matters, his neighbor - the feisty, dark-haired woman of his nightmares - refuses to follow the rules and he's the one called in to enforce them.

It's an instant clash of wills.

Only the more Brooks gets to know Meredith, the more he realizes that there's a lot more to the fierce warrior than meets the eye.

SNEAK PEEK:

Meredith
November

Let's pretend for a second that I'm the type of person who would go to a psychic, and that at that visit while gazing into a crystal ball I'd been told that someday I'd buy a six-foot tall, inflatable turkey wearing a Pilgrim hat, and spend an entire Saturday after dark trying to stake its stubborn bubble-like feet into my front lawn . . .well . . . I'd have asked for my money back and called her a kook while loudly proclaiming my disbelief to anyone within ear shot.

Yet, here I was.

Holding a stake while a stupid six-foot bird tried to blow away in the truly annoying east wind that came flowing over the top of the mountains and straight into my yard. If I didn't know better, I'd think a cosmic funnel existed upwind from my property and that someone was having a laugh at my expense. My neighbors' leaves appeared to be hardly blowing, while my trees were attempting to fall to the ground.

"Do you think we could try again during daylight tomorrow?" Lizzie asked, her voice muffled by the turkey's gigantic plastic feathers shoved up against her face.

"The goal is for everyone to wake up to this little surprise," I replied with some effort. I had a stake between my teeth and was trying my best to tug the bird's feet back toward the ground. "If they see me doing this I'll have to answer too many questions."

"I think you'll be answering questions regardless," Ruby piped up from my front porch where she was sipping something steamy.

She'd flat out refused to get involved in this battle, but definitely wanted to watch it all unfold.

"My yard, my choice," I stated, a mantra I'd been saying to myself all afternoon.

Did I really want a gargantuan turkey, complete with an LED light-up bow tie, towering in my yard? No. Did I really, really want to passive-aggressively get under the skin of my HOA board? Yes. I had a point to prove, and if it took a little bit of tacky yard decor to accomplish it, well, I was game.

Another gust of wind hit and I heard Lizzie squeak as she tumbled to the ground. She was now being mauled by the turkey, which made Ruby laugh out loud and I bit my lip to keep from joining her. All I could see of poor Lizzie was her mittened hands and her kicking feet.

"Ruby, a little help?" I called as I grabbed one of the winged, arm looking things and heaved it toward me.

Ruby thankfully sat down her mug and joined me, lifting from the other side. Before too long Lizzie's head popped around and the look she gave me was anything but amused as she straightened her cap and tucked her springy curls back into place.

"I'm done here," she grumped. "I was on board with making your yard into a haunted house last month. And I'll definitely be back to set up Santa's sleigh and reindeer next month. But this turkey crossed a line with me and I'm out." She huffed a little as she marched to the porch to retrieve her purse and then headed toward her car. "You'd better pray I don't have a black eye from that stupid battery pack that just tried to knock me out cold. I have my bridal pictures next week."

Ruby and I watched her drive away as we held onto the wings and struggled against the beast. When Lizzie's taillights were out of sight I turned to Ruby who had been unusually quiet for the past couple of minutes.

"I feel like I shouldn't enjoy her anger so much. She just bounces around like an irritated oompa-loompa and I can't take anything she says seriously," Ruby giggled.

This time I didn't bite my lip, but laughed out loud. The description was spot on. "You want to help me finish this?" I asked.

She reached out a hand and I gave her a stake and the small hammer I'd been using. "Well, this may have gone easier if you didn't have a toy hammer," she said as she bent and gripped the spastic cord. "Where did you get this?"

I avoided answering, slightly embarrassed that I'd somehow picked out the wrong hammer. "Just get this sucker staked, please."

Ruby made short work of it, staking the bird as competently as I'd known she could. Ruby had a strange and varied set of skills that made her quite handy to have around. We stood, both of us putting our hands on our hips and taking a few steps back to see the end result. The end result was that the bird was facing the house and its tail feathers were facing the street. With the breeze blowing, it looked like it was wiggling its bum at the neighborhood in a taunting and sassy manner.

"Oops," Ruby laughed.

"No, leave it," I said as she started moving toward it to fix the situation. "It's perfect."

*****

A knock on the door sounded right as my toast popped up the next morning. I smiled smugly to myself, buttering it and spreading on some homemade preserves I'd gotten from my dad last time I'd visited. A second knock came as I rounded the corner out of my kitchen into the small entry area of my home. I opened the door and held out the toast in offering. Brooks van Orman, HOA president and pain in my back side, looked at the toast and back at me with an inscrutable expression. His dark hair was still wet from his shower and his beard looked freshly trimmed. As usual, he was wearing a button-down shirt with the sleeves rolled up over his forearms. Today it was a washed-out denim.

"You're right on time," I said, wiggling the toast. "So predictable, as usual, that the toast popped up just as you knocked. I made it for you."

His dark eyes looked at the toast again before moving up to my face. "I don't want your toast."

I ignored the involuntary way my traitorous ears seemed determined to love the sound of his voice. He always spoke slowly, carefully, his voice deep and almost hypnotic — as though he'd been taught how to speak by a grandfather sitting on the front porch with all the time in the world. Yes, I liked how his voice sounded, but I hated how slowly he spoke. Sometimes, during HOA meetings, I had to cross my toes back and forth over each other to keep myself from trying to finish his sentences.

"What do you want, then?" I asked, both of us knowing exactly why he was here.

He jerked a thumb over his shoulder at my turkey, standing proud and wiggling its bum at the world. He sighed, already weary of this conversation. "Miss Atwood, the HOA bylaws clearly state you can't have horrendous turkeys twerking in your front yard."

I raised my eyebrows and took a bit of the toast he wasn't going to eat. I didn't bother with good manners, talking through my food as I replied, "Could you please explain what twerking is? I'm unfamiliar with this term."

He blinked the slow blink of deep skepticism. "You don't know what twerking is?"

I took another bite. "Sure don't."

He nodded and stuffed his hands into his pockets, the movement giving me a sneak peek of that mystery tattoo on his collar bone before it disappeared again. He took in a deep breath and focused on me as I continued eating. I held his gaze as he tilted his head, watching him try to decide what angle to hit this from. Brooks Van Orman was a lawyer of some sort. I wasn't really clear on what his specialty was, or whatever, but he was probably used to having to face down difficult people and argue his case.

"Miss Atwood," he started, and I grinned.

"Meredith. Miss Atwood sounds so formal."

"This is a formal complaint."

"From whom?" I asked, eyes wide as though I didn't know that Hazel next door, loyal HOA board member and snoop extraordinarre, had to have called him at sunrise.

Hazel was in charge of distributing tickets to people who'd broken bylaws, and she loved her job with a rabid commitment I begrudgingly admired. She also loved her blue hair - on purpose - and telling everyone that her seventieth birthday was coming. Two things I admired less.

"Hazel," Brooks answered. "She also texted me a picture of the exact bylaw you're breaking."

I brushed the toast crumbs off my fingers and chuckled lightly. "Hazel knows how to text pictures?"

"She does," he muttered.

I was suddenly intrigued by just how many text pictures Hazel had sent him, and what they were of. From where I was sitting, Hazel didn't do anything but snoop and knit. I doubted Brooks was interested in pictures of her latest hot pad.

"Hmm. Maybe she's the one I should ask about this twerking thing then?"

Brooks rolled his eyes. "Look, you and I both know, that you know, that this turkey thing is completely ridiculous. You did it to once again irritate me and waste my time. Are you going to take it down or do I need to set Hazel free with her ticket book?"

"First of all, Mr. Van Orman, I don't spend all my time thinking up ways to irritate you, and I don't care how you spend your time."

"Right." His tone was clipped, suspicious and annoyed.

"Second of all, I happen to love Thanksgiving and this is how I choose to honor the day our great nation came together to . . ."

He held up a hand and I stumbled to a stop. "Meredith?" He leaned slightly forward, close enough for me to catch scent of his toothpaste. "The turkey is tacky and you know it. What will it take to get you to remove it?"

Maybe stop treating me like road kill at the HOA meetings, is what I wanted to yell at him. Instead, I balled my hands into fists and met him head-on. "You veto the idea of charging overnight guest fees."

His head bobbed once, sharply. "Done."

"See, that wasn't so hard."

His hands came out of his pockets and he tugged at one of his sleeves, adjusting the fold. "It would be great if we didn't have to do this every month."

I smiled sweetly at him. "You're the one who wanted to be president so bad."

"Actually, I didn't want it at all. But I've heard that you did, and that explains a lot."

Before I could respond, he spun on his heel and was off my property in a matter of seconds. I watched him go next door to knock on Hazel's door, but I wasn't able to see her or hear the conversation thanks to one very large bird and his inappropriate dance moves.

A Class of Her Own is available for preorder on Amazon now

Acknowledgments

As always, I have to start with my husband, Steve. When I was told that my publisher was no longer going to work with fiction authors I was like a deer in headlights. I'd either need to find a new publisher, or try my hand at self-publishing. Steve was the first person to tell me there was no doubt in his mind that I could self-publish. He's been my listening ear, my calm when I wanted to pull my hair out, and consistent in his belief that I can do whatever I put my mind to. Thanks Goose!

My four kids. You're patient when I'm deep in a manuscript, and love to tell everyone how cool mom's job is. I hope someday you'll chase your own dreams, and when you do, I promise I'll be the one doing the loudest cheering of all!

To my family and friends who check in regularly, who ask about characters, who share their funny stories, and who wait anxiously for the next book -- thank you! You make this entire process so much more fun, because happiness shared is the best!

Lastly – thanks so much to my women friends. I can write realistic, deep, funny and supportive female friendships because you live that way each day and allow me to benefit from your amazingness!

ABOUT THE AUTHOR

Aspen Hadley loves nothing more than a great story. She writes what she wants to read: clean, sassy, romantic novels that give you a break from real life and leave you feeling happy.

Outside of writing, Aspen's number one hobby is reading. Number two is sneaking chocolate into and out of her private stash without being caught. Other favorites include: playing the piano, traveling, a good case of the giggles, kitchen dance parties, and riding on ATVs.

Aspen shares her life with a patient husband, 4 hilarious children, and 1 grumpy dog in the foothills of her favorite Utah mountains.

You can find Aspen on social media at:

FB: Aspen Hadley Author

Instagram: aspenhadley_author

Website: www.aspenmariehadley.com

Made in United States
Troutdale, OR
04/01/2024